Mattaponi Queen

Mattaponi Queen

Stories

Belle Boggs

GRAYWOLF PRESS

"Good News for a Hard Time" first appeared in *Glimmer Train*.
"Homecoming" first appeared in *At Length*.
"Imperial Chrysanthemum" first appeared in the *Paris Review*.
"Jonas" first appeared in *Five Chapters*.

Publication of this volume is made possible in part by a grant provided by the Minnesota State Arts Board, through an appropriation by the Minnesota State Legislature; a grant from the Wells Fargo Foundation Minnesota; and a grant from the National Endowment for the Arts, which believes that a great nation deserves great art. Significant support has also been provided by Target; the McKnight Foundation; and other generous contributions from foundations, corporations, and individuals. To these organizations and individuals we offer our heartfelt thanks.

NATIONAL ENDOWMENT FOR THE ARTS

MINNESOTA STATE ARTS BOARD

WELLS FARGO

TARGET.

Published by Graywolf Press
250 Third Avenue North, Suite 600
Minneapolis, MN 55401

www.graywolfpress.org

Published in the United States of America

ISBN 978-1-55597-558-6

2 4 6 8 9 7 5 3

Library of Congress Control Number: 2010920765

Cover design: Christa Schoenbrodt, Studio Haus

Cover photo: Frances Pelzman Liscio/Punks and Roses

For Richard Allen and Jumbo Wilde

Contents

Preface

I'm not easy to please. So I've been told. I don't like it when bits and pieces of stories strike me as false or easy. I don't like it when writers try to compensate for lack of story and ideas by ladling on adjectives and useless descriptions of things that need no description. I don't like work that fails to address the complexities of language and the whole business of making meaning. And I don't like stories that have no guts, no strength, no sense of place or world. That said, I really like the stories in *Mattaponi Queen*. I'll say this before it gets said someplace else. It's wonderful that in these stories we get a rare glimpse of Indian and reservation life in Virginia. There is not a lot of literature from eastern tribes. I write this in order to point out that none of this is why these stories are good. It is always good to hear new voices, but the newness of a voice alone carries no literary value. These stories are good because they are strongly imagined, finely controlled, and well crafted. These stories are good because they are true, true in that way that only good fiction can be. The last thing a reader or this writer needs is my clumsy attempt to synopsize any bit of any story. I will not do that to good work. If you don't know me well enough to trust me about the value of these stories, you will after you read them.

Percival Everett

Mattaponi Queen

Deer Season

On the first day of deer season the high school is deserted by all the boys. This is expected by the teachers, who will chat with the girls and show movies all day, and by the principal, who shrugs and laughs, looking out at the empty student parking lot. He was once a boy too; just last year he bagged a ten-point buck. Tomorrow he will give out stern looks and admonitions while inviting the boys to tell him all about what they shot. But today is an easy day—with no fighting to worry about, a general air of femaleness takes over the building. A softness and gentleness. He thinks they dress more casually on this day, no boys to impress. He likes the space between their sweaters and their jeans, soft pale expanses of spilling flesh that were always covered when he was a boy, when he used to take off school days for hunting.

But it is a harder day than most for the secretary, who must bubble and bubble all the absences on the Scantron forms—so many absences! She thinks of all those boys out there in the woods with their rifles, thinks about their test scores, which she must also compile in forms, and hopes her own children at the elementary school, all of them girls, are safe inside. Also there is the principal with nothing to do, who stands over her drinking his coffee. He slurps as he sips it, though it is surely cold by now, and there will be the faint sour smell of coffee on him all day, stuck in his mustache where he doesn't wipe his mouth. He is smiling privately as if remembering something funny that probably soon he will tell her and will not be funny but instead will be arrogant, bragging; for the satisfaction of slapping him she sometimes thinks she would give her job.

Down the hall Jenny is glad to have the day away from her boyfriend. He is always kissing her in the halls, embarrassing her, or putting his hand in her back pocket as they go from class to class, which makes it hard to walk or even to feel like a person. He is taking art, like her, even though he hates art and makes fun of the slides their teacher shows them of Pollock, de Kooning, Klee. Even Monet: he doesn't get *Monet*. Jenny is working on a charcoal still life of the roses he brought her on her birthday; they are dried up and brown, which makes them harder to draw, which is the point. She is working on the curled shriveled lip of the rose nearest her when she hears a shot, distant and echoing, and looks up. The rest of the class, a few girls and nerdy guys, are all bent over their own still lifes. The teacher walks from person to person, murmuring advice or appreciation, and Jenny is suddenly and unexpectedly filled with happiness. It is a warm, fleeting feeling; it will dissipate in a moment, leaving her with the poorly drawn roses, which are beginning to look like a mass of long-stemmed prunes. She thinks of her boyfriend and hopes he has not killed anything; she is an animal lover, only eats meat on holidays and when her parents nag her. She imagines the deer with their moist eyes and soft fur and hopes they run like hell.

Two seats away, at the end of the long, scuffed table, sits Jason. He is shading in an aluminum skateboard truck and he is also glad, so glad that Jenny's boyfriend and the rest of the rednecks are missing school today. He hadn't expected them to take this class, Art I; they are juniors, seniors, and not exactly into art. They give him shit about his clothes, his hair, the music he listens to; it's easy to think of things to say back, but he keeps them mostly to himself. He can't quite capture the metal's shine; he sees now that he should have brought something easier, like feathers or leaves or roses. The art teacher stands behind him, leaning over his shoulder and nodding. She smells suspiciously like mouthwash; he knows what that means. She pats his shoulder and he can feel a transmission of sympathy coming from her, but he doesn't want it, doesn't want Jenny next to him to see the teacher's hand on his shoulder. Anyway, Mrs. Hayes probably thinks Jason wishes *he* were out hunting, ha, what a joke. Jason's dad offered to take him; he left a message on their machine, but then he never called back when he said he would. He was probably waiting for Jason to call *him* back, and Jason was busy. Later, maybe later in the season or maybe not at all. Jason doesn't think he could shoot something as helpless as a deer anyway.

Mrs. Hayes is tired today, hungover after a night of drinking and fighting with her husband. She'd forgotten all about the first day of deer season—how fortunate it came now, when she needs it. She was planning to show slides of Futurist art but thinks how much better it would be to let these kids work for a while, to let them draw uninterrupted by jeering and teases from those boys with their model trucks and deer antlers. Jason with his wheel thingy and Jenny with her bunch of dried-up roses, they seem as though a weight has been lifted from them. It has not really affected their work, which remains lumpy and coarse and badly composed. Their shoulders seem less tense and constricted though; without thinking she puts her hand on Jason's shoulder and feels him flinch under her touch.

She and her husband are fighting over a hole on their property—a sinkhole, her husband claims, but Mrs. Hayes thinks it is actually an ice hole, dug a century ago or even earlier for the purpose of storing ice cut from the frozen lake in winter. Her husband wants to fill the hole with sand and dirt; it has a depth of almost twenty feet and he says it isn't safe or right to keep it, what if it gets bigger and bigger, degrading the value of their land? Mrs. Hayes has found things inside the hole—a beautiful little hand-blown glass bottle, an arrowhead, a Confederate belt buckle, a bone toothbrush without any bristles. How did you find those things anyway? her husband wanted to know. I dug around a little, she said, remembering descending the sloping sides into the hole's cooler air, brushing away the layers and layers of leaves and scraping the damp clay walls with her fingers. Next time you'll likely find a copperhead, he said, meanness in his voice. Their fights escalate over nothing, become a reason for shouting and crying and making a bed on the couch. Her head burns with a dull ache; she wishes she could lie in the hole now, unseen under a big pile of cool, golden leaves.

The glass bottle, the arrowhead, the belt buckle, and the toothbrush sit on the windowsill above the heating vents. Their images bend and waver in the warm, billowing air. No one has chosen to draw them; even the girl who forgot something to draw dug around in her book bag until she found something of her own—a pencil, nervously bitten during last week's trigonometry test. It is hard to render all the tiny tooth marks, the barest scraping away and flaking of smooth yellow paint, but at least it is hers and not someone else's. Those are her tooth marks, after all; she bought the pencil herself at Walgreen's. She has made no mark on the glass bottle, the arrowhead, the belt buckle, or the toothbrush, nor does she know where they came from. Better to leave them there on the windowsill, mysterious and wavering and fragile-looking.

Two more distant shots open into the overwarm air, but no one looks up this time. If they did, and stood looking through the window where Mrs. Hayes's excavations appear to tremble, they might see something. A white-tailed deer has wandered from the cross-country path behind the school onto the track, has tripped across the pale crunching gravel to stand near their double-glass window in a forgotten and overgrown patch of brownish chickweed. Long dry fronds brush against its limbs and it holds as still as a gasp. It is a young buck with a small rack of newly hardened antlers, bone for locking against bone. It has found the safest place in the county, but of course it does not know this and soon will run off again into the woods, where shots will be fired throughout the day and into dusk.

Good News for a Hard Time

It wasn't his car or his house or his clothes that told you Ronnie's father had made it, but the way he treated his dogs. Walking through the tiny airport's automatic doors into April sunshine, Ronnie spotted him pacing before the muddy green Subaru, cell phone to his ear, Tiparillo cigar in his mouth, and knew the dogs were why he hadn't met her at baggage claim. He liked to keep the engine idling, to power the specially installed, oscillating fan that cooled the two fat mutts, Brooks and Dunn, passed out in the sun-hot backseat.

When she was a little girl, before her mother left, their various dogs had slept outside and rarely made trips to the vet. Lola, a favorite, was let in on the coldest nights to warm herself next to the stove; her fur was so long and fine that she had to be watched carefully lest she catch fire. Bruce, Ronnie's dad, still lived in the same house she'd grown up in, a defunct hunting lodge on the Mattaponi Indian Reservation. From the outside it looked much as it had when Ronnie was little—a square, one-story log cabin with creosote-black logs and pale chinking—but inside, everything was different. The kitchen had real tile floors, the drafty casement windows had been replaced, and he had central air conditioning, not to mention forced-air heat that clicked on with satisfying regularity. Brooks and Dunn slept under his bed, on big, cedar-scented pillows he'd ordered from a catalog. They rode with him everywhere, to job sites and on vacations, and they had a standing appointment each month to have their fur groomed and nails clipped at the poodle shop in Tappahannock, where Bruce made the old ladies blush and giggle with his stories and easily overheard cellular conversations.

He saw her and waved, but didn't stop his pacing or talking. She shifted her carry-on to her other shoulder, smoothed her blouse over her stomach. She had not told her father yet about the baby, two months along, nor had she even told her husband, who would the next day return Stateside to Walter Reed, right arm gone to just above the elbow. Her scalp twitched just thinking of his poor arm, so she put it out of her mind, smiled wanly at Bruce.

"All right," he said, tossing down the cigar to give Ronnie a half hug. "My daughter's here, gotta go."

"Dad," she mumbled into his scratchy pullover. She yanked open the back door, shoved in her luggage. "Hey, Brooks. Hey, Dunn," she said, like they were sullen younger siblings and she was home from college instead of an army base. Dunn lifted his head an inch off the hairy carpet and thumped his fat-heavy tail. Privately, she thought the dogs' names stupid—Brooks was a bitch, after all, and Bruce was no fan of contemporary country music—but they had been named by Bruce's friend Skinny, who loved country music and was slowly dying of hepatitis C and painkiller addiction. Skinny lived on the reservation too, and was a real Indian, unlike Bruce, who lived there because no one had the heart to kick him off after Ronnie's mom moved to California.

"It's chilly, Dad," Ronnie said, as she slid into the front seat.

"Georgia's spoiling you," he said. "Turning you into an old lady."

Ronnie frowned. "I don't look—"

"No, you don't look like an old lady," Bruce said, with exaggerated annoyance. He lit up again, and Ronnie cranked down her window and leaned toward fresh air in what she thought was a subtle way. "I'm just saying, it's a retirement place. For people who can't deal with life anymore."

"That's Florida," Ronnie said. "Nobody retires to Georgia." In truth a perpetual dissatisfaction with the weather, begun in childhood winters warmed by a too-small woodstove, was one reason she hadn't dissuaded Jeremy from joining the service. The overserious recruiter—he talked on and on about *9-1-1,* like it was a call to the police—said a base in the South was likely, and Ronnie had pictured warm winters, palmetto trees, all the time she needed to herself. Okay, she'd said, a decisive firmness in her voice. Jeremy and the recruiter had looked up from their Cokes as if they were surprised to find out that all along it had been her decision to make. In fact, they'd looked surprised to find her in the room at all.

"I should never have let him join up," Ronnie said, as I-64's newly green trees swished by on both sides of the highway. "I should have said no."

"Probably you're right," Bruce said. "But how could you have known what was coming? Three weeks babysitting a tank's gas gauge and then this?"

"I should have stopped him," she said again. She didn't buy her dad's surprise—he'd had buddies in Vietnam, spent three years in college until his draft number came up low—and so a growing part of her blamed him now too.

"Well, you are the smarter of the two of you."

Ronnie had gone to an expensive art school in Savannah, and even though Bruce, with his contracting business, had kicked in what he could, and with scholarships from the Kiwanis and Rotary clubs, she'd had to drop out, thirty thousand dollars in debt, at the end of her second year. She told Bruce that she'd taken all the important classes already, and that the actual piece of paper that said you graduated was not really so valuable when it also said *painting and printmaking.* Bruce hadn't tried to talk her out of it, though she'd wished he would; he tended to believe what was most convenient at the time.

She didn't mind dropping out, not really. Savannah had not exactly been a welcoming place, and she'd been homesick and lonely most of the time, though she hated to admit it. People always wanted to know *where are you from?* and *who are your people?* and Ronnie found herself perversely referring to the reservation and growing her thick, near-black hair long and wearing it in a single braid. She lived by herself in an unheated basement apartment that was perpetually damp, and cold three seasons of the year, and after a while her clothes and her long hair and even her skin smelled of mildew. She missed Jeremy, though she'd dumped him before starting school. He still wrote her letters on lined notebook paper, which he folded into little squares and mailed inside envelopes he made from the local newspaper.

Hey what's up? most of the letters began.

He told Ronnie about shows he'd seen in Richmond, about working as a dock builder in West Point, about friends they had in common. He recommended CDs she'd never buy, movies she had no interest in watching.

Alarmingly, the letters also told of a growing friendship—was that the word? *apprenticeship?*—with Bruce. *Bruce has aquired for me an Indian hunting license. Bruce is taking me on a deep-sea fishing expidition. Bruce put me on his crew.*

Ronnie had always found Jeremy's predilection for formal words he could not spell to be an endearing trait. He was sweet. He was funny. He was even handsome—tall, with sandy blond hair he had to brush out of his blue eyes and a wide, easy smile. He'd been a senior when they started dating during her sophomore year; once he graduated she was happy to keep him around to drive her places, make mix CDs for her, and provide an easy exemption from high school social events. But she did not want to date him past her own graduation—she knew, all along, that she would wind up pregnant and poor. Married.

So she mailed warning letters back to Bruce:

I don't know what you're doing with Jeremy but it needs to stop.

An Indian hunting license? Out of the three of us, I'm the only one who should have one of those. Let him hunt with his own dad.

Seriously, Dad, don't you have friends your own age?

Of course, Jeremy was there when she came home, waiting. She accidentally got drunk and slept with him her first night back, accepted a marriage proposal within the year. They rented a house, went to jobs, barbecued alone or with their families on weekends. Once or twice a week he played guitar in their basement, sending up the muffled, twangy notes while Ronnie lay awake, listening. It was a life that offered so little surprise that Ronnie didn't get involved when her husband stayed up all night watching C-SPAN, when he got all worked up about al-Qaeda and making a future for them, when he decided to join the army and move the two of them to Columbus, just a few hours from where she'd dropped out of school. If she was really honest with herself, anger with Bruce, who all along just wanted her back the way he wanted her mother back, was also part of what made her say, to the surprised recruiter, *Okay.*

She told Bruce about the baby as they crossed the metal drawbridge that divided King and Queen County from King William County. The wheels thudded against the loose wooden planks. Brooks struggled to stand and sniffed the air.

"It's his?" Bruce said, as the wheels gripped smooth asphalt again.

"Goddamn it, Dad."

"All right, sorry," he said. "I was trying to be funny—"

Ronnie felt her eyes begin to sting, but let him continue.

"I'm sorry," he said again, running a hand over his face. She saw how old he looked, just for a minute, the skin on his hand as leathery as an old man's. "I was kidding. No, this is good news," he said slowly. "Good news for a hard time."

"He thinks there'll be money," Ronnie said. "His disability rating is pretty high. I looked it up and there'll be more once we have the kid. I haven't told him yet."

"What we need," Bruce said, "is a special occasion. This is a special occasion, I mean, and we need a way to, let's say, commemorate and announce it."

"I don't think so," Ronnie said, looking out the window. They were crossing onto the reservation. Last year's hurricane had broken down all the pine trees. Despite the faint buds and new leaves, the woods that in her childhood she'd known as forests, palaces, looked bare and gray-brown. "I think you'd better let me deal with telling him."

But Bruce was already planning. "What we need," he said in his loud, decisive voice, turning on the radio to the classic rock station, "is a shad feast." Zeppelin. He cranked it. "A shad feast for spring."

The biggest fault Ronnie found with Brooks's and Dunn's names was how they linked them, eternally, made them into a pair. If something happened to Brooks—if she were hit by a car, say, or got cancer—where did that leave Dunn? In the year her mom left them, Ronnie and Bruce brought home three domestic goslings from the Southern States hardware store to raise on the river. They'd named them Larry, Darryl, and Darryl after characters from a television show. Before spring turned to summer, both Darryls were gone—one killed by a fox, the other run off by dogs—and Larry was left so mean Bruce had to borrow a gun to shoot him.

Ronnie looked at Dunn, curled next to the new French doors that led out to the deck, with a deep and sorrowful pity.

"Supper," Bruce said, loudly shaking kibble into their matching bowls. It was not until he got out the can opener that both dogs struggled to their feet, tails wagging.

"Green beans?" Ronnie asked, as he spooned some over their food.

"For their diet," he explained. "The doc says they're too fat, but they won't eat the kibble dry. So I put this on top, they eat it so fast they hardly taste it."

"I don't think a shad feast is such a good idea," Ronnie said, staring at the mass of gray-green beans. "I'm gonna drive up to see Jeremy tomorrow. I don't think you should be planning some big thing."

"How do you feel about it?" Bruce asked as he set down the bowls, not looking at her. "You happy?"

Ronnie shrugged, embarrassed. "I suppose."

"Shad is good for expecting mothers."

Brooks and Dunn gobbled the food, pushing their bowls across the floor as they ate. Soon they raised their doggy heads, looking for more.

After a supper of eggs and toast, Ronnie put on one of Bruce's golf windbreakers and went for a walk. The airs she put on at school, you would have thought she lived in a teepee village, but really the reservation was just like anywhere else, trailers and double-wides and clapboard ranchers set on weedy lawns far off the black asphalt road. Pickup trucks with expired license plates. Girls who wore tight jeans and hair spray. It wasn't exotic or special, just a big bunch of acres on the river.

But the river was beautiful, even a mere silvery glimpse of it here and there through the thick growth of trees. The road Ronnie followed traced its steep banks. Skinny loved it so much he kept his house there, really just a few duck blinds modified and tacked precariously against the crumbling soil. When it stormed or the weather got especially cold he had to stay with Bruce. They stayed up late, drinking beers and listening to Tina Turner records and crying about how much they both missed Ronnie's mom. It disgusted Ronnie how her dad wasn't even mad about it. He just missed her, wished her the best.

Ronnie drew in a deep breath, quickened her pace. She wondered what Jeremy's arm would look like, if she would have to see it before it healed, or scarred up, or whatever the stumps of amputated limbs did. She shuddered and started a slow jog. The asphalt stung her feet through her thin Converse soles, so she switched to the gravel shoulder.

On the tinny line from Germany, he'd tried to make the best of it.

It ain't so bad, he'd said. I can do a lot with just the one arm.

Her throat had tightened to where she couldn't say anything back, not because of the injury itself but because of the insistent, desperate tone of his voice.

Really, trust me, we'll be alright.

She knew he was afraid she would leave, just like her mom had.

Ronnie was ten when Susanna left. Disney had flown her out to their studios in Glendale as an animator's model for the movie *Pocahontas*. That was how beautiful she was—it was shocking that it had taken so long for her to get discovered. She was tanning leather in a teepee in Colonial Williamsburg when an agent came by on vacation. Of course, she never came back, which was what Ronnie feared would happen all along. Two years later all the kids were wearing plastic Halloween costumes with big-eyed, anglicized drawings of her mother on them, and Bruce had wept, handing out candy at the Central Garage hayride, while Ronnie had wanted to scream.

She tucked her braid inside her sweatshirt and began to run.

She didn't tell him. She was tempted, just to see how it improved things—he looked so depressed, dark circles under his eyes, his shirt-sleeve already pinned up like a veteran's—but she just sat there, holding his one hand. Jeremy had insisted on being dressed and out of bed when she got there, no self-pity for him, and something about his forcefulness made her want to keep it a secret, her secret. Well, hers and Bruce's.

Because more and more, when she thought of the baby, she was filled with a crazy, happy feeling that she didn't want to share with anybody. Sitting in the lounge area of the hospital, mothers and wives all around surreptitiously pressing Kleenex beneath their eyes, she should have been sobbing. But she felt strangely good, alive, her body working like it should. And guilt, for that.

But not as much as she should have felt.

"Let's take a walk," she suggested. There was a tall stack of CDs with cracked jewel cases on his bedside table. The Dead Kennedys, the Rolling Stones. He used to be so exacting about his collection, sheathing each disk in a square plastic sleeve, alphabetizing the liner notes, that Ronnie hardly ever listened to any of his music. She pulled out Neil Young's *Rust Never Sleeps* because the name sounded familiar, then remembered it had been one of Bruce's favorites. She slid the CD back into its same spot, stood up. "Come on."

"I can grow my hair out again," Jeremy said as they made their way into the hallway. He walked slowly, like an invalid, and Ronnie kept having to adjust her pace so that she didn't leave him behind.

"That's true," she said. "I like you with long hair."

After a while, they somehow made a circle to the lounge, where a wall of vending machines beckoned. Ronnie stood next to him while he fumbled with wrinkled dollars pulled from his jeans pocket. Everyone there was talking about how much money they were going to get—so much for a leg, so much for a hand, an arm below the elbow, to the shoulder—and how they had no regrets. Don't look back. Can't look back. In a hopeful tone, Jeremy said he would get more for a right hand than a left hand, since that was his writing hand. Oh yeah, you're real lucky, Ronnie had snapped, then spent the next hour apologizing while he ate three candy bars right in a row, not even wiping the chocolate from his lips. Ronnie realized, sitting next to him, that he would never play guitar again.

It did not go well, and still she kept her secret. She felt a kind of mean pride in that. She noticed how the landscape turned gradually from brown to a brown tinged with green the farther south she drove. She thought of her little apartment in Savannah, the green mildew smell, canvases leaning enticingly against the damp, chilly walls.

Ronnie's mom was eighteen when she met Bruce at a Dylan concert where she was selling jewelry. Bruce was a motorcycle hippie, and he bought one of Susanna's goofy beaded necklaces—he still wore it to tribal meetings sometimes—and was smitten. They had to settle down soon after, when she got knocked up. The Mattaponi River was as good a place as any. Better, when you considered that the land was Susanna's.

Ronnie had photos of a very pregnant Susanna, hair in two glossy braids, wearing cutoff men's jeans and open-necked shirts and looking kind of put-upon and faraway. Bruce was almost never in the frame. Ronnie assumed he was the photographer. Susanna took few pictures of Bruce.

It was late when Ronnie got home. She found her dad sitting at the dining table, writing intently in a notebook. Brooks and Dunn were at his feet, sleeping.

"Guests," he told her. "Guests to the shad feast."

"Long list," Ronnie remarked. She didn't feel like arguing.

"A shad is a big fish. What did he say?"

"Nothing," Ronnie said.

"*Nothing*," Bruce said. "Nothing?"

"I didn't tell him, Dad."

"Oh," Bruce said, crossing a name off his list, adding another. "You want to wait for the shad feast."

Ronnie stood behind him, rested a hand on his shoulder. "It looks like a guest list to a Little Rascals reunion," she said.

"Be a bunch of knee-walking Indians, hope you don't mind," he said. "Only people you can get to eat shad."

"*Native Americans*," Ronnie corrected him, because she knew the term annoyed him. "We prefer to be called knee-walking Native Americans."

"Bah," he said.

Bruce wanted to catch the shad himself, even though it was cheap enough to buy them.

"Come on," he said to Ronnie. "Let's you and me have a crack at it."

Ronnie couldn't say she had anything better to do. She'd spent part of the morning talking to Jeremy, part of it to his doctors. They said he could come home in two days—Saturday, it would be—and told her a little of what her responsibilities would be, mainly just making sure he got to the doctor for physical therapy, something about watching for alcoholism and depression. When she asked if he would have to go to the base at some point—to get their things, to sign the paperwork—the doctor had said he'd need to speak to his case manager, that was all.

But I'm *pregnant,* she'd said. I think that makes a difference. In the paperwork, I mean.

Congratulations, ma'am, the doctor said. He didn't mention.

He doesn't know yet, she said quickly. So don't tell him.

Bruce wouldn't let her drag the johnboat out of the rushes, and he wouldn't let her row, either. She didn't have a fishing pole, so she just sat there, hands in her lap, and looked at the scenery. The river was low, revealing wide swaths of black spring mud along the banks. It smelled rich and old and oily, like shad meat.

"You *are* going to tell him, right?"

"Yes, eventually," she said.

"Because you have to tell him."

"I know," Ronnie said. "I'd just rather wait until he's had a few days to adjust to me again. I'd rather, if we have to have a shad feast, that it be a sort of welcome-home, isn't-life-a-bitch feast."

"That doesn't sound as good," Bruce said. "But okay."

They were quiet for a long while, and then Bruce asked if she had thought about names. Ronnie shook her head.

"You know, I was the one who named you Ronette."

"Yeah, I've been meaning to thank you for that."

"No, really," Bruce said. His people were from West Virginia; Ronnie was named for a great-aunt. "I wanted to give you a solid, feet-on-the-ground name."

"Seriously, Dad."

But Bruce ignored her, looking up into the sky as a flock of geese passed overhead. "Now, Susanna, that's a beautiful name. All those curvy, soft Ss. But flighty. Not a name you can pin down. But Ronette, Ronnie, it's a solid, dependable name. Rs and Ns." He looked at her hard, as if pinning her down with his eyes. "And that's what you are."

Ronnie blinked and looked away. She found she cried about once a day lately.

"Painting and printmaking aside," her father said.

Bruce didn't catch any shad until after he'd dropped Ronnie off at the pier so she could run up to the house to pee. From the house she could hear him shouting something from the boat, so she walked to the edge of the bank and saw him holding up a large, silver-brown fish. She wondered if it had spawned already; she hoped so.

Ronnie gave him the thumbs-up and headed back to the house with a heavy feeling. She guessed that now there was no way to avoid the dinner. Bruce wouldn't pass up the opportunity to show off the first shad of the spring.

She grabbed her toiletries bag from inside and dragged a lawn chair into a sunny spot on the deck. She loosened her hair from its band and slowly unbraided it with her fingers. She flipped her hair over her head and began to brush it in long, smooth strokes. Through the dark strands, as thick and straight as fishing line, she could see Brooks and Dunn sniffing at something in the yard.

Bruce liked to joke that Ronnie had been raised by dogs. Susanna would put her outside in the morning, along with Criminy, their collie. Criminy was the smartest dog they ever owned, and he would follow Ronnie around the yard and the garden, barking if she got too close to the river or the road. It wasn't too difficult a chore, even for a dog, because Ronnie never strayed far from the house. Around noon Susanna would call Ronnie inside to feed her lunch, and would empty her pockets of whatever strange detritus she'd picked up. Ronnie was told, but didn't remember, that she liked to bring her mother the plastic tips of her father's cigars, which she would line up in her mouth like a row of phantom smokes. Even now, she could picture her mother's irritation. "Thanks, Ron," she'd say, holding the chewed ivory tips in her flattened palm as Ronnie spat them out. "These are real nice."

Ronnie got out her nail polish—Gypsy Red—and shook it. She wondered what kind of mother she would be. She'd hardly ever held a baby and was nervous around children. She held on to grudges and didn't filter the mean things she thought of saying. It was less difficult to picture Jeremy as a father—he was patient and kind, quick to forgive. He would have made a good teacher or coach. Ronnie could see him even with just the one arm, or with one arm and a prosthetic, outside with some little squirt, lazily tossing a pop fly high over the trees while she watched, jealous and alone.

Part of her wished that she could just stay pregnant.

The one professor who'd taken a shine to her warned Ronnie of the dangers of trying to have a normal life. She was divorced, and smoked cigarette after cigarette in a tiny, windowless office when Ronnie would visit her for office hours. "Don't do it," she'd said. "At least not until you've had a show. A solo show."

"Don't worry about it," Ronnie said proudly. "I don't even have a boyfriend."

"Find yourself a nice gay boyfriend, it'll keep the others away," the professor had recommended, blowing smoke sideways away from Ronnie. "That should be a cinch around here."

Almost three years out, Ronnie knew that she didn't care as much as she hoped she would about art. She wasn't going to New York; she wasn't going to L.A. She got married in her dad's backyard to a boy she knew in high school, and now she was going to have his baby, a soldier's baby, probably in the county she'd grown up in. Probably on an Indian reservation that advertised on its weathered sign: *Stone Age Relics: 1,000 years old!*

She wondered what Susanna would think. Although Bruce would never admit it, Ronnie knew that Susanna hated the reservation, hated making beaded jewelry and dancing in the annual tribal dances. Hated their little cinder block museum with its Stone Age relics.

Good luck with that, kid, she pictured her saying.

When what she really wanted to hear was this:

Jesus, Ron, I really let you down.

Around seven, Skinny brought over spaghetti and meatballs. It was one of those spring nights when the air just gets warmer, even as it grows dark, so Ronnie spread the picnic table with a cloth, set out candles, and opened a bottle of wine for Bruce and Skinny. Skinny, who was not skinny at all, had been shy around her ever since she left for college. Ronnie wondered if Bruce had told him about her being pregnant, and if it would make any difference.

"Skinny was telling me his ideas for the supper we're gonna have," Bruce said, nodding at Skinny. "Tell her."

"Well," he began slowly, not looking up from his plate. His voice was rough and gravelly from the emphysema. "I was thinking we'd go with the spring theme. Asparagus, wilted salad, spoon bread, deviled eggs. Coleslaw. Maybe," he said, chewing thoughtfully, "an asparagus frittata."

"A what?"

"He's been watching the Food Network," Bruce explained. "*Molto Mario.* That's his favorite."

The tribe's big luxury, a while back, had been paying for the county to lay cable on the reservation. This was an effort led by Bruce, who wanted the sports channels and HBO.

"Well," Ronnie said, smiling at Skinny and spearing a parsley-flecked meatball, "I guess it's worth it if he brings over food like this all the time."

"Bah," Bruce said. "Mainly we eat sandwiches."

Bruce and Skinny had been friends, Bruce maintained, since they met. In Ronnie's early memories, Skinny was sort of a distant acquaintance—

someone who fixed their car when it broke down, someone they'd nod to off the reservation, at the 7-Eleven or NAPA Auto Parts—until Susanna left for California. Then he was over all the time.

Skinny had never dated Susanna, but he said she knew that he loved her. According to Skinny, she always said that it was a cliché for them to go out, whatever that meant.

Skinny and Bruce treated her absence as if it were inevitable, like death or the equally poignant loss of a hometown girl to Hollywood. Ronnie remembered bringing this up in annoyance when she was sixteen and off to the prom in a shiny green debutante dress, two braids down her back, and they said how they wished Susanna could see her.

"She *did* leave us for Hollywood, Ron," Bruce said. Skinny had nodded sagely, Coors Light in one hand, cigarette in the other.

"She went to *Glendale*," Ronnie said. She had decided on the two braids at the last minute, self-conscious over the dress, a consignment shop find that felt uncomfortably bare and grown-up with the updo whose instructions she had torn, surreptitiously, from *Seventeen* magazine. The dress was supposed to be *funny,* she'd thought, but it had surprised her by also being sexy. "And I don't remember seeing any of her movies."

"Glendale," Bruce had said wistfully, not looking at Ronnie anymore. "It's definitely in the Hollywood vicinity."

And the boy waiting on the doorstep, that was Jeremy. He had picked every rose in his mother's garden until he had a tight, fragrant bouquet twice the size of Ronnie's head. When she opened the door, he'd proffered it like he was fending something off. Delighted, she'd carried it all night.

Driving to D.C. the next afternoon, Ronnie found herself wishing for a friendship as good, or at least as reliable, as Bruce and Skinny's. The other wives on the base seemed so busy, with their children and errands and keeping up with relatives in other states, that she hardly felt like bothering them with her loneliness. And they didn't seem to *get* her, either, when she made jokes about marriage or the commissary or called the base the rez.

The only time they had seemed to understand her, or had wanted to understand her, had been when she got the call about Jeremy's arm. Someone brought over a casserole, and someone else had washed her dishes and cleaned out the fridge and taken out the garbage. Her next-door neighbor, Trina, had found the EPT package in the bathroom trash.

"You expecting, honey?" she'd asked.

"No," Ronnie had lied. "Negative."

It seemed to Ronnie that there were two types of women in this world—those who collected female friends like curios, and those who sort of drifted on the outside of those relationships, stuck primarily associating with men. Ronnie was one of those. Other women's motives seemed too mysterious, opaque. Men were annoying and stupid, but at least you knew what they were thinking almost all the time.

Take Jeremy, for example. Ronnie knew that tomorrow, when she picked him up, he would start out sort of quiet and moody, worrying about what she thought of him, afraid he'd be a burden. He'd search for a decent radio station in the borrowed Subaru, and that would make him think about the F-150 he'd sold before they moved down to Columbus and about getting a new truck, an automatic so he could drive it. He'd be thinking about their bank accounts, what was left of their small savings, and about getting a truck loan and how he'd miss those guys at Walter Reed and where to stop for lunch. It would be thirty minutes before he warmed up and would start talking, and those things—what he'd been thinking about—would form the content of his conversation. She yawned, imagining the long next day, the shad feast. Telling him.

Ronnie used her credit card to splurge on a room in the Hilton instead of the Motel 6 close to the hospital. She hadn't told Jeremy that she was coming up a day early, and she thought it would be good to take a bath and get changed before she saw him.

The room was bland and comfortable, with a window that looked out on Georgia Avenue and a writing desk and an armoire that hid the television. Ronnie dropped her overnight bag and collapsed on the king-sized bed. She imagined bringing Jeremy here from the hospital, holding his good hand, riding the elevator with him. She imagined bringing him into the quiet, curtain-drawn room and telling him about their child in a shy, proud way.

No, she thought, that was stupid. The world didn't work like that. Before any of that could happen he would say something to annoy her, or her mood would shift that small amount that would make her not want to tell him.

Sometimes she let herself imagine what would have happened if he had been killed instead of wounded. She pictured herself grieving for a time at home, then heading west, to Arizona or New Mexico. Somewhere dry and warm, where she could start over. Maybe she could have worked in a gallery or framing shop, like most of the people she'd been in school with, or maybe she could have gone back to school. Nursing school, she thought. That would have been handy. She had heard that nurses could move wherever they wanted, there was such demand for them.

Or what if, instead, he had never joined? He could still be building docks in West Point, working with demolition crews on Bruce's latest project.

Trina had said, to Ronnie's "negative," "Well, it's just his arm. You can try again."

She walked to the window, parted the sheers, and looked out at the busy street in the direction of Walter Reed. Somewhere in that hospital, Jeremy was playing cards or chess or eating an early dinner. Laughing with his mouth open. She opened the armoire and turned on the TV, then turned it off again before the picture materialized. She decided to take a nap before driving over and surprising him.

Ronnie slept through visiting hours, woke up in bewildering, silent darkness. When finally she remembered where she was, she sat up and looked at the phone to see if the red message light was blinking. Then she remembered that she hadn't told anyone where she was staying.

When Jeremy was a teenager and they'd begun dating, he had a habit of sleeping with headphones on, music blaring. T. Rex, Sonic Youth, Bad Brains—Ronnie remembered lifting the headphones from his ears as the music poured out, angry and loud, while his long lashes barely fluttered. She'd never been able to tolerate any noise while she slept; these past couple of months alone had given her the most restful sleep she'd had in what felt like a long time.

The next day was warm, edging toward seventy by ten o'clock, when Ronnie sat outside waiting for Jeremy in the hospital's circular drive. Other soldiers milled about, smoking and shooting the breeze. Ronnie had to roll her windows shut, just to keep from breathing the cigarette smoke. She turned on Brooks and Dunn's oscillating fan.

Finally he emerged, looking sheepish and awkward, his jacket draped over one shoulder. He came around to Ronnie's side, knocked on her window. She rolled it down, squinted up at him. "Hey," he said. "I can drive."

Ronnie drew in a deep breath. "I don't think so," she said. "No offense, but I think you'll be riding shotgun awhile."

"Seriously, Ron, I can manage," he said. "I bet you're tired."

Ronnie leaned over, popped the passenger door open. "Get in," she said.

On the road, things were better, and Ronnie found herself almost telling him about the baby, and the shad feast that was waiting for them. Instead she exited the interstate to a Waffle House and told him they were having an early lunch.

They sat in a booth, and Jeremy flipped restlessly through the mini-jukebox on the Formica tabletop while they waited.

"Want a quarter?" Ronnie asked.

"Nah," he said. "You know, I just wish I could have stayed longer. Finished a tour, at least."

Ronnie crossed her arms, looked out the plate glass window. A thick and sloping stand of birch separated the Waffle House parking lot from the interstate below.

"You probably think that's stupid."

"I think you gave enough," she said quietly. He'd hardly been overseas long enough, she knew, to even feel like a soldier. Most of the stories he told in his letters were about the people he'd met, their lives Stateside. "I think you gave plenty."

Jeremy picked up the napkin-wrapped silver like it was something he had never seen before, began unrolling it. They sat in silence, and Ronnie thought about having to use her left hand for everything.

"Well, eat up," she advised when their food came—a stack of pancakes with sausage for Jeremy, a waffle for her.

It seemed that they were, at least for a time, going to be more awkward around each other in public than when they were alone. She imagined that Jeremy was worried about what other people thought, worried they might feel sorry for him or, worse, for her. The waitress had been a little too chirpy, a little too solicitous.

"You know, I'm used to people looking my way," Ronnie said, wiping her mouth and looking squarely at her husband. "It doesn't much bother me."

"Yeah, 'cause you're pretty, right?" Jeremy said morosely.

"No-o-o," Ronnie said, drawing out her answer. "Because my dad talks so loud."

Shad had been a fixture of Ronnie's springs since she could remember. The local paper each year told of the good-old-boy shad plankings, where shad were smoked on cedar planks for hours while local who's-whos got drunk on rye whiskey. The Indians cooked shad too, and took long, smoked pieces of it, prettily packed into woven baskets, to the governor's mansion in Richmond. It was a fishy fish, and no one much liked it—the good old boys' joke was that when they were done smoking it, they threw away the shad and ate the planks—but for a certain kind of person, and Ronnie guessed she was one, it was something that had to be eaten, like collards and black-eyed peas on New Year's.

Ronnie's mom used to make shad roe for breakfast this time of year. Ronnie loved the rich, grainy roe, fried in butter and cornmeal and served with eggs and ham, but she had never learned to make it and hadn't eaten it since. Eating the roe was illegal, anyway—antienvironmental, a disruption of the shad's natural spawning process.

Making the turn at Central Garage, Ronnie thought about how far each shad she'd eaten in her life had traveled to spawn, from the salty bay to the fresh waters of the Mattaponi, the same place it had been spawned. She wondered if, to the shad, it had all been worth it, if after spawning it looked around at the shallow, mud-bottomed river and thought with its tiny thoughts, *Oh, yeah, I remember this.*

"Look, Ron," Jeremy said, craning forward and pointing to the top of the windshield. "Geese."

A wide V formation of Canada geese was passing overhead. Through the open windows, they could hear the cacophonous honking. Jeremy leaned his head out the window like a dog, his bristly hairs stiff in the wind, and Ronnie imagined she could feel him thinking that the air felt warm and good.

Bruce's mailbox was decorated with partially deflated Mylar balloons, and cars and pickups lined both sides of the road for about a quarter mile. She recognized Jeremy's mom's car and his dad's dented pickup. Two of Skinny's cars were parked along the road for some reason. The chief's big truck was there, and so was a station wagon belonging to Bruce's sometime girlfriend. Ronnie parked and they got out.

"Don't be alarmed," Ronnie said. "Bruce loves you."

She held his hand and led him across the road to Bruce's driveway. From the backyard, she could hear laughter, glasses clinking, someone picking guitar. She heard the back door opening, country music pouring out. Jeremy stopped in the driveway, and Ronnie stopped next to him, still holding his hand. He crouched down, and Ronnie panicked, afraid he was going to be sick. He clucked his tongue, and out of the bushes came Brooks and then Dunn, wagging their fat tails. They were all over him, licking him and whining.

He smiled and held his face up, slightly out of their reach. "What's that smell?" he asked.

"Shad," Ronnie said. By now, it would have been baking for hours, the bones soft and gelatinous in the tough salty flesh. Ronnie could almost taste it, intense and rare, not like food at all. It was like love, she thought. Something you thought you should have until it was right there in front of you and you realized you were committed to it whole.

Overhead, a few straggling geese, separated from their flock, honked by. Brooks and Dunn lifted their doggy heads briefly, then trotted off to join the party. They seemed to know that today was special. There would be scraps for them, all night and into the morning.

Imperial Chrysanthemum

Mrs. Cutie Young lives in two rooms and drives a 1982 Ford Country Squire with the wood stickers peeling off, but her silverware collection used to be worth forty thousand dollars. I say "used to" because three weeks ago it was stolen right off the mahogany breakfront while she was out visiting. I also should qualify that her house has plenty of rooms she isn't using, and it is not Cutie Young who drives the Ford but me, Loretta, her nurse. I drive her to the Food Lion, to Aylett to go to the doctor, and lately to antique stores and pawnshops, to look at silver asparagus servers and ice tongs and oyster forks and what all, glinting pieces of metal as lacy and useless as doilies. The State Farm man offered her the forty thousand, or to replace what she had with new pieces, but the new pieces don't approach in quality—it's all hollowware now—and besides, her silver was not monogrammed but had her married name, Young, written out whole in scripty letters. They came down four generations of Youngs.

We have been all over: to Tappahannock, to Deltaville and Urbanna and Richmond and Gloucester. Her idea is that she will find the set piece by piece at the shops. I say good luck. Just getting her out of the car in some pawnshop's weedy parking lot and walking her through the caged door really takes it out of me.

I do not know why Cutie has a nurse, or why, for that matter, people call her Cutie. She's mean and stubborn and takes a long time in the toilet, but other than that there's nothing much wrong with her.

The pattern is called Imperial Chrysanthemum. It has a bumpy, spiny surface that hurts your hand to hold and is a royal pain in the ass to polish. They don't make it anymore, though they make plenty of other patterns just as tacky.

Maybe simplify, I told Cutie, picking up a simple Revere pattern with plenty of room for her name—first and last. The insurance man had brought a whole suitcase of patterns from Richmond to show her. I wanted to open up the dining room for his visit, so he'd have a place to lay them out, but she said the sunporch was good enough for an insurance man. I do not know a soul who has been good enough for that dining room, or either of the living rooms, since I have worked here. That includes grandchildren, her son, his wife, and the minister. She won't let him in at all.

She shook her head. Ridiculous, she said, like I was suggesting she eat with plastic forks and knives, or with her toes. You criticizing my taste?

No ma'am, I said, thinking, I am criticizing your husband's great-great-somebody's taste.

The Imperial Chrysanthemum was a beautiful pattern, said Mr. State Farm. He had on a suit. It was so hot on the sunporch that I think he had armpit stains through the wool. One of a kind, he said.

I had to admit, the new stuff had a cheap feel. Light as popcorn, compared to that Imperial Chrysanthemum.

Have I said that I have a good idea what happened to it? About a month ago my great-niece's husband and some others came and painted the sheds and outbuildings for Cutie. I let them in to use the bathroom— just once, while Cutie was napping, but it was enough for them to get a look around. They took their time, I remember. Her husband runs with a no-good crowd; I told Tamara as much myself and wasn't even the one to recommend them for the job. It was Horace, Cutie's son, that paid them to come over and do it. I just looked out the window one morning, stirring coffee, and there they were. I'm sure he paid them diddly-squat.

Not that they were owed forty thousand. When the sheriff's deputy came to ask who had been where, I didn't tell about letting them into the house. Don't ask me why. There has been a wave of juvenile-

delinquent crime in the King William subdivisions—white kids steal-
ing from neighbors, joyriding cars. Rumors of drugs. Go with that, I
guess I was thinking.

I am old—though not as old as Cutie—too old to get into this
mess. I've been here eight months; I wear my own clothes to work, and
I am here six days a week. My nursing degree came from the Medical
College of Virginia. When I was younger I worked in the NICU at the
hospital in Tappahannock. Holding all those tiny babies, small and
sweet as pastries, made that my favorite time of life. Also my husband
was alive then, and all my sisters.

I work for Cutie to pay on my boat. It has a name—the *Mattaponi
Queen*—and a sleeping bunk and a ladder to a high perch where you
can stand, and it needs a lot of work. It's a riverboat. I remember a
boat like that from when I was a little girl growing up nearby. It would
go up and down the river like a floating wedding cake, always a party
of white people drinking and waving their fans in the summertime.

Cutie's two rooms are the kitchen and the sunroom, where she
has her daybed and her desk and two sitting chairs. There's a ceiling
fan and a little table where I serve her a cold lunch, Monday through
Friday, and an early hot supper. Saturday her daughter-in-law brings
a lunch, or has her over to her house. On those days I drive her the
half mile, listen to her complain the whole way, go back to my house
for a while, then pick her back up. It's criminal the way her family
won't drive her anywhere, though I can understand their reluctance.
Sundays she fends for herself.

The rest of the house is quiet, the drapes drawn, some of the better furniture covered in bedsheets. I don't spend time in there for any
reason, not to dust or sweep up the mouse droppings or wash the
pollen-yellow windows. I am not a maid.

This morning Cutie says, after I check her blood pressure, "We're
going to Petersburg to look at some silver."

"Petersburg," I say. "Hmmmf."

"What, hmmmf?"

"I don't think the Squire will get us to Petersburg. I also don't think we're gonna find your silver there."

"I have a feeling," she sniffs. I know that you are thinking: why doesn't that fool pick up the telephone? Her *name* is written on the silver. Well, the answer is that her name isn't on some of the serving pieces; the pattern's too crowded. Also, Cutie doesn't trust anyone. "I have a strong feeling we will find something."

In another six months I will have enough for the boat and its repairs, and I will quit. When I get that boat working it will not be for any parties. It will be just for me.

On the way to town, Cutie holds the two pieces she has left, a spoon and a napkin ring, in her lap. She presses her pink, wrinkled thumb into the concave surface of the spoon and closes her eyes as if that spoon could tell us where to find its mates. I think she will fall asleep, right here, and prevent me from having to talk to her.

As we pass King William Estates, a parking lot of cheap little ranchers they knocked down all the trees to build, her eyes pop open like she was stuck by a pin. "White trash," she pronounces, the *sh* like gnashing her teeth.

"Yes ma'am," I say.

"Stole Mother's silver."

One reason I think it is my niece's people is because I haven't heard a peep from her, and usually she calls me on Sundays. Also they would know, from her, that I always take Cutie over to Andrea's on Saturdays, and that is when it got taken. I say it is a lucky thing I stayed in their drive waiting, reading a book, or else the police might think I did it. In fact, they questioned me, right there on Cutie's back porch.

Loretta, Cutie said, would not know what to do with silver asparagus tongs or cucumber forks. She feeds me colored food.

She doesn't mention that this is the food she *requests*: collards and fried chicken and cornbread. I'd just as soon boil an asparagus.

What about selling 'em, the deputy said, looking at me. He

had another cop, a lady cop in training, waiting halfway down the steps, and she looked at me too. I just kept on watering the hanging bougainvillea.

Loretta, Cutie said, has a pension.

"So what'll you do with it?" I say, since she is awake. Today we are pretending we will find it. "When you get it back."

"What do you mean?" she says. "I will count it, and I will put it away in the chest."

Three times I have seen her count the silver in neat, fanned rows spread on the mahogany dining table, its leaves opened for just that reason. Every time we polished it, both of us out of boredom, she would make two counts. It was like the tired old gears in her brain made visible. She counted them by twos, barely touching them with her two shaking fingers.

Tamara lives just a mile down the road from me with a husband and no babies. I am hoping she will have some babies soon, to focus the both of them. I never had any babies, but that was not my choice. And besides, I was always focused.

Her grandma who raised her was my oldest sister. She died of a heart attack a year ago, which is a good thing, I guess, because she would hate to see the way Tamara keeps her little house or her yard or her husband, the way she runs around. She tells me she goes to night-clubs in Richmond where I am sure all kinds of rough people go.

Most days, she wakes up after 12:00 noon. I was taught, just like I know she was too, that nothing good can come of a day that starts after eight.

The Petersburg trip is a bust. The yellow-toothed man who owns the shop pretends to go looking in some back rooms for the silver, and when he comes out tries to sell us some chipped old pink and white Spode he says came down through A. P. Hill's family. Cutie leaves in a huff, but I can see that her eyes are watering in the corners. Before we leave town she makes me drive up and down the cracked cement road looking for more shops.

"I had a dream about it," she says. We have all the windows rolled down, front seat and back, and Cutie is pressing a dampened rag to her forehead. "My dream told me we would find the coffeepot in Petersburg, and the sugar spoons."

Now Cutie, I want to say, we could both of us be sitting on your screen porch under a ceiling fan. You could be having your afternoon glass of whiskey right now. What do you need the silver for except to leave it to people that won't appreciate it?

"I think your silver's gone," I say finally. "I think you need to look again through the State Farm catalog."

"No," she says. "What do I want with that trash?"

To make her feel better, I stop at a Dairy Queen on the way home. The sun is blazing in the gravel parking lot, and I wait by the open passenger door. Cutie doesn't like me to help her out of the car. She frowns down at her purse, willing herself, I guess, out of the seat. I tap my foot, bend down, and yank her up by the elbow. She is still clutching the spoon and napkin ring, all folded up inside a ratty piece of linen.

I settle her at a wooden table beneath some shade trees. I know what she wants, so I don't bother to ask. A hamburger with ketchup and a strawberry milk shake on the runny side. When I come back she has spread the ratty cloth and laid the spoon and napkin ring on top of it.

I give her the tray and sit down across from her, unwrap my cheeseburger. I like the salty, greasy thinness of a Dairy Queen hamburger, but it's not something I eat often. My husband used to take me to the Dairy Queen in Tappahannock for soft serve on Friday nights. We would sit on the cement benches and eat our cones like a dating couple, never mentioning that it would have been more fun if we had children with us. Cutie pulls the paper wrapper off the top of the straw, rolls it up into a little ball.

"Loretta," she says, after she has had a sip of the shake. Sometimes when she says my name it has a melody, almost like singing. *Lo-ret-ta.* It is one of the things that keep me from hating her. She bends over the burger, unwrapping it slowly. The spoon is glinting in the light, not showing any tarnish. It must be three o'clock by now; the spirit is gone out of her. "What'll we do tomorrow?"

The way she says it I can tell she doesn't want an answer.

After I drop Cutie off and fix her something to drink, I decide to go by Tamara's on my way home. She's not the easiest person to visit, either. She lives at the back end of a dirt road that the state doesn't maintain. It gets muddy and rutted in the spring, banked up with snow in the wintertime. No big deal to her, since neither Tamara nor Charlie has a car. They need to go somewhere, they walk themselves to the main road and hitch. On the days Charlie works, he gets picked up by a truck with a white man driving it. He and all the others ride in the back like dogs.

I have a 1990 Chrysler New Yorker—last thing my husband bought me; I expect it to last—so I park along the main road, half in the ditch, and get out. My hip is sore from driving. I take my shoes off and roll up my jeans to keep them out of the dust.

The nice part of me is thinking that when I get there Tamara will have some iced tea to offer me, and we'll sit on the front porch and talk, and I'll tell her stories about her grandma. How summertimes when we were little we went everywhere except church in our bare feet, so tough on the bottom we could run down a gravel road without it hurting. How I still like the dry, clean feeling of dust under my toes. Overhead, the pine trees sway a little in a breeze I can't feel.

But then the mean part of me is reminded that I will have to tiptoe over crushed bottle glass and cigarette butts to get onto her porch. I scuff my shoes back onto my feet to walk down her driveway, weedy in the middle from the scarcity of cars to pack it down.

Their house has two windows in the front, and a porch that sort of leans off the house into the gray dirt yard. That's it. There's nothing planted, not a single bulb or bush. Tamara's grandfather was the finest gardener I ever knew. Planted my asparagus patch and the deep-green boxwoods in front of Cutie's house, too.

Pulled up in front is a neat little silver car. It's one of the cheap kinds you can get now with a million miles on the warranty, all the parts made of plastic. Great, I think, somebody's visiting, but then I notice the temporary red and white tags on the back.

"Auntie," I hear Tamara say from behind the darkened screen door. "I thought that was you coming up the drive."

I climb up the rough steps she doesn't have sense to sweep. In front of them she has laid out a flat of pansies, all purple and yellow and white.

"Whose car is that?" I say, stepping around.

The screen door creaks open and snaps shut behind her. Tamara has her hair tied up in a scarf and a flowered sundress on. She's smiling real big at me, like the cat that ate the canary.

"It's mine, Auntie."

"Yours," I say, looking back at it. "It is not."

"Sure it is," Tamara says. She squats down to fuss over the pansies, snapping the flat apart into rows. "Charlie got it for me."

"Charlie," I say. "Where'd he get the money for a new car?"

"It ain't new," she says. "It's got miles on it."

"Even still. It wasn't free."

"It won't," she says back smartly. My sister Ruth was not the one to teach her to talk common. That she learned outside the home. I think she does it to get my goat. "Charlie's been working."

"He has?" I ask, surprised. "Where?"

"For Mr. Young," she says. "And some big jobs in Tappahannock. We owe on it still."

Tamara disappears inside the house and comes out with two sweating cans of beer. I accept one and sit down heavily on her porch swing. It's not like they installed it; it was there when they moved in. She sits down cross-legged by the pansies, resumes ripping the flat apart.

"I drove it into town this morning. Bought these flowers at the Walmart."

"You did," I say.

"Didn't Grandma used to plant these same flowers every spring?" she said.

I say nothing back, so she adds, "At least I thought I remembered them. She told me, you know, some things about that Cutie Young." Her voice is offhand and pointed at the same time.

"Things," I repeat warily, sipping beer.

"More about Horace Young, *Junior*," she says. "But also about Cutie."

"Your grandma had a lot of ideas," I say. "She had a big imagination too."

"Way she told it, that big ole estate is part mine."

"Oh Lord," I say. "That old yarn."

"Way she told it, them Youngs have some making up to do."

What I want to say is: why would you want what they can give you? They have nothing you can use.

"I suppose she did plant pansies," I say instead. I have a vivid image of Ruth's slate walkway at Easter, bordered on each side by pansies. "In the springtime."

It's summer now, and they'll wilt in the ground, but I don't say so.

Tamara's mother was young when she had her—nineteen—and my sister was none too pleased. Ruth, who'd raised chickens for her living, wanted something better for her daughter, an only child. She thought Carolyn should go to school like I had, get a nursing degree. But Carolyn didn't like school—started cutting around the sixth grade, I believe—and she got held back twice along the way. It was the end of her senior year when she had Tamara, and I remember we had a hot early spring that year, and Carolyn grew fat and mopey and impossible waiting for the baby. She cried and slept a lot, and she cursed anyone who tried to shake her out of it. Worst of all, she wouldn't tell her mama and daddy who the father was. Ruth would beg and wheedle and threaten, and her husband, William, would threaten some more, but that girl wouldn't budge. Ruth used to say, *If you think I'm raising some baby you won't give a name to, you're sore mistaken.* She must have said it a dozen times a day, to Carolyn or just to herself, folding clothes, sweeping, feeding her hens. But I knew she was bluffing, and Carolyn must have too.

Carolyn was allowed to do her schoolwork at home in the last weeks of her term. She'd take off in the middle of the day, just walking, tell Ruth she was going to work at the library. The library, a one-room place with no air-conditioning, only open Thursday through Saturday. Ruth just let her go, it was such a relief to get her out of the house. She'd come home with things for the baby or for herself: a blanket or a nursing bra, little onesies in pastel colors, little socks. Ruth figured she must have gotten them from the baby's father and was encouraged. She let the schoolwork go.

Then in the last week before Tamara was born, it rained. I mean it poured. Thunderstorms every day and hot. Steam rose from the streets under the constant patter, a rolling white fog that looked eerie on the cloud-dark mornings when I used to go over there to check Carolyn's blood pressure on my way to work.

With all the rain it was impossible for Carolyn to go off in the daytime, and I guess Ruth had stepped up her questioning. Still Carolyn wouldn't budge. This baby is *mine*, I heard her say once, and that's all there is to it. Finally it was her due date, and I brought over some hot pickles—one of the nurses from my shift said spice hurried babies—and a present, a small crocheted afghan I'd been working. I remember holding it against my chest as I dodged the great puddles that had collected in Ruth's drive. Ruth was standing just inside the door, holding a dish towel.

She's gone, Ruth said blankly as she opened the door to me. Rain pouring from the downspouts.

To the hospital?

She shook her head. I made her tell me, she said, her voice flat and faraway-sounding. Last night. I made her say it. It's Horace Young.

Ancient history: that's what a lot of this town is. Houses, rented or owned, passed down father to son and mother to daughter. Silverware older than the people eating with it. Traits traced back into the uppermost branches of the family tree: well, you know his great-granddad was mean as a snake.

Carolyn showed up three days later at the hospital in Tappahannock, gave birth to a healthy baby girl, and tried her intermittent best to raise her for four years. Horace never claimed her, and I gradually began to believe that Carolyn had said his name in desperation more than anything. She looked so much like Carolyn it was hard to picture a father, and you couldn't tell from her skin tone. Ruth held on to the idea, though, and I think it about ruined her life. Not her outside life, not the one we could see; no, she still laughed and loved and went to church and did her best with Tamara. What I mean is she spent a lot of time thinking, after that, about unfairness.

She and William had rented their house from the Youngs, William worked for the Youngs; the only thing she had separate from them was Carolyn. Horace had a reputation, so I knew about how he'd been kicked out of three boarding schools, and I knew he ran around. Back when Carolyn's trouble started he was unhappily married, drove a little red convertible. I can see Carolyn sitting up in that car, thinking she was on to something.

But children can be cruel, and I wondered then if Carolyn sensed that this story was the only way to ensure that her mama wouldn't press the issue any further.

Ruth blamed herself. What did I do wrong? she used to ask me, after Carolyn left.

Sometimes I was too tired to answer any way but honestly: I don't know.

Andrea drops off Cutie's granddaughter Sammy first thing. She wanted to spend the day with her granny, Andrea says. Cutie, you don't mind watching her?

Sammy is six, and a handful, and I can tell you the person who will be responsible for her will not be Cutie. I'm also certain that Andrea just wanted to be shut of her for the day so she can do her shopping or get her hair curled.

Sitting in the wicker sunroom chairs, Cutie and Sammy have a stare-off as soon as Andrea's car pulls away. It's not my business, but ladies as old as Cutie are no use as grannies to young ones. Andrea is Horace's second wife, and she wanted a child badly enough that he let her have it even though he has four other children grown and married. Sammy is as spoiled as you would guess she is.

"Here," I say, and give them both biscuits I've split and toasted with butter. "Give me your arm, Cutie."

I take her blood pressure and her pulse: normal. I'd feel more useful if she at least had diabetes.

As soon as Sammy is done with her biscuit she starts kicking her shoe against the white wicker chair bottom. "Where's my mama?" she says. "I didn't ask to come here."

"Doing errands, I suppose," I say. Cutie is still working on her biscuit, but I see her casting a sharp eye at Sammy.

"I hope she buys me something," Sammy says. "I have to go to first grade next year."

"You cut that out," Cutie says, pointing at Sammy's feet. Her reflexes are slow but sure. "Or I'll make you walk home. When I was little I didn't expect to get something every time somebody came to get me."

"You can't make me walk home," Sammy says.

"I can," Cutie says, picking up her dish and heaving out of her chair.

"I'll go," Sammy says, "but you won't know where."

"Where'll you go."

"To the store to get a Popsicle," she says. "I have fifty cents."

I bend down so I am at eye level with her. Her eyes are blue, like her hair ribbon, and hard. I think about her being half sister to Tamara; it's not impossible. "I better not hear of you leaving here to cross that road, miss," I say. "Or you will have to cut me a switch."

Sammy blinks at me like she knows I'm serious, and I can tell that she is thinking about crying. After a minute she asks, "But how will I get my Popsicle?"

"I'll walk you after lunch," I say.

There's not much for a six-year-old to do in two rooms and a yard that hasn't had a child to play in it for twenty years. It's already too hot to play outside anyway. Cutie keeps a narrow drawer of broken toys, doll heads and Lego scraps, but Sammy has no interest in these. I give her a deck of cards and tell her to play solitaire on the screen porch. She spreads out on the Astroturf carpeting, starts lining the cards up by suit. I suppose she doesn't know how to play.

"Like this," I say, and I show her how to deal out the cards fast in a row, and how to scan them for movable cards. I show her how to build up her row stacks, and tell her about how my sisters taught me to play solitaire so I'd stop bugging them to braid my hair.

Sammy looks at my short, straightened hair skeptically.

"Used to be long enough to braid," I say.

Solitaire is sort of a complicated game to teach to a six-year-old, but I see that she is smart and she picks up fast. Before long I stand up, watch her start to play. Right away she starts cheating.

"Now that's not playing the game right," I say, "when you dig under the piles like that. If you cheat, what's the point?"

"The point is I'll win," Sammy says, not looking up at me.

I turn around and see Cutie frowning in the doorway. She is wearing a housedress today and looks out of sorts. Her hair needs combing. She has the catalog from the State Farm man under one arm and a cup of coffee in her hand.

"Don't you cheat," Cutie says. "Loretta, if you see her cheating, take the cards away from her."

I roll my eyes. "She's six," I say.

Cutie settles into her rocking chair. "We'll both of us sit here and watch you," she tells Sammy. Sammy just looks scornfully up at her. I think about the temper tantrum she must have thrown when her mama told her she was coming over today.

"Well, maybe I don't want to play anymore then."

She adjusts her game to the made-up one she was playing earlier. I can hear soft little mumbles as she makes the queens talk bossy to all the rest of the cards.

Cutie licks her thumb and starts paging through the catalog. She shakes her head at what is offered.

"Maybe you should just take the money, Mrs. Young," I say.

"What do I need with forty thousand dollars," she says. "An old lady like me."

At the mention of money Sammy's ears perk up. "What money?"

"Never mind," Cutie says.

"What's it for?" Sammy asks. "Why won't you tell me?"

"If I told you everything I know, you'd know more than me," Cutie says, but she spreads open the catalog and sets it on the floor next to Sammy. "Why don't you tell me which of these patterns you like the best?"

Sammy seems pleased with her assignment, and right away starts looking real close at the catalog. I sit back in my soft-cushioned chair and look out at the boxwoods. They are a deep, lush green-black and more than eighty years old, just like Cutie.

"My husband was born in this house," Cutie says, "and the silver was here then. His daddy was born here, and it was here then too."

It used to depress me to think of being born so close by—the idea, I guess, was that I hadn't gotten anywhere—but now I don't mind as much. I'm able to see what has changed and what has been the same, even if those are not all good things. Somehow it's a satisfying feeling, like staying to the end of a party to make sure you don't miss anything.

Andrea picks Sammy up looking like a poodle. She keeps her sunglasses on in the house. She always looks straight ahead inside Cutie's house, like she's afraid if she looks around she'll find something she has to do something about.

"You have fun?" she asks Sammy.

"I picked out new spoons for Granny," Sammy says. "So she won't have to eat with her hands."

"That's nice," Andrea says. "I got held up." Sammy walks out the door without saying good-bye and isn't scolded a bit. "Thank you for watching her, Cutie. I'm sure it was a treat."

"A treat for who," Cutie says. She has the catalog with her, but Andrea doesn't ask to see it. Andrea gives us and the place a quick once-over, and I can see Cutie, her freckled pale legs beneath the housedress, reflected in Andrea's glasses. I can smell her permanent solution from where I stand, by the stove.

When I leave I decide to go by my boat. I like to go there when I feel down. The man who's letting me pay on it keeps it docked at his pier, and he doesn't mind if I go and sit beside it for company. Well, he might mind, but he doesn't say anything. I walk down the steep and creaking steps and feel the reassuring, good feeling of seeing it sitting there. *Mattaponi Queen* is spelled out on the hull, in peeling black letters. The first thing I'll do is go over them so people don't mistake: Loretta is the Mattaponi Queen now.

I lower myself slowly to the pier, let my legs swing down. They don't touch the green surface of the water, as smooth as glass. The water reflects my legs back to me, and I think about Cutie's poor, veiny legs sticking out from under her dress. Anchoring her wherever she stands, white and stubborn as she is.

Cutie, not Horace, was the one Ruth focused her bitterness on. The way she hardly ever left the house, not even to grocery-shop; she had "girls" to do that for her. Ruth would have hated to see me working for her, I know that much, and I wonder sometimes why it doesn't bother me more than it does. Maybe it's seeing Cutie reduced and weak, or maybe it's just the easy money.

When Tamara was six, Ruth finally got the nerve to go over there. Put on her best clothes, her town hat and gloves, walked right up the front steps. Even the Jehovah's Witnesses knew not to do that.

Cutie opened the door and looked at Ruth with a start.

Your son, Ruth began, and my daughter—

Cutie looked her up and down like she had never seen her in her life—you know the look—and then she shut the door in my sister's face.

The boat is as still as a house. The windows inside the cabin part, where you steer the boat, are frosted over with dirt and dried spray, so all you can see inside is darkness. Not a ripple disturbs the water; it is like a new-paved road.

I know a boat can't tell you anything you don't want to know. All it says is get away, get away.

It's finally coming on fall, but still hot. My riverboat is still flaking paint into the river; I've made a practice of visiting it on Fridays. The sycamore leaves are curling up and falling into the street. At school, Sammy is already on warning for being sassy, Cutie tells me. On warning, I laugh. What are they gonna do about it?

It's time to put away the tomato stakes and can what's left. When there's a cool day, Cutie and I will put up some pickles and stewed tomatoes. She says I can have some to take home too, like she's doing me a favor.

I should think so, I say.

By December, I'll have enough to make my final boat payment and the repairs besides, and I'll stop working for Cutie. Thank God, Tamara says. I can't imagine.

You do what you have to do to get what you need, I say to her. Isn't that right? It's what my father did, and your grandfather and everybody's mother.

I go to her house more often, now that she is expecting. We're painting the second bedroom yellow and bordering it with a purple paper we found at Walmart. Tamara knows somebody who says she can paint pansies here and there for an accent. We don't know, but I hope it's a girl. A sassy one.

She's mostly stopped drinking and running around, and Charlie has a state job working road crews. He's actually a foreman. Tell him to get a crew on your old road, I say. Lay some asphalt down here. I am still parking my car in the ditch and walking to get to her house, but like I said it's still warm out.

Sometimes he has to be gone for a couple of days at a time, and on those days I stay the night with Tamara and tell her stories about her grandma and me. How we used to run around before we got married, which was something I'd forgotten until she showed me this old sparkly dress of Ruth's. Also about being kids and fishing and playing in the woods, all that stuff. Cakewalks. Church picnics. The old days. We don't mention the Youngs.

When Charlie comes home Tamara makes a big meal and sets a place for him at the head of the table. She goes to a special drawer in the kitchen and gets out a fork, a knife, and a spoon. Imperial Chrysanthemum, heavy as lead. We don't ever speak of it, but I guess he saved those pieces just for himself.

Cutie keeps the check she got from State Farm on her dresser, under a jelly glass. I've told her a bunch of times I'll drive her to the bank, but the Squire is in the shop, and she says she doesn't like to ride in my car. I think it embarrasses her to need something material of mine. I also think she doesn't want to cash that check.

When I am feeling nice I think about me and Cutie doing something together with the money, going to South Carolina to the beach for the winter maybe, or taking a trip to Italy, away from all these fools. On my meaner days I go to the drawer at Tamara's. I like the cold, briny taste of a silver spoon in my mouth.

Opportunity

Lila cursed herself for getting talked into hosting a Career Day at the elementary school. Now, with two weeks to go, she had lined up only four speakers, a meager column even in her own voluminous, slanting script: the zealously Christian editor of the *County Crier;* a hard-of-hearing, government-subsidized soybean farmer; a breeder of Labrador retrievers; and Ricky Davis, owner of the McDonald's franchise in West Point and brother-in-law to third-grade teacher Brenda Davis, who came up with the whole stupid idea of Career Day. Ricky Davis cleared a quarter million a year and Ms. Davis had just wanted to show him off.

Lila did not often let herself get talked into things, but she had been distracted by the effort that went into Ms. Davis's typed memo (albeit on her kitten stationery) and had honestly thought their county could produce more careers than four. Now she had to scramble, perhaps look as far away as Tappahannock and Mechanicsville or even Richmond to find suitable speakers, a task that somewhat defeated the theme she had chosen and spelled out on the school marquee: Careers in the Community. But she didn't want her students to think the only profitable job was running a McDonald's, and besides, she was scheduled to talk about the results at an upcoming principals' conference. At their last meeting, it had been the only accomplishment she could think of on the topic of "outreach." The other principals, in their jeans and sweaters and clog shoes, disheveled, happy women who let their children's parents call them by their first names, names like Shirley and Marge, had nodded eagerly and encouraged her to *share*.

"Oughta ask Byron to come speak," her father, Moe, said at their weekly dinner, cooked and served by Lila in his house, using recipes from Lila's mother's paperboard file box. Mentioning Byron's name perked him up. "He could play his bass."

Lila had shrugged. The children would have gone wild for that. Even his hair would give them a thrill, she was sure. "Not much of a career, if you ask me. Not much of a thing to put in front of *children.*"

Now she made a paltry list of other businesspeople nearby:

Feed & Supply Store owner?
Tire Shop guy?
Pharmacist?

Nowhere on that list was there a spot for "tour musician."

Byron Charles was Lila's last boyfriend, a man too handsome to stick around for long. They had dated, off and on, for five years, mostly in the summertime, when he was playing bass at local shows for Patti LaBelle and Lila had time to spend with him. Byron had dreadlocked hair he wore tied back, muscular arms under printed-silk shirts, and a smooth, soothing voice that sounded especially good on the telephone. They could talk for hours. He lived in Oxon Hill, Maryland.

He was not a regular kind of boyfriend, Lila allowed to her friend Donnelle when they first started seeing each other. He didn't call her on weeknights, ever, and she didn't have any of his things stored in her house. But then she was too tired for phone calls on weeknights, and she didn't have closet space for anyone's things but her own and her mother's.

How about the grocery store? Donnelle asked. Has he ever gone with you to the grocery store? Donnelle had once told her she would prefer the old days, when you might have married someone distantly related, some sort of cousin. At least then you knew what you were getting, she said: that was the kind of romantic interest she took in men.

Once, Lila said. They had gone to the Food Lion in Tappahannock to get steaks for the grill.

He push a cart?

No, Lila remembered. He had not. Instead he gathered their things awkwardly in his arms, as if he were going to run off with them, leaving her standing alone and embarrassed. She had grown panicked then, standing in the checkout line. She had been afraid of being deserted. That part she did not share with Donnelle.

His fingers, she said. They were strong from plucking the heavy bass strings, and it was nice to be touched by such strong fingers.

Outreach. A stupid, invented word, white and mealy and weak. Lila was forty, never married, the only child of an aging parent. Her teachers were paid the lowest wages in the state, and it showed in their teaching, which like their paychecks lacked vigor and energy and dignity. It showed in the students' test scores, also low. It was a matter of time before the parents of her few gifted students figured things out for themselves and sprung for tuition at the country day school. It was always the slightly better-off parents whose kids did better; Lila watched for proof to the contrary but was mostly disappointed.

Her mother died of cancer of the breast and sometimes Lila felt that she was carrying the cancer around too, in her own full and heavy breasts. They ached. They had pangs, sharp stabbing pains as she sat at her desk or walked the halls with her stapler, fixing torn bulletin board borders. She had them checked by a doctor twice a year. Donnelle said this was from never having children; sometimes her breasts felt that way too.

Lila had graduated cum laude from the teachers college at Longwood, and had gotten her administrative degree from Mary Washington College after only a few years in the classroom. Her dream had been to move to Washington, D.C., and deal with tough high school kids, straightening them out with her own tough country smarts. She would move up the ladder from there. But that was not how things worked out. Her mother got sick and needed her nearby; then she died and Lila bought a house near the river and let her father fill every weekend with his own needs. There was no ladder to climb, not really, despite her beautiful suits, her timely paperwork, her careful and immaculate speech.

It was not so bad, her job. It was there whether test scores went up or down. The students had their challenges, even if they were not so exotic: parents who beat them, lice and general lack of hygiene, absent dads who skipped their child support, mothers with drug problems, though the main problem, Lila thought, was a lack of perspective, a failure of imagination. Each year they held a 4-H fair and a science fair, and each year the very same projects—algal blooms in Mason jars, bottle-fed baby goats, volcanoes made from baking soda and vinegar—were on display. Each grade had a field trip in spring, fixed so that no one saw the same thing twice: the volunteer fire station for kindergarten, the Indian reservation for first grade, the science museum in Richmond for second, and so on, farther and farther away from the school until the fifth grade took their class trip to Virginia Beach. Many of the children had never even been to Richmond, except on field trips, and they always squealed and made a ruckus going into the unfamiliar marine darkness of the Hampton Roads tunnel.

Lila's home was a tidy brick rancher with an attached garage a little ways off the Mattaponi. There she had a closetful of apple and chalkboard-themed knickknacks given by parents and teachers. She had, from a child whose father was a taxidermist, a turkey-foot key holder whose claw gave you the finger. Its middle claw was where you hung your keys. It was the only gift Lila displayed.

What she missed most out of life was her mother. Byron had lost his mother, too. Lila thought this might bring them closer, but instead it left a sort of wall between them, as if in their mutual understanding they couldn't do the pretending necessary for love. No one will love you like your mother did, he told her sadly. Nobody's never gonna love you like that again.

"It's getting on time for Kings Dominion to open," Moe said. Lila had stopped by to bring him his vitamins. He was waiting inside the doorway with his fingers hooked into his belt loops.

Kings Dominion, a treeless amusement park with an amphitheater next to its decaying safari village, was where the big R&B and country acts performed. The list of seasonal names and dates appeared on the marquee around opening weekend at the end of March each year.

"That's enough of that," she said.

"You should call him up," Moe said. "I bet he'd be pleased. How many acts have you got lined up?"

"They're not acts."

"Talkers, then. How many?"

"Only four definite," Lila said breezily. She reached into her shopping bag and brought out the amber jars of vitamins and directions handwritten on index cards. He scowled at them.

"You didn't treat him well enough," Moe said. "Your mother treated me like a king every day we were married."

When Lila didn't say anything back, he repeated, "You should call him."

"I don't think I have his number anymore," Lila muttered. "Your forsythia needs pruning." Moe belonged to the let-wild-things-be-wild school of thought. Lila liked a neat yard.

"But you do have his number," Donnelle said, when Lila told her about it. Donnelle came over once a week for the Parker House rolls Lila got from the school cafeteria. They came frozen on a foil tray. She heated them in the toaster oven with butter brushed on top and they ate them with honey or ham by the dozen.

"I suppose I do," Lila said. "So?"

"It's been a while, but you look the same."

"He could have a girlfriend."

"So?"

"Maybe *you* ought to look him up."

"Maybe I will," Donnelle said. "My birthday is coming."

They laughed and popped more rolls in their mouths. It seemed to Lila that they dissolved on the tongue. The kitchen had a sweet, close, yeasty smell. From the bay window where they sat they could see warm sunset colors reflected on the Mattaponi's surface. Lila liked to think of Donnelle as Toad to her Frog. The *Frog and Toad* books were her favorites and she often carried one around with her at school in case she had the opportunity to read to a class. See? she would say. It's good to have a friend to talk to. Or, good friends always help each other out. Though it felt a little forced to her, she really did love Frog and Toad: their cozy homes, their steady friendship.

If she really thought about it, she was not much like Frog at all. Frog was always quietly right. He was self-contained; he didn't gossip. He went barefoot and swam with no clothes on.

"You could do a talk, couldn't you, Donnelle?" Donnelle owned half of a Slender Lady workout club in West Point and sold Avon products out of her house.

"Oh no," Donnelle said. "You wouldn't want me."

Byron, once mentioned, began to seem more missing. Moe did not talk about him at their next dinner, but Lila could feel her father *thinking* about him. He would pause his slow chewing and smile to himself. What? Lila would ask sharply, and Moe would say, Nothing, still smiling a little. Stop that, she wanted to yell across the Formica table, never as clean as when she'd last left it. You let me do the remembering.

Byron knew the best places to go, even around here. He took her dancing at a black club in Ashland and to a restaurant she'd never heard of in Tappahannock. They had eaten oysters and drunk champagne on a screened-in gazebo overlooking the river. Once they even went to church, but just to stand outside near the gravestones and listen to the choir. Always, they wound up back at her place and for as long as he was there Lila kept the ringer off. Except for the times when his visits coincided with her weekly dinner with Moe, Byron kept her either in the bed or in the kitchen cooking when he visited. He sang her little songs and washed her back with scented soaps in her sunken Jacuzzi tub, which she'd had installed with the money her mother had left her. Admiring her house and her newish car, he said he liked a woman who worked for a living, like he was used to another kind. She had never visited his house, but he said it wasn't as nice as hers. It needed a woman's touch, he would say, and then he'd kiss her neck and there would be no more talk of that.

At around four o'clock on a Monday, after everyone at work had gone home, the county sheriff's deputy called Lila at work. She was sitting at her desk, shoes off, massaging her insteps with a rolling contraption she'd ordered online. Moe had been picked up for driving without a license. Did she know that he had no license? That he had never had a license?

"No," Lila said. She had no idea.

"Well, he doesn't," said the deputy, and waited, as if Lila were supposed to say something to atone for this.

"I asked him if he'd ever had one and he said no," the deputy went on. "So I asked him why not, and he said he never went anywhere.

"So I said, 'Looks to me like you're headed somewhere,' and do you know what your father says?"

Lila waited for him to continue.

"He says, 'I'm not. I'm just going to Riley's store.'" Then the deputy laughed until Lila interrupted him to ask what she needed to do, and he thought for a minute and said, "Nothing." They'd called ahead to Riley's store, and Riley had called his brother, an attorney for the state. He was arranging, as a favor, for Moe to take the driver's exam at a DMV in Deltaville.

"So you see that your father has friends," the deputy concluded.

"I suppose he does," Lila said.

"Even me," said the deputy. "I'm the one that called Riley."

Lila thanked him for taking the time. He stalled for a while longer before halfway asking her out. He had seen her around and wanted to know if she had plans to go to the fire department's pancake supper.

Lila told him she always went to the pancake supper, but only for a little while. She didn't want to specify a time when she would be there. She was a busy woman.

Sometimes Lila pictured Byron at home. She imagined that he ate takeout every night and had an empty fridge and corners that needed sweeping, but for all she knew he had a full-time girlfriend cooking for him and keeping the house clean while he was away. For all she knew, though she hated to admit it, he was married. She'd been out with his band a few times and they never mentioned it, but wasn't that the way with men? They never would have said a word.

Lila didn't like to watch Byron perform for a crowd. It just reminded her how he did not belong to her any more than anyone else. Patti LaBelle and her music, brassy and synthesized and insistent, swelling at the high notes, had a stronger claim to Byron than did Lila.

Lila went to only one of his Kings Dominion concerts, on a sweltering August afternoon in the year they first met. To enter the park she had to pass through metal detectors, which were set up specially for black acts. Park officials blamed the problem, the need for precautionary measures, on a "D.C. crowd" when Lila questioned them at the ticketing window. They said it apologetically, conspiratorially, as if Lila would understand. After passing through the temporary plastic gates into the bright unfiltered sunshine of International Street, Lila felt suddenly trapped and out of place, awkward in her slacks and blouse. She held her backstage pass in her hand, ladylike, instead of wearing it around her neck.

Teenagers in baseball caps and oversized sports jerseys thronged the Belgian waffle stand, the tissue-flower vendor, the cotton candy and kettle corn machines. Lila searched their faces for a former student, but they were unfamiliar. As usual, she was early. She could go to the amphitheater, but it wasn't shaded and she hadn't brought anything to read. It was possible, she supposed, to look for the trailer, but she'd rather that Byron look for her at the end.

It was nearing dusk when the concert started. The teenagers who had filled the park and caused the extra security measures sat respectfully on stone benches, waiting. Lila took her seat off to the side and craned her neck to see Byron's tall, handsome shape.

"How y'all doin' tonight?" Patti LaBelle asked, and everyone stood and cheered. She was wearing a shimmery gold pantsuit, big gold earrings like saucers. Lila narrowed her eyes at Ms. LaBelle; it seemed to her that Byron was following her around the stage with his eyes. You're being ridiculous, she told herself. That's his job. But then she could not help thinking mean thoughts about Patti LaBelle.

Surely that's not her hair.

What black woman needs hair that color?

They played about a dozen songs—"If Only You Knew" and "Lady Marmalade," "New Attitude," "When You Talk about Love." She stayed alert for people she knew and didn't dance much during the show, though she loved to dance. The whole time she tried to catch Byron's eye but failed. He would be looking at his hands on the bass strings or at the guitar player or the keyboardist or at Patti LaBelle.

To keep her mind occupied, Lila tried to count all the people associated with the band. There were ten people onstage performing, then there were the lighting people, and the roadies, even the drivers of the buses. How strange their lives must be, Lila thought, never staying in the same place long enough to unpack a suitcase. She wondered if it got boring, all the going and going, if it made travel for fun impossible. She wondered what their houses were like. Were they as glad to see a full refrigerator as Byron was? Maybe, Lila thought, all those men in the band had women here in the crowd somewhere, foolish women like her, waiting to cook for them and love them.

And then the concert was over. Lila moved against the tide of fans, her pass held aloft, toward the backstage area.

"Hey baby," Byron said when he spotted her. He was slick with sweat but still smelled good, as always, when he went to hug her. She blushed as he held her chin and kissed her on the mouth. She was already thinking of what they would do when they got home. "What you want to eat?"

"I've got you something fixed at home already," she'd said, which was code for let's get out of here.

After that she mostly met him after shows, in the parking lot or at her house.

They didn't see much of each other in the winter.

Moe was not keen on taking the driver's test. "It's a far way to go for somebody who never goes nowhere," he told Lila. His car was seventeen years old and had only twenty-three thousand miles on it.

"Riley said he would drive," Lila said. She had brought over a KFC dinner, which Moe pretended to be offended by even though he loved KFC. She felt morose because Career Day was in a week and a half and it seemed, at this point, too late to call Byron. A few more people had come through, a nurse and an occupational therapist and a high school basketball coach and gym teacher. The owner of the kitty litter factory across the river. The sheriff's deputy, who promised to bring a suitcase of confiscated drugs and firearms to show.

Moe shook his head. "I don't want to drive no one else's car for my test. My car is the only car I know."

Lila rolled her eyes. "They won't make you take the driving part of the test, Daddy."

"And what if they do?" he asked. "I don't see why I need a license, when I've been driving safe in this county since I was fourteen. I drove a truck full of chickens for five years and I never lost a chicken."

"If you don't take the test," Lila said, "you'll owe a fine. And you won't get to drive anymore."

Moe frowned into his mashed potatoes, wet with butter and gravy. "I never go nowhere anyway."

Lila started to get calls on Monday, the day of Moe's test, at a little after noon. We're about to leave now, the sheriff's deputy said. His name was Ben. He would follow behind Moe to make sure he made it there all right.

"Okay," Lila said.

"We're in West Point now," he said, an hour later. He was calling from his car. Lila could see how this was going.

By the time they reached the DMV, it was closed. Lila felt bad for the deputy. "I should have thought to warn you," she said when he called to tell her about it, "how slowly he drives."

Ben brushed off her apologies. It was a nice drive anyway, he said. Next time they would leave earlier.

Next time? Lila asked.

Sure, he said. He's not gonna give up now, you think?

Lila felt him angling for a date and so she got off the phone. Ben was younger than she, and skinny and white and a policeman. That might have done for someone like one of the teachers at her school, someone who wore sweaters when it was warm out, who liked things safe and plain, but it would not do for her.

That Ben fellow, Moe said later. Nice but a little dim. He must have pulled him over four times to tell him to drive faster, or to keep off the shoulder. They might have made it without all the pulling over.

Lila and Byron had met at a flower show in Richmond. It was an annual thing, and she'd been walking aimlessly for about an hour when his pace fell into step with hers. They walked around and around the orchids without talking, sneaking sly glances and brushing hands and shoulders. The theme of the show that year was porches, and all the displays were set up to look like front porches, with picket fences and porch swings overgrown with flowers. The convention center was dim and high-ceilinged, so the whole effect was like walking around a pretty neighborhood at night with a beau. It would have made a nice story about the magical beginning of a relationship, an old-fashioned courtship for modern times, except that they wound up that afternoon in a Howard Johnson motel. By then she could mostly tell how it was going to be. It only occurred to her later that Byron had gone to the flower show to pick up a woman like herself, and that made the advantage his; she had only gone to look at flowers.

The last time he called was before a big tour. They were going to all the cities in the Midwest: Chicago, Cleveland, Detroit. He had sounded excited on the phone, and also slightly drunk. He would call her when he got back home, he said. There were dates booked at Kings Dominion in the spring; he would surely see her then.

Those dates came, and then they went. Lila didn't go because he didn't call. She was mean by June; she put letters of reprimand in six teachers' files. Two quit, then came back the following September when they could find no other work.

Her mother had taught her to let the man call her, Lila explained to Donnelle.

She didn't teach you to do some of those other things you do with men, Donnelle said. Did she?

"I told him you'd go out with him," Moe said. "I told him Friday night."

He had returned from Saluda the second time with a driver's license and some nonsense about a date with the sheriff's deputy. He'd shown Lila the license before he told her about the date. He looked both surprised and tired without his glasses; his height and weight were all wrong.

"I told them I never go nowhere *without* my glasses," he was saying. He held the license in his hand and stared at it. "But they said I had to take them off because of the glare. Now it don't even look like me."

"You said I'd do *what?*" Lila asked. She breathed in slowly, set her bag down on the counter, picked it up again and hung it on the back of one of Moe's chairs. She pressed her fingers against her eyelids.

"I said I thought you'd go out with him," Moe said, pretending to look through some mail. "He went with me all that way. Plus when's the last time you even went somewhere with a man?"

Lila just stood there, seething.

"Now don't get all excited," Moe said. "It's just a date. He's taking you to Outback. You like Outback.

"You can't go being lonely all your life," he said.

"This is barbaric," she finally sputtered before grabbing her bag and marching out the door. She tripped on the step but kept her pace all the way to her car and did not turn around once to see her father standing there.

Ben called to confirm on Wednesday. He didn't have her phone number at home so he called her at work, leaving a message with the secretary while she was on the other line.

"He's *cute*," the secretary squealed, setting the message down on her desk and smiling. Ben had come in the week before for an unnecessary meeting he'd scheduled about Career Day, and all the office staff had ogled him in his deputy's uniform. Lila rolled her eyes. She might as well get it over with, she thought. There were worse things than being taken out to dinner on a Friday night. She'd have to listen to some boring law enforcement stories and suffer his flattery, but it was true that he'd helped her out with Moe. She would explain that she just wasn't looking for a relationship. She had her work to think about, her career.

On the night of their date she was surprised to see him pull up in an Acura sedan. She thought all men like him drove pickups in their off time. She didn't invite him inside.

"You've got a great place here," he said as they left her driveway. "Brick house, riverfront property, right near the boat landing." He whistled.

"I've lived there for ten years," Lila said. She didn't want him thinking she'd paid the house's current value. In the past few years everything near the water had doubled in price; now you'd be lucky to get something near Moe's place for what Lila paid.

"Smart," he said. "Me, I don't own. I rent."

"Oh?" Lila said. It didn't surprise her; he probably made about as much as one of her teachers.

"I like to be free," he said. "I like to travel. How about you?"

"Travel?" Lila said. She looked at the side of his face. He was wearing polarized sunglasses but she could see now that he was younger than she even guessed, maybe thirty? Smooth skin, just a couple of smile lines, a tiny bit of stubble. He had the kind of skin that flushed easily. Pink. He was skinny but he had good shoulders. "I guess I like it as much as anybody. I don't have as much time as I'd like."

"Time?" he said. "Don't you have summers off?"

"Not really," she said. "I do get more time off than most people."

"Man," he said, stopping at the light at Central Garage. "I've been to Amsterdam and Paris. Last year I went on this tour to Laos and Cambodia and Thailand. You ever been anywhere like that, Lila?"

No, she allowed. She had not.

"You gotta go," he said. The light turned green and he crossed the intersection instead of turning onto 360, the way she always went. "You gotta see the way the people live there. It's just *different*. I'm telling you, growing up, I never thought I'd go places like that. I thought the Eiffel Tower looked just like the one they've got in Doswell."

"You grew up near here?"

"Yep," he said. "Proud product of the King William County school system. You don't mind if I take the scenic route, do you?"

She said she didn't mind.

Over their fried-onion appetizer, Ben told her about some of his favorite meals: a picnic of bread and sausage on the Champs de Mars, coconut rice wrapped in banana leaves eaten standing on a sidewalk in Bangkok. He couldn't believe that a woman like Lila had never even been to Paris. Lila didn't ask him how he afforded his trips or with whom he shared them or when he'd graduated from King William, what he'd done after that. She didn't want her surprise to show so she focused on the food, deconstructing the anemone-like onion with a knife and fork, nodding. The lamps cast a warm yellow light on the fake rough-hewn table. Finally she asked him where he'd gotten the travel bug: Was it a teacher or a relative? A book?

He shook his head. He couldn't narrow it down to one thing, he said. He said he just started with that first tour of Europe—he'd had a girlfriend who wanted to go—and after that it became a habit.

"A habit," Lila repeated. "And the girlfriend?"

"She's married now," he said.

"So you go alone?"

"Pretty much," he said. Their steaks arrived. Ben tucked into his with the energy of a teenager, and Lila felt herself thinking about other things. She flushed, looked at her plate.

"But you always come back," she said.

"Sure I do. I live here."

Lila had never kissed a white man before. She didn't know what she expected—a different taste, like vanilla cookies? A movie-scene softness and slowness? But kissing Ben in her driveway was the same as kissing any man she'd chosen to kiss; she just closed her eyes like always, let it take her where it was going to take her.

Ben was quick and eager, leaning over to her side of the car. He cradled her neck with his hand and made little appreciative noises: *mmm, mmm.* She ran her fingers through his short, straw-dry hair. It was a good thing she had a long driveway, bamboo and cedar planted all around her property line for privacy. The moon was high overhead. The crushed oyster shells shone white in the driveway like something out of a fairy tale, crunched softly under their feet as they made their way toward Lila's house.

Monday morning Lila had to push her good mood down, ignore the secretary's questions and sly looks. She gave herself distasteful tasks to keep her mind off Friday night, to keep herself from thinking about him. She cleaned out her in-box, started to work on her summer school budget. The day passed slowly.

Right as school let out she left for the party store in Doswell, where she would buy paper napkins and plates for the refreshments she planned to serve at Career Day. While she was there she would check out Kings Dominion's marquee.

The trip was a straight shot thirty-five miles down Route 30, a road populated mainly by truckers hauling timber and, in the wintertime, hunters in pickups looking for empty woods and fields. You passed through Central Garage, with its three gas stations and its loitering teens—the big brothers and sisters of her students—then there was hardly a turnoff until you passed Route 1, the old-fashioned way to Washington, D.C. Route 30 to Route 1, that was the way Ben had driven them Friday night to Outback Steakhouse. It was the same way her mother had driven Lila on their annual trip to the Smithsonian. They would stop to eat in Fredericksburg, always at the same place, where they split a sandwich and drank iced tea. Lila remembered that Cita had worn gloves, even though they were going out of fashion by then. It was something Cita's mother had taught her.

Cita was only fifty-seven when she died. The illness was short, just a few months, and terrible. Lila had to throw away all the sheets and towels, even some of the rugs, when it was over. She got the metal hospital bed out in a hurry, arranged the funeral herself and to her mother's exact specifications: the flowers, the hymns, everything. The worst part was that she had been alone; Moe left for his sister's when the chemo started and Cita couldn't so much as hold her head up or get to the bathroom. He didn't take any of his things, not even the car. Just up and left. Hitchhiked, Lila guessed.

He'll be back, her mother told her. He couldn't watch your birth either.

Lila called her aunt Rose and told her to bring him back. She had a job, she said, and he was retired and he was her daddy, and Cita's husband besides. Rose was truly country—more so than Moe—and she just hemmed and hawed. Some mens is built one way, and some mens is built another, she said. Moe Perkins never could stand the sight of blood.

He came back for the funeral and never left the two counties, King William or King and Queen, again. He was older when he came back, and Lila was too. She forgave him because her mother told her to. But when Rose got sick with diabetes and had to have her feet cut off Lila didn't go. She didn't even send a casserole.

She had wanted to tell all of these things to Byron, especially the part about her aunt and about the metal bed. It had always seemed like there was time for getting serious.

After Route 1 the landscape changed abruptly—it grew hilly and pastured, with fields of horses lined by freshly painted white fences. Then, to spoil the view, there were the signs of Kings Dominion: the stilled metal roller coasters, so much taller and more unnatural-looking than the old wooden ones; the squat, blue Eiffel Tower, only ten stories high and topped with its graceless, bubble-shaped observation deck.

It was a gray day; the sky matched the cracked asphalt of the empty parking lot where Lila pulled in. She read the dingy marquee list three times, her mouth drawn in a tight line.

All country and Christian acts. No Patti LaBelle. Maybe they lost the lease on their metal detectors, Lila thought. She closed her eyes and thought about Byron's long dreads, their smell and feel against her face. *I kissed a white man Friday night, you damn fool. I brought him into my bed on our first date.* She wished she could tell him. She knew he slept with plenty of white women.

The next morning, soaping up in her Jacuzzi tub while she sipped coffee in the doorway, Ben had said she was different. He grinned like a puppy dog, splashed water everywhere. She didn't take any crap off people; he liked that. She was independent and smart.

And fast, she thought. You probably like that too.

She gave him cold cereal and coffee and kicked him out around ten. Don't go getting any ideas, she said, standing there with her arms crossed. She was wearing a silk kimono, her hair was loose and shining. In the hall mirror she was surprised by her looks; she was what some people call beautiful.

And what ideas would that be? He had bent to kiss her cheek before he left.

She sat staring at the marquee for a long time, hands on the steering wheel, as if she could will someone to come change it. Far off, she could see a single test car slowly climbing one of the coasters. How long are you gonna stay lonely? she asked herself.

Just 'cause you're alone, her mama always told her when she was little and had no one to play with, that doesn't mean you have to be lonely.

It was a chilly, damp spring. She'd told Ben not to call her. She was so busy, she said, getting ready for this Career Day.

"Opportunity," Ricky Davis was saying to the gymnasium of students. He was speaking into a microphone, pacing inside a large, imaginary rectangle. He let the word hang there for a minute. "Opportunity comes knocking, you've got to answer the door."

Lila could feel the gym teacher looking nervously at Ricky Davis's cowboy boots. His rectangle extended beyond the brown paper cover taped over the gym floor. She held a cup of coffee in her hand and stood behind where he was speaking, at her own podium. To the side was a table with all the other guests seated in a row: the Labrador breeder, the newspaper editor, the nurse in her uniform, the occupational therapist, an auto mechanic, the high school basketball coach, the owner of the kitty litter plant, Ben with his suitcase full of contraband. The soybean farmer's rheumatism was acting up and he couldn't come.

Ben looked over at her. He gave her a long stare, a smile in the corners of his mouth.

Lila shifted her gaze to the audience of listless but well-behaved students all slumped in the bleachers.

"It doesn't knock twice!" Ricky Davis was shouting now. Ms. Davis sat rapt in the first row, her feet planted neatly on the floor. He must have thought they needed a motivational speaker; so far the mechanics of buying and operating a fast-food franchise had not come up.

Lila would interrupt him momentarily to guide him with questions, which she jotted quickly on her notepad. Did you have to go to school first? What degree did you take? Do you have any partners? What are the challenges of operating a fast-food franchise?

She took a sip of coffee and it scalded her tongue. It was bad coffee anyway, burned and oily-tasting, ordered from the Fas Mart along with a few dozen doughnuts. They looked pale and unappetizing on their white plates. That morning Moe had called to tell her he was going to Saluda and did she want anything? Saluda, she'd said. What's in Saluda?

I don't know, Moe said. That's the point.

Now that he had his license, he was driving more places. He said there was more to see than he thought.

"Don't let it pass you by!" Ricky Davis fairly screamed.

The scald would be there for days, Lila thought, as rough as sandpaper in her mouth. She glanced at her watch; Moe was probably halfway to Saluda now. Byron was on the road, she felt sure of it. In a few months, Ben said, he was off to Alaska for a week to see the humpback whales. He was working nights as a security guard to save up. Maybe next time she could ask Ben to talk to her students about one of his trips. He could bring photographs, they could have a slide show. They could see rice fields and houseboats, whales cresting the cold Pacific waters. They could see the real Eiffel Tower.

She bent down to her microphone to ask her questions, but the words came out wrong.

"What road?" she said, too loudly.

Ricky Davis turned to her, startled, and looked ready to answer her question before she apologized and began again, working from the list.

It Won't Be Long

Wayne "Skinny" Littleton lived with the expectation of not living much longer, but this had been going on for years now. Why don't you just get on with it? his friend Bruce would ask. Bruce's two mutts, Brooks and Dunn, had been digging a trench next to Bruce's house for almost as long as Skinny had been dying. Flanked by high mounds of excavated gray-brown dirt, it approached the width of a grave. You wouldn't want to hurt their feelings, Bruce teased. They've worked so hard on it.

Skinny didn't mind joking about his death. He had a drug-resistant strain of hepatitis C, he'd been an alcoholic and a painkiller addict for years, and he never expected to live this long. Sometimes, when the ache that collected his joints and muscles and organs into its tight net got really bad, when he couldn't throw it off with Percocet and Budweiser, he even looked forward to dying. He imagined, by comparison with the ache, that it would be a relief.

But the truth was he had gotten used to living. He had his regular customers with their steadily deteriorating vehicles, all dependent on him; he had his friends, his cooking shows. He had his house to work on, to finish; he wanted to put in a hot tub and a second bathroom. He had his kids, Erin and Tyler, who could hardly be called kids anymore and with whom he communicated mostly by telephone. He looked forward to small things: Friday-night bluegrass on the public radio station, driving across the reservation to Bruce's house for supper, fishing the Mattaponi in his dented aluminum johnboat. His first beer of the morning, his last beer of the night, and all the beers in the middle.

Sometimes he caught himself looking forward to these things, anticipating them, and he'd feel a terrible, helpless sadness at the very smallness of what he would miss: phone calls to Erin, the smell of garlic cooking in olive oil, even work. Then he'd tell himself it wasn't sadness, after all, but self-pity. In July his skin was jaundiced, his belly distended and tender and hostile to any solid food. The doctor told him he should get his affairs in order, it wouldn't be long. He said it so casually, leaning back in his office chair with a clipboard on his knee like a newspaper, that Skinny wasn't sure, at first, what he meant.

"Won't be long until what?" he said.

"I'm sorry," the doctor said, putting the clipboard down and leaning forward, a pained but professional expression on his face. He'd known Skinny for years, but he must have known dozens of other guys just like him. On his desk family photos—a smiling blond woman on a boat, a thin shirtless boy holding a fish—faced out at Skinny like a rebuke. He had no framed family photos, no desk even.

And now he was dying.

His Indian name was Lone Fox, for the way his birth—he was an only child—crept up on his aging parents, but nobody used their Indian name anymore, not even the chief. His mother was Mattaponi, his father Pamunkey; they'd lived on the Mattaponi reservation in a small tin-roofed farmhouse on the way in to the main part of the village. Now a completely different family lived there, a husband and wife and their two teenage kids; they'd called for the lot after Skinny's parents died. Skinny was in rehab then; he wasn't even warned, though he doubted that back then anyone would have stood up for him at the council meeting to say he was an upstanding tribe member, a shepherd of tribal lands. He'd been living off and on in Richmond, renting rooms from friends for twenty-five a month, picking up what work he could, and shooting heroin. His parents' deaths, one right after the other, helped him shake it off; he went into rehab after that and traded junk for methadone.

As a boy he'd loved to fish for shad and trout with his father. They could sit in their boat for the length of a school day and barely say ten words between them. He must have been thinking of this when he moved back to King William County after he got out of rehab; he was so tired by then of talking and listening. There were no lots to call for then, and no one to stand up for him anyway, so he bought a little rancher on Route 30, the old Indian road connecting his parents' two tribes, with some of the money they'd left him. He met Sandra through an ad she'd placed in the paper. It said *Please be clean, no games*. She was a hairdresser from Warsaw, but he heard a kind of plaintive, old-fashioned poetry in her simple requests. Writing to her was like a test for himself; he passed and they married after what Bruce called a lean, mean courtship. After the divorce—she took their kids and the last of his money to a new condo in Lorton, up in northern Virginia—he called for a lot. They gave him three acres, vertical. There are no other lots, the chief said solemnly. Your father was a good man and I am sorry I don't have more to give you, but this is all there is. They were standing there at the edge of the riverside cliff, looking down into the winter-black water below. The chief had a formal way of speaking that made Skinny want to cuss.

At least you can fish here, the chief said. You can build a dock for your boat. You can build steps down to the water, and a pier.

Hell, Skinny said. I'm gonna live here if I have to build a goddamn teepee.

I don't think you'd like living in a teepee, the chief said thoughtfully. He was old, with creased sun-brown skin and thick tinted eyeglasses; he had a split-level brick house with wall-to-wall carpeting, central heat and air. But do what you like.

Skinny built his house, after all, on the idea of the teepee. There was a little building for sleeping, and a building for cooking and showering, and a building for hosting guests. Small cedar-clad shacks, they looked more like duck blinds than like teepees, but their size and close grouping suggested readiness, temporary shelter for someone on the move, just the way teepees had for Powhatan's tribe. He built them that way out of necessity—the steeply sloping cliff would not support a regular house's foundation—but over the years he'd found ways of adding small measures of comfort: a small, screened-in gazebo for summertime dining, new double-paned windows, a solar-heated water tank, cable television, a stove. Meanwhile he saw the new family on his parents' lot pull up his mother's azaleas and blue hydrangeas and replace them with plastic flowers, yellow and black, spinning in the wind on metal stakes. Skinny took the azaleas and planted them on his own banks, tended them carefully with fertilizer and pruning shears. In his memory the flowers were pale yellow and white, but they surprised him by blooming bright pink and orange, early the following April. His mother could make anything grow—she'd cultivated orchids in her sunny kitchen—and Skinny allowed himself to imagine that the success he had was due to her, that she was speaking her forgiveness through the sturdy roots and delicate, colorful blossoms. He found that he liked to look at them at a distance from his johnboat. Scattered across the brown, leafy banks, they were like the last remaining beads on her old moccasins, which he kept packed in tissue to give to Erin one day. He wanted to give them to her here so someone could show her the dances, but Erin and Tyler wouldn't come down to King William anymore.

Trips to see them, which he made once a month, took two hours each way, more with traffic. They usually met at Denny's or Applebee's and then he'd take them to the mall and buy them the things they needed—shirts and jeans, backpacks, notebooks, video games. Apart from when he was buying them something, Skinny sometimes thought they acted like they hardly knew him anymore, and he'd get mean and impatient with them. Then the whole way home he'd feel like hell, and the next time he'd remember just to buy them things.

He imagined taking the moccasins out at the mall or handing them across a table at the Olive Garden. How incongruous they would look, how removed from Erin's life. He imagined her brushing their dirt from her hands, reminded himself that he was once like her; all he had wanted to do was get away.

He told Bruce he was dying.

"Sure you're dying," said Bruce. They were sitting in rusty lawn chairs on his back porch, passing a joint back and forth. It was early evening, the sky a light gray-blue over the river. Skinny liked to smoke after his monthly doctor visits; he usually went straight to Bruce's. "You've been dying for years."

"No," Skinny said. He'd thought about it on the hour-long drive back from Richmond, and he realized the doctor was right. It was getting worse now, the tiredness and aching. And he could feel a tenderness in his belly that wasn't like that before. His liver, when he pictured it, was something extra and poisonous and unnecessary inside him, a soft, rotting fruit or lifeless piece of meat, like the actual liver his mother used to serve him, pan-dark and acrid. "Soon, I'm dying."

"Bah," Bruce said. "Doctors. You're a human cockroach, you'll outlive them all."

"Tyler turns eighteen in November," Skinny said. "He can call for my lot then. I want you to stand up for him at council."

"Tyler wants to move back here?"

"No," Skinny said. "I guess he doesn't yet." There was a rule about calling for lots; you had to live on a lot if you were going to call for it. This kept people from reserving weekend places, fishing lodges. "I want to be able to leave him something."

"That house he lives in with his mama, that was your money that bought it."

"I want to leave him something good," Skinny said. "Something he'll care about twenty years from now."

He disapproved of his ex-wife's condominium townhouse and of Tyler's choice—influenced by Sandra, no doubt—to go to the nearby community college. He helped them move in himself, though, drove the rental truck and carried his old furniture, some of it his parents', up the front steps. Inside he opened and shut closet and cabinet doors, rapped on the windowpanes, bounced his heavy frame on the stairs. Everything cheap and hollow and new. He'd told her what she could get by staying in King William or Caroline or King and Queen—a decent old farmhouse or a mid-'80s split-level or brick rancher. They could even live on the reservation on account of the kids, or keep their old place on Route 30. But she was done with that backward place, she said. She wanted to start fresh. He'd saved the real argument for the community college plan.

Let him go to a real college, he'd pleaded with her over the phone last spring. I can get him the money.

He wants to be near me, Sandra had said. He wants to look after me and Erin, and I can't fault him for that.

You can take care of yourself, Skinny told her.

Oh, can we? Sandra said. I guess that's what you always counted on.

The tribe has scholarships, programs—

You've been drinking, she said, which was her smug, smart way of saying *this conversation is over.* He could see her thin lips, her legs drawn up under her on the couch, the phone held loosely in her manicured hands.

"I hate her," Skinny said to Bruce.

"Nah," Bruce said. "You don't hate her."

"For breaking up our family, I do. You mean to tell me you don't hate Susanna, ever?"

"Susanna made her choice. Sandra made her choice. You and me, we made choices."

He got up, went inside, and put on a Tina Turner record. The needle jumped, scratched. Brooks and Dunn, their snouts covered in freshly dug dirt, whined at the screen door. Skinny let them in, killed his joint with a long slow inhale. It hadn't made a dent in the aching.

"You can't die yet," Bruce said, easing himself back down into his lawn chair. "I'm gonna be a grandpa in a couple months."

"I'm thinking about calling Susanna," Skinny said. "I think she'd want to know."

"Susanna," Bruce said sadly. "Wonder how she's doing. I guess she'll be a grandma. You have her number?"

"No," Skinny said. "I thought I'd look her up."

"That might work," Bruce said. "Then again, it might not. What if she doesn't want to talk to you?"

That hadn't occurred to Skinny. He was used to taking forgiveness from people like it was an easy thing to give, a handshake or a cup of coffee. He never thought it cost them something too.

It was growing dark. Next to the screen porch the wide trench yawned open, its cool depths darker than the air around it. Fireflies gathered, blinking, near the tree line; the black shapes of buzzards hulked above them.

"The kids," he said. "I've got to get them down here."

"Then it's Sandra you should be calling," Bruce said.

"They're old enough to make up their own minds," Skinny said. "I don't want the last place I see them to be some northern Virginia strip mall."

"Well, they sure won't come if you don't tell them," Bruce said. "You gotta be honest."

This was an easy thing for Bruce to say: earlier in the year his daughter and son-in-law came home to stay, and Bruce hadn't even needed to ask. The son-in-law lost his right arm in Iraq, but at least he wouldn't be sent back, and his daughter Ronnie was pregnant: a trade-off. They were renting a house in the next county; they ate dinner at Bruce's house every weekend, simple things like takeout pizzas, spaghetti, hamburgers, fish. Sometimes Skinny brought over stuff he'd cooked, though he didn't usually stay. He didn't want them thinking he was jealous of what Bruce had: a whole life stretched out in front of him, no end point in sight. A long string of bachelor meals served on his porch overlooking the Mattaponi.

"Aren't you sad, Bruce?"

"Course I am, damn it."

He made arrangements for Erin and Tyler to come next month to homecoming, a week of revival meetings and traditional dances on the reservation. Sandra couldn't say no—she was a sucker for anything religious—and the kids seemed to understand from his tone that it was important. He didn't say anything about dying.

After that he lay in bed and waited. He made his breath shallow, the barest scooping of air, and closed his eyes. He was weaning himself off the Percocet, taking one pill less every day, so that he would feel the pain he was supposed to feel. He'd read somewhere that dying was the most delicate art: you had to get it right the first time. Actually, he hadn't read it but had heard it in his doctor's waiting room from a transvestite with a carved, ageless face. The final curtain call, she said to no one in particular. Everyone's last memory of you. Your last memory of you.

Today the pain was twisting his bloated middle and filling him with nausea. He hadn't eaten anything more than soup for days, though he continued to cook, every night, on his little stove. Usually he took whatever he made over to Bruce's, came back home to his crackers and broth and beer.

It was a hot, bright day. Outside a Ford pickup awaited a new catalytic converter, a Volvo station wagon had been brought by for a tune-up, and the bottle-green MG he'd picked out for Tyler's eighteenth birthday present needed its entire engine rebuilt. These cars, and a few others he kept for parts, were parked on the narrow gravel lot that stretched between the roadside and the line of trees that sheltered Skinny's house and drooped with thick curtains of wisteria and kudzu. His bedroom had two windows, one facing the lot and one facing the river; through the blinds he could see sunshine glinting off the cars' windshields.

His double bed took up most of the bedroom. At the foot, atop his bureau, his television cycled mutely through Emeril, Rachael Ray, Paula Deen, and *Molto Mario* as the leafy green light passed from one side of the tiny room to the other. Every now and then Skinny looked up to tell the time. Mario was his favorite: he came on at four, a time that was late enough to be beyond work. Back when Skinny ran a shop he used to call anytime after four beer-thirty.

He sat up in his bed, propping himself on pillows, and turned up the sound with the remote. Mario was sliding sausages into a pan greased with lard. His ruddy skin shone with sweat. He looked like he might die soon too. The room was chilly; Skinny had the AC unit turned on high. He pulled the covers up around his bare chest. The pillows were soft, and he sank deeper into them. They'd been purchased a long time ago by his wife, who would sleep on nothing but down. He was surprised when she left them. I'll buy new ones, she'd said after inspecting the old ones without their cases. They were splotchy and yellow with years of his sweat.

"Hello? Skinny?" Someone was calling him, knocking on his kitchen door. Skinny slid out of bed, pulled on a T-shirt over his shorts, and peered out through the blinds. It was Bruce's daughter, Ronnie, holding an empty casserole dish and facing the kitchen door.

Skinny was embarrassed for her to see him in his bedroom. Maybe she wouldn't know he'd been in bed all day, feeling sorry for himself. He quickly walked outside and said hello.

"Oh, hi," she said, turning around. It was always a surprise to see someone pregnant when you'd known her as a child. Like her mom, Ronnie didn't wear maternity clothes, just low carpenter jeans and large men's shirts. And she was beautiful, like her mom, with the same thick black hair and dark eyes, the same perfect skin. Skinny wondered if that was some consolation to Bruce or if it made him sad. He wondered if Susanna looked the same or if the California sun had wrinkled her.

She thrust the casserole at him. "This is from my dad. He said to tell you it was good, and I agree. He let me have the last piece."

Skinny peered into the clean white dish, thinking of the squash-and-eggplant timbale he'd baked just a couple of days before. He hadn't been able to eat even a bite. "His legs broke that he has to make you do his errands?"

"I'm hanging out there today," Ronnie said. "I told him I needed a walk."

"Well, thank you," Skinny said. "You want some iced tea?" He looked at her belly. "I guess you don't want a beer."

Ronnie laughed. "I actually have to get back soon. I'm doing a painting, and the light is right at five."

"A painting, huh?" Skinny asked. "Like your mom."

A cloud passed over Ronnie's face. Of all of them, she was hardest on Susanna. Skinny figured she had every right to be.

"Sorry," he said. "You're like the good parts of her, I mean. The way you look, and the painting. Your mom was a good artist, probably not as good as you, but she never went to school for it."

Ronnie blushed. "That's sort of why I came over," she said.

"To talk about your mom?"

"No," she said. "It's the paintings I'm working on. They're all about Pocahontas, in one way or another. I'm painting scenes from her life, using the natural parts of the river as the background, and then I'm also painting her descendants, so that means people on the reservation as it is now.

"I'm only painting full-blooded people," she continued. "Which leaves a lot of people out. Me, for example. I can't paint me."

Ronnie held out her hands, spreading her fingers as if examining the whiteness—Bruce's whiteness—in them. Her nails were crusted with paint, bits of blue and green and brown caught in the cuticles.

Skinny allowed himself to think that if he'd been Ronnie's dad, instead of Bruce, her blood quantum would be $\frac{1}{1}$ instead of $\frac{1}{2}$.

"So I was thinking about you," she said. "I'd like to do your portrait, if it's okay."

"I don't know why you'd want to do that," he said. "Pocahontas—I don't guess I resemble her too much."

"I don't guess you do either," Ronnie said. "But that's not the point."

"You're not gonna steal my soul, are you?" The joking—it was a thing between them since she was little. Somehow he missed that with his own kids. They didn't like to be teased.

"Ha, ha," she said. "If you're lucky."

Skinny said again how he didn't know why she'd want to paint him, but he didn't say no. After she left he stood for a while in front of his tiny bathroom mirror—a narrow rectangle inside the door, the only mirror in his house—and regretted it. Most of him did not fit inside the mirror but he could see, in the dimming afternoon light, the bloating in his joints, the yellowness in his skin, his thinning, graying hair. You're a mess, he thought meanly. You're fit to die.

Skinny brought old photographs to the first sitting. Though he was not handsome, he was vain and over the years he had saved the pictures of himself that flattered. There was one of him sitting astride a motorcycle and wearing a tight leather vest. In another he was standing in the kitchen of his old house wearing dark aviator glasses and smiling slightly, like he had a secret, and there was another—his favorite—that showed just the top of his head bent over an acoustic guitar. He held the small pile nervously in his hands as he waited on the community pier for Ronnie. The day was warm and overcast, muggy. It was low tide, the yellowish stalks of weeds and lily pads exposed where the water had receded. The smell of mud hung in the air.

She showed up a few minutes late, struggling to carry the canvas, easel, and small leather case down the steep hill. He put the pictures in his shirt pocket and held out his arms to take what she was carrying, but she waved him off, annoyed.

"Sorry," he said. She got to work setting up the easel, screwing its parts into place. He took the photographs from his pocket to show them to her. "Here."

Ronnie looked up, surprised. "What's this?" she said. "Oh. Thanks."

"Artistic license," Skinny said. "That means you can paint me in my better days."

She flipped through the pictures quickly and handed them back. "That's okay," she said. "I prefer to paint from life."

Skinny squinted at the gray sky, put the photographs back in his pocket. He felt the beginnings of a sinus headache and wished he'd brought a beer. "It looks like rain," he said hopefully.

"Not supposed to rain," Ronnie said, not looking up. She finished with her adjustments and set the canvas in place, took up a pencil and smiled. "There," she said. She pointed with the pencil at the rusty metal porch chair that was a permanent fixture of the pier. "Sit," she said.

Skinny sighed and sat down, tried to suck in his gut so it didn't spill so obviously over his belt. He was wearing a long-sleeve button-down shirt, both to hide the sores and bruises that had begun to appear on his arms and also to keep them out of the sun. He'd started sweating, ticklish trickles running down his back and his sides and dampening his armpits. Ronnie got right to work, her pencil scratching the primed canvas as she quickly sketched. Maybe this won't take too long, he thought. Skinny sat stiffly, his breath held, his hands on his knees.

"Relax," Ronnie said after a while. "Just be natural."

"Natural means I'd have a beer about now," he said.

"You could've brought one."

"Now you tell me," he said. "Actually I think this is better. Don't want my final portrait to be something to embarrass my kids."

"Your final portrait," Ronnie repeated distractedly. "It's so bad already?"

"You mean Bruce didn't tell you?"

"Tell me what?"

"That I'm . . . not gonna live that much longer," Skinny said, exhaling. His belly flopped over his tight jeans. He couldn't believe Bruce hadn't mentioned it, but now that he thought about it, that was just like him to be so blind. So self-absorbed. "I'm sick, and I'm dying."

Ronnie stepped out from behind the easel, crossed her arms over her stomach, and frowned. "He probably doesn't believe it," she said finally. "Or else he doesn't want to believe it. I think you're right, though—this isn't natural for you, this setting. Where would you normally be this time of day?"

Bruce looked up at the sky. It was about four o'clock. "Up at the house, I guess," he said. "Working on a car or the house, or cooking maybe."

"Let's go look around your house, then," she said. "I've always liked that spot, anyway. We used to play there when I was a kid."

This time Skinny carried most of her things himself, huffing up the hill. He liked thinking that Ronnie used to play on his lot. She'd been a quiet child, tomboyish and smart, devoted to her mother. He didn't remember a lot of other kids around, but there must have been someone to play those games with her. Skinny used to worry about Ronnie after Susanna left—every girl needs her mother—but she'd turned out all right.

They set up on the side of the kitchen building, Ronnie positioning herself at an angle that would catch the buildings and a little of Skinny's car lot, with a glimpse of the river through the trees. Skinny set a chair in a spot in front of her, got a beer from the fridge, then checked the view from her vantage.

He was pleased. "That'll work."

From then on Ronnie met him at his place in the afternoons. It took her a few false starts to get comfortable, and by then Skinny had given up trying to hold his face or his body in a particular way. He usually had something to eat waiting for her—a sandwich or a plate of homemade hummus and tabouli, cheese and apples—and it made him feel good to watch her eat. She told him stories about the other tribe members she was painting, their vanities and quirks, and Skinny hoped that she didn't say as much about him.

"There's one lady, Nellie Wynn, you know her?" Ronnie asked one day. "Lives over near the post office?"

"Yeah," Skinny said. "That's my parents' old place she lives in."

"Oh," Ronnie said. "It's a nice house. Every day she offers me a cookie out of this enormous Aunt Jemima cookie jar. Blackface and everything, polka-dotted kerchief, big gummy smile. You pull her head off and there's cookies inside."

"She gives you cookies?"

"They're not *homemade,* like yours," Ronnie said. "It's the Aunt Jemima jar. It's so strange. And then she wants to talk about Pocahontas, how she was raped, and I just sit there."

"My mom was stuck on Pocahontas too," Skinny said. "Matoaka, she called her. She said it meant 'naughty one.' I guess in hindsight she probably shouldn't have stepped in like she did. Then my mom would talk about how she broke her father's heart, running off to England to get put on display."

"You think she was trying to tell you something?" Ronnie said.

"What do you mean?"

"About women," she said.

"Hell," he said. "Where've you been all my life to translate this shit?"

Sometimes Skinny forgot it was Ronnie and not Susanna, they talked so easily. She would paint almost into dusk, the dry bristles swishing loud against the canvas as the bullfrogs and cicadas started up, and Skinny would close his eyes and imagine her dabbing and dragging her brushes over his own yellowing, sore-bound skin. He imagined her painting a new surface there, smooth and tan from working in the sun. He could tell she was really concentrating when she stopped talking and stared right at the canvas. She held her mouth open, the tip of her tongue resting between her teeth. Sometimes he wanted badly to kiss her, but instead he'd sit reminding himself who she was. That's Ronnie. Daughter of your two friends, twenty-five years old. Keep your dirty old self away from her.

"You ever call your mother?" he asked her once.

"No," she said. "Not ever."

"You know her number?"

She'd closed her eyes and repeated it from memory. He'd gotten up to write it down on a box of crackers. "Might call her sometime," he said. "For old times' sake."

The homecoming grew closer, and Skinny continued to think about dying. They never talked about it, even though he wanted to, and he was often on the verge of bringing it up when her cell phone would ring and it would be her husband, telling her he was at Bruce's. Skinny would offer her a ride and she'd say no, she liked to walk. She'd taken to leaving her things at his place—the canvas and easel and brushes, which he'd talked her into letting him clean. Don't want the baby breathing in any of that poison, he'd said.

After she left he washed the brushes slowly and thoroughly in the aluminum sink, pouring turpentine over them and forcing the sticky pigmentation out of their bristles with his fingers. He ran the hot water and leaned over, breathed in the strong, astringent smell. It felt cleansing and good in his nose, his chest. He dried the brushes on paper towels, blotting away the colors—blue and green and brown and orange—that continued to bleed no matter how carefully or how long he washed them.

Once she had asked him, in her offhand way, Have you made a will?

It all goes to my kids, he'd said, not mentioning how little he had to leave. He'd been to the lawyers' office right after his last doctor's appointment. Wrapping the whole thing up had taken under an hour.

No, she said. A living will. For the doctors.

Sure, he said. I've got one of those.

Good, she said, nodding in satisfaction. I have one too. I wouldn't want any, you know, artificial or extraordinary measures.

Yeah, Skinny said. He'd known his lawyer for years, through DWI cases and possession charges, divorce—he was intimately acquainted with Skinny's recklessness—and had noted his surprise when they got to that part. He'd surprised himself even.

Yes, he'd heard himself saying. I want every measure taken.

Ronnie's work went slowly and was still unfinished on the night Skinny expected his kids for homecoming. The easel, canvases, and paints took up half of his bedroom and filled it with the smell of paint and linseed oil. He was starting to like the smell, waking to it in the mornings. For a long time he avoided the portrait, but he'd finally looked at it, just the other day—a fair likeness, neither harsh nor flattering, but the best part was the way she'd captured his house. As she'd worked he'd described building each part to her, how he'd decided the structures' placements to maximize sun and shadow, how he'd laid the plumbing between the kitchen and bathroom, the choice of wood and window and cabinetry. She must have understood it was important because she'd rendered every detail, down to the very grain of the cedar siding. So much detail you could forget to see the man that sat in the foreground, shoulders slumped, beer cans at his feet, a worried look on his face.

Skinny had the portrait covered with a sheet because he meant it to be a present to his kids and he didn't want them catching a glimpse of it. Ronnie was giving it to him. It looked done, but Ronnie said it wasn't—there was more fine-tuning she said she needed to do.

Skinny resisted at first but soon understood her perfectionism. It was the same way, when a customer tried to pick up a vehicle after Skinny got it running, he'd have to sometimes put them off. Hold on now, he'd have to tell them. He'd maybe want to make some final adjustments or test the air compression. Let me do this right and you won't have to come back. He figured his portrait was like that—if he didn't let her finish her way he'd notice some imperfection, some branch of tree or turn of the house she had missed, and it would stop working. He knew it was working because he could stare and stare at it and still see something. He hoped his kids would feel that way too, that the portrait would be a way of keeping his lot even if they didn't call for it. He wasn't going to show it to them until it was all-the-way finished.

He had plenty of other things for them, though. He'd made up the couch for Erin and a cot for Tyler with new sheets bought at Kmart. He'd washed the starch out of them at Bruce's. He had supper cooking on the stove, spaghetti and meatballs, Erin's favorite. He made the meatballs himself with lamb and beef, fresh Parmesan, and seven different spices. He had the moccasins wrapped up to give Erin, and the still-unfinished MG covered in a tarp for Tyler.

They said they'd be there around six, and by six thirty Skinny was pacing his house, wandering from the kitchen, where he stirred the thick red sauce, to the living room, where he straightened the sheets and gave the TV screen a final dusting. He called Tyler's cell phone and got his voicemail, left an unworried message. Then he drank a beer, and another beer after that.

He called Sandra at seven. "What time did they leave?" he asked. He'd poured himself a glass of wine from the bottle he'd bought for the sauce, held the phone shoulder to ear as he sipped.

She sighed. "I guess a while ago. They probably hit traffic. Maybe they stopped to get something to eat."

"Dammit, I told them I was making supper. I *told* them."

"I didn't say they definitely stopped," Sandra said. "I said maybe. The traffic, it's bad sometimes. Are you drinking?"

"No," he said. "I had a glass of wine when I made the tomato sauce."

"A glass of wine," she repeated. "Call me if they're not there in an hour."

He hung up, poured another glass. Beer before wine, doing fine, he muttered to himself, leaning over the pot to smell the sauce. He could hardly smell anything from breathing in the paints and turpentine. A small taste would twist his stomach into cramps. The wine did almost the same thing, but it kept his mind off the kids. He called them once more and got voicemail.

By the time they arrived it was growing dark and he was dozing in the living room on the cot, his boot-clad feet propped on the carefully folded blanket. Tyler's knocking startled him from a dream about a dog he had when he was little. A Labrador retriever, it had fallen through the ice one winter and drowned.

"What?" he said into the air. The television was on: racing.

"It's me, Dad," Tyler said, standing over him. "Don't you ever lock your doors?"

"Hell," Skinny said, belching softly as he sat up. He shook Tyler's hand, then pulled him into a hug. Tyler stepped back quickly, folding his arms over his chest. Skinny could see he was trying not to look at his arms, where the sores had crusted over with purple-brown scabs. He pulled on a long-sleeve shirt over his T-shirt and went to hug Erin. He thought he felt her wincing, patted her back gently as he released her as if to say, it's okay, I know.

"Where have you been?" he asked, switching off the television. "I made spaghetti and meatballs."

"We stopped at Wendy's," Tyler said. "Sorry."

"I told you, Tyler," Skinny started. He felt his voice getting loud and stopped. "I tried to call you, too."

"The phone gets bad reception as soon as you get off Ninety-five," Tyler said.

"Then you should have called on Ninety-five," Skinny said. "I worry. Don't roll your goddamn eyes at me, I'm your father and I've got a right to worry."

"I could eat some," Erin said.

"Okay then," Skinny said. "Follow me."

But in the kitchen he saw he hadn't lowered the burner enough and the sauce had cooked down to a thick paste that clung like cobwebs to the meatballs. The water he'd simmered for the pasta had almost all boiled away. Above the sink, the window was fogged over with steam.

"Shit," he said, turning off the burners. "It was good at six. It was perfect then."

"Maybe you shouldn't have drank until you passed out," Tyler said.

Skinny sucked in his breath and stared at the low ceiling.

"Huh?" Tyler said, as if expecting an answer. Like *he* was the father. Skinny just shook his head. "Why do you think we stopped at Wendy's? Why do you think we didn't want to rush down here?"

"Tyler!" Erin said. "Jesus!" She left, slamming the door behind her. It shook the whole kitchen.

"You upset your sister," Skinny said calmly.

"I'm tired, Dad," Tyler said. "Let's just go to sleep."

Skinny found Erin sitting at his boat landing, cell phone clasped to her ear. He stood at the top of the hill watching her chatting lightly with someone—a boyfriend?—as if nothing had happened. She turned and saw him standing there and waved, put a hand over the receiver. "I found reception," she shouted up to him, like that was the thing that had worried her.

"Okay," he said. "Good."

The moon shone round and white on the water, glassy and full at high tide. Erin dangled her long bare legs over the water, admiring them. The frogs were deafening. He felt as stoically helpless as Powhatan.

At sunrise they stood tired on the banks of the river, just down the hill from the church. Bruce was there too, and Ronnie and Jeremy. A black woman was singing "Life's Railway to Heaven" in a big resonant voice. It was a song Skinny's mother had liked; she'd had it on a Patsy Cline record and sang along with it sometimes.

They'd already sung "Shall We Gather at the River?" and "Calvary" and "The Eastern Gate"—all songs about dying and heaven. Skinny didn't believe in heaven. He thought when you died, that was it. His mother had believed in heaven, had him baptized in the chilly river water just feet from where they stood. His father had stood beside her then, had followed his mother most Sundays to their little church, professed his faith in God and heaven mostly through acquiescence. But he'd also told Skinny once that, just in case, you should live your life like it was all you got.

The small crowd was mostly stout older women, the kind whose bodies looked like they'd been made for choir robes. Their long black hair hung straight down their backs, the way Skinny's mother's had when she stood in this same place to sing and be sung to. The singer's face glistened with sweat and the effort of her singing, which was beautiful and pure, the notes at once heavy and light, like herons gliding above the water. Skinny's kids shifted from foot to foot, checking their watches and stifling yawns. When they were babies he'd been afraid to hold them. He was on the wagon then and his hands shook so bad he was afraid he would drop them. It was worst with Tyler, who was colicky and tired his mother out; he would squall in his crib and Sandra would say, *Pick him up, for godsakes,* and Skinny would hang back, afraid.

He hadn't told them, wouldn't tell them. It was an unfair burden, his dying, too much for two kids who'd already seen more than their share. Poor Tyler, Skinny thought. Poor Tyler and poor Erin.

But as he listened to the woman's voice, the notes opening wider and wider, he started to get angry. No one wanted to think about it—not Bruce or Sandra or Ronnie—much less talk about it with him. He *had* to think about it: the when and where, and who would take care of his things, his kids. It was overwhelming, the things he had to think about, the planning, while everyone else just lived their lives. He thought of his doctor and his smug family photos. The anger tightened in his chest like a fist.

> *Blessed Savior, Thou will guide us*
> *Till we reach that blissful shore*
> *Where the angels wait to join us*
> *In that great forevermore.*

He looked over and saw Bruce's head tipped back to hold in tears, saw Ronnie and Jeremy swaying to her voice.

You make your own family, Susanna had told him a long time ago before she left, when he asked what Ronnie and Bruce would do without her. Don't you?

After the morning services, they ate a fish-and-pancake break-fast on the church's damp, mossy picnic tables. People made a point of stopping by Skinny's table, reintroducing themselves to Erin and Tyler, saying how much they'd grown and asking about school. They bore it pretty well, Skinny thought, though they didn't say much. Bruce and Ronnie and Jeremy sat across from them.

Erin ate everything: fried roe and apples, pancakes and fish and hash browns all mixed together on her plate. Tyler just stacked pan-cakes and ate them plain, like medicine. Skinny sat sideways next to Erin and smoked. His mother would have asked him if he had a train to catch.

"I guess this'll be the most preaching I've heard in a while," Skinny said. "I haven't come to homecoming since I was living at home."

"I've been a few times," Bruce said. He'd cleaned his plate and was going back for more.

"Ha," Ronnie said. "You come every year. You used to *drag* me, and then when I was gone you dragged Jeremy."

Jeremy nodded. "That is true. I have been dragged."

Bruce turned and grinned. "I like shad roe, what can I say?"

"So what made you get religious, all of a sudden?" Tyler asked, not looking at Skinny. "Free food or something?"

"I'm not religious, all of a sudden," Skinny said. "I've always been in touch with my spiritual side."

Tyler snorted. Erin gave him a look.

"You should eat something, Dad," she said, pushing her plate toward him. "It's good."

"I know it is, honey," he said, blowing smoke up and away from the table. "It would make your grandmother happy to see us here. It honors her spirit. She danced at homecoming until she was seventy."

"It's just weird," Tyler said. "All this church stuff, like a regular Baptist church, and then you put on feathers and do these dances to honor the spirit or whatever. It seems contradictory."

Skinny shrugged. "How many things in life don't contradict each other?"

Bruce returned from the buffet with a heaping plate. "Jimmy says they're having a council meeting tonight. You going?"

"Yeah," Skinny said, finally accepting a bite of roe from Erin's plate. He chewed it thoughtfully, rolling the salty grains around in his mouth before swallowing them. They stuck to his tongue, and he reached for Erin's water to wash them down. "Me and my kids'll go so they can see it."

"You and Tyler can go," Bruce said. He pointed his plastic fork at Erin. "But it's no squaws allowed."

"They're afraid we might take over," Ronnie said. "You can go if you want to, though, just to watch."

"That's okay," Erin said. Skinny had the feeling she'd be on her cell phone anyway. He smiled at her, patted her back. He should have had more kids like her, a bunch of easy, unquestioning girls. He didn't know why things were so much harder with Tyler. He was a real grudge holder, Skinny thought.

Council meetings were held in the back of the museum and gift shop. Skinny wished they had somewhere more like a TV courtroom, with dark wood and columns and a high domed ceiling, a place that might impress his son. Instead they had a cement floor, a few rows of metal folding chairs, lamps made from deer antlers. About twenty-five people had come to the meeting, more than usual because of homecoming. Bruce was there too, though as a non-Indian he couldn't vote.

The meeting had been requested by two sisters. They were calling for their parents' lot, a nice piece of land with a tiny strip of river frontage and a double-wide trailer. The sisters, Rose and Sarah, had lived apart and off the reservation for years, but they wanted to retire together on their parents' land. One had been a teacher and the other had worked for the phone company.

"See," Skinny whispered to Tyler. "Now somebody's gonna have to stand up and say something about their character. It's the same as when I got my lot."

Tyler didn't say anything. Skinny was picturing his kids calling for his lot, all the people who could stand up and say that they were good. Neither one of them did drugs as far as Skinny could tell; they got good grades and stayed out of trouble. He thought what a good system the reservation had, letting people honor their parents by taking care of their land and preventing them from selling it. He liked to think about giving his kids something on those terms.

Bruce leaned over and whispered, "Those two hate each other, they just can't agree who should get the lot. If it was a single-wide they sure would be in trouble."

Three people stood to say that Rose and Sarah were good tribe members, fine upstanding citizens, and then it was over.

On the way out Skinny made Tyler stop in the museum to look at a yellowed newspaper clipping taped to the wall, one among many above the glass cases of tortoise shells and moccasins, decaying canoes and endless dusty arrowheads. The black-and-white photograph Skinny pointed to was of Tyler's grandmother, dancing in a powwow in her long deerskin dress.

Skinny checked the date on the paper. "She was sixty when that picture was taken. Hair still black and everything."

"Good genes," Tyler said. "I guess you didn't go to that one."

"No," Skinny said. "You're right. You know, I really regret that I didn't call for her lot. She and Dad loved that house. The family that lives there now has plastic flowers stuck out front."

"So call for it when they die."

"It doesn't work like that. Their kids have a right to it now. Just like you and Erin will have a right to my lot. You could live in it and go to school at William and Mary—"

The way Tyler looked at him, Skinny saw that he knew. He must have known when he saw him.

"Dad," he said. "I'm glad all this is here for you, but it isn't my life. It's your life."

Tyler's voice was tight and angry. Skinny imagined that it was anger at him for dying. He felt his eyes stinging, peered closer at the picture of his mother. Even in the grainy photograph you could see the mix of concentration and joy on her face, like she was dancing for God. That's what she believed anyway. Skinny thought that he would ask Bruce to tack up a photograph of him somewhere in the museum, maybe in a corner where you had to look to find it.

"I wasn't the worst father, you know," Skinny said as they were leaving. "I tried, and I'm trying."

"I'm sorry," Tyler said. "I try not to be mad."

"It will be hard on your sister," Skinny said. "And on your mother, too. I want you to take care of them."

"I do," Tyler said. "I do take care of them. And it's already hard. It's been hard all along."

Skinny reached to put his arm around Tyler's shoulder, a half hug, but Tyler shrugged it off. They walked the rest of the way home in separate silences, the moon a little less full than the night before, a little of it sliced away into darkness.

Erin was down the hill again, talking on her cell phone, when they got home. Tyler said he wanted to sleep, so there was nowhere for Skinny to go but his bedroom. He sat on his bed, turned on the Food Network. A woman he didn't recognize was icing cupcakes. He turned it off; he hated to see people he didn't know on television.

Next to the television was the box of crackers with Susanna's number scratched on it. He'd thought of calling her last night while Tyler slept and he waited for Erin to come up from the river, and now he was thinking about it again. He got up, held the box in his hand, and tried to imagine what he would say to her.

I'm dying.

That was as far as he got.

The portrait leaned against its easel, still covered in a sheet. Skinny didn't want to look at it. He'd found that it made him tired. Instead he turned out the lights and lay in the dark on top of the covers, the box of crackers next to him. He thought he could hear Erin's far-off laughter, light and unworried, through the open bedroom window. His stomach growled, but he was suddenly too tired to go to the kitchen for a beer and some soup. In the dark he reached his hand inside the box of crackers and drew out the last unopened packet. He ate them, slowly chewing each dry cracker into paste, until they were gone.

Erin and Tyler left without the portrait, without the moccasins, and without the bottle-green MG. Skinny gave them each one hundred dollars and lay in bed for two days after they were gone. The next week he had his monthly doctor's appointment.

"Well," the doctor said, shaking his head over Skinny's charts. "Your liver function is up, and your white blood cells are closer to normal. It looks like you've made something of a recovery for now."

"Okay then," Skinny said, blinking hard. He shook the doctor's hand and left.

A panic came over him in the elevator—sixteen floors down—and he was breathless when he stumbled outside and into the summer afternoon. The Ghostbusters building, that's what Tyler used to call the clinic when Skinny had first gotten sick. He'd liked the parking deck and the elevator and the fierce stone gargoyles that clung to the buttresses. He imagined his father fought battles inside.

Skinny lowered himself onto the wide stone steps. Broad Street's cars and buses and frowning businesspeople went about their business like he wasn't there. The recently paved street threw off a shimmering haze. Sunlight caught door handles and windshields and hubcaps, briefcase latches and windows, bits of glass ground into the pavement. It was hot, too bright, too loud: like coming down from heroin, or getting born.

He thought of all the dinners stretched out before him, a long line of them flowing like a road or a river, just like they did before anyone else. And he sat there, hands resting on his knees, like someone having his picture made.

Jonas

It came as almost a relief when Melinda's husband told her that he wanted the operation. At first, all she could think of was the thing itself—as pink and ugly and tender as a face crumpled from crying—and how she would never have to see it again. She thought not of what would replace it but only of its absence, a blank space, *missingness,* like the infinite and mysterious black hole space she had seen on *NOVA.*

Melinda resolved her features into a look of utter surprise as Jonas, coached in his words no doubt by that Richmond therapist, carefully unspooled his case like the most ordinary and obvious yarn.

"So what you're saying . . . ," Melinda repeated, slowly, not looking at her husband. They were sitting in bed on a Sunday morning. Yellow sunlight streamed onto the unread newspaper. "What you're saying is you've never felt right . . . down there."

Jonas explained, patiently, that it was not about *down there*—it was less about that than about his whole body not feeling right. Could Melinda imagine what it would feel like to have never felt like a girl? Like a woman? If every time she put on her cheerleading uniform she felt more like putting on football pads, cleats, a helmet?

"No," Melinda said flatly. She could not. She had coached state championship cheerleading teams eight of the last fifteen years, hot-rolled her hair every morning of her life past age thirteen, carried twenty-odd shades of eye shadow in her purse. But she had been thinking lately that if anything ever happened to Jonas she would never seek another man's company, less out of loyalty to Jonas than out of mere tiredness.

He was already taking the hormones, he told her. Already he could feel changes in his body, a softening of something, coarse hair turning fine as silk.

"Tell me about how you felt, in that moment." Melinda had agreed to see Jonas's therapist in private sessions, to help ease the transition. Seeing a therapist made her feel sort of stupid, but she agreed with Jonas that it was good to know what she was in for.

Melinda shrugged, afraid to say too much, of sounding country or simple. She was also afraid she might start crying for no reason, though she felt fine. That happened sometimes at the gynecologist's. The therapist had long brown hair pulled into a low and glossy ponytail, white-white teeth. Under other circumstances, Melinda might have felt jealous that her husband was spending so much alone time with such a smart and attractive woman.

"Jonas says you are taking it quite well. That you are unbelievably supportive, in fact."

Melinda smiled.

"Did you feel that this was somehow inevitable?"

Melinda thought for a minute, then said, "No. I mean, I have always known that Jonas was sort of different. The quiet type. My first husband was loud." She looked up, waiting for the therapist to say something, but she was only waiting, expectant, so Melinda continued.

"I think partly I took it so well because I'd just come home from my sister's. Her husband bosses her so much. Get-me-a-beer. Where's-my-pants. Et cetera."

She said, in a quieter voice, "And my last husband. My daughter's daddy. He drank. And he cheated."

"But Jonas has been a faithful husband for ten years," the therapist said. "Is that not right?"

"No, it is."

"Then there is no reason to believe . . ."

"Well, it isn't that, not really. It's more the other thing. I'm tired of being bossed by men. And I'm used to taking things as they come."

The therapist nodded with a concerned and gentle frown, but Melinda thought she did not understand. She did not look like she had ever been bossed by men.

Before Melinda left—on the hour to the minute, she noticed—the therapist asked her in a delicate way if she had questions, of any kind, about the process. The procedures. Melinda shook her head vehemently. She did have questions, primarily about what would be expected in the bedroom, and about down there, but she was too shy to ask them. She could not help thinking, as she left, that if the therapist had been truly good and smart, as Jonas said, she would have known that and made her ask them anyway.

Telling Jessica, her daughter, was the hardest part. For one thing, Jonas had been the primary daddy that Jessica had known, past age ten, and Melinda thought that this was probably the hardest news you could hear about a father. It didn't seem right, Melinda said, for Jonas to tell her. She would do it herself, just as she had talked to Jessie about her period and boys and sex. This fell into that category, she felt. Jonas had done the normal dad things—he'd taught her to drive, had chaperoned dances at the high school. Had told Jessie's dates to have her home by eleven, then twelve as she got older. He had even walked her down the aisle, which was possibly the proudest moment in Melinda's life. It had been Jessie's choice to give him that honor, and Melinda had been the one to choose Jonas.

Melinda did not want to tell anyone else first, and she could not imagine not keeping such an important piece of news a secret. When it was not competition season, she spent half her mornings on the telephone, and the person she talked to most was Jessica. She called her when she found a funny piece of news in the local paper, and when she was feeling down, and when she had heard gossip about the neighbors. She'd told her when Jonas had irritable bowel syndrome and had to sit on that funny, doughnut-shaped pillow for a month. Jessie was the first to know anything Melinda knew.

Later, Melinda would wish she had told Jessie in a more properly formal way than how she did it, over the phone, spooning sliced peaches onto a pan of chicken. It just came out:

"Jonas is getting an operation to become a woman. A sex change."

She had hoped that telling Jessie would finally give her someone to talk to about it, someone to be concerned about *her*, but what she heard from the other end of the line was Jessie's phone clattering to the floor.

It took several calls before she would answer again, and by then she was crying, and *she* was the one who had to be consoled.

"But what will people *think*, Mama?"

Melinda shrugged, licking peach syrup from her fingers. "This county has had to get used to a lot of things," she said. There was the Arab-looking country store owner who'd married the sixteen-year-old and set her up working the counter. Countless teen pregnancies, a few of them from Melinda's own cheering squads. An accounting scandal with the county supervisors. A professor who moved here from Richmond and flew a rainbow flag. Her best friend had her ski boat sunk by a jealous ex-husband. The way Melinda saw it, this was a small and superficial change, no more unnatural than the fertility pills Jessica had been taking for six months, the half-dozen fertilized eggs she'd had implanted in her womb. "He still loves me, honey. Just the same as he did."

"But Kevin's congregation," Jessie wailed. "They *will not* get used to this. Oh, it's easy for Jonas—he's *retired*—but some people still have to work in this town."

Melinda did not mention that she still worked, and that high school cheerleaders were not known to be the most open-minded bunch. Jessica had married the county's most popular Baptist church's self-righteous and smirking youth minister. Neither Melinda nor Jonas liked him much, though Jonas wouldn't say so, but it had been clear all along that Jessica was smitten. Melinda wanted to explain something about that, how when you loved someone it didn't matter what other people thought, but on reflection she realized that wasn't it, exactly. There was something more complicated that she herself barely understood, and expecting a twenty-two-year-old to understand was probably pointless. It was more like, you come into this world alone, and you go out alone, but it wasn't exactly that either.

"Well, I wish you wouldn't take it so hard," Melinda said. "But I understand why you are. It was a shock to me too."

She could hear Jessie sniffling. Hopefully, she asked, "Do you want me to come over?"

"No," Jessie said in a calmer voice. "The doctor says I should not get upset. He says stress is the enemy of conception."

"All right, sweetie." Melinda felt her own tears starting, tipped her head back. You mustn't cry, she told herself. Think of your grandchildren.

"He says I should isolate myself from my stress factors," Jessica said ominously. Melinda could not help wondering how such a smart girl could have married a man who put vanity plates on his truck.

REV KEV, they said.

A sex change is not an overnight thing, Melinda learned. First there are months of hormone therapy, coaxing the body into its new self through small and incremental changes, small surgeries leading up to the big one. Before you even have one surgery there is a period of dress-up, drag they called it, so you get used to the feeling. Of being different. Of being looked at.

The first time Jonas went out in drag they took the doctor's sensible advice and made it an out-of-town and not overly formal or overly long appearance, shopping for pillow shams at the Ashland Walmart and dinner at the Ashland Ponderosa. Melinda bought Jonas a smart new mint-green pantsuit—none of her clothes would fit him—helped him style the ash-blond wig he'd bought, and powdered his face and eyelids and even gave him a touch of blush and lip gloss. She was careful not to overdo it.

When she was finished he looked, rather as she expected, like an older, mannish woman. She realized, rubbing a bit of thick gloss away from his bottom lip, that she had probably never touched him there, not with her fingertips, never touched his soft and crepey eyelids, or the high sharp ridge of his cheekbones.

"Am I beautiful yet?" he asked, his voice still manly, husky. He laughed, as if to dismiss the notion.

"You'll do," she said.

"You do the talking, okay?" he asked in a whisper voice, on their way out. Melinda nodded. She even drove.

Melinda did not think she'd had so much fun in years. First, shopping at Walmart, Jonas meek beside her in the brightly lit aisles. With a new and keen interest, he watched her finger the fabrics, place flowered pattern next to solid rug or curtain material, and did not once check his watch. He wasn't wearing a watch; his watch was a man's. No one seemed to notice his large, still-hairy hands, or his Adam's apple; Melinda told her sister later that was because women from Caroline County were so damn ugly.

At dinner, he ate slowly, carefully, cutting his steak and bringing it right to his mouth in the continental style. Melinda was put in mind of a delicate, long-lost aunt come to visit, or a sister you didn't have to compete with in looks. She smiled at him across the table, but they didn't speak. They spent an entire hour and fifteen minutes at the Ponderosa, lingering over black coffee for Jonas and an ice-cream sundae for Melinda. Normally, Jonas would raise his finger for the check before she'd taken her last bite. To save time, he always said.

Time for what? She used to wonder. At a table across from them, new parents took turns feeding their baby. She thought of Jessica and Kevin, said a little, useless prayer for a grandchild. She was sure it was prayed for plenty.

Later, in the car, she asked him what he wanted to be called. Joanie?

"Joan, I think," he said. He put his hand over hers, which rested on the gearshift, and patted it. Even his palm felt softer to Melinda. "You can call me Jonas still, Melinda. I don't have to always—"

She gave him her sweet-martyr look. "Like I told your therapist, I am used to taking things as they come." When in bed he reached for her, she kissed him chastely, then turned over.

"But clearly, you would prefer he stay a man," her sister Pauline said over the telephone.

"Well," said Melinda. "It's not up to me."

"But secretly."

"I want Jonas to be happy." Melinda had come out with Jonas's news to just about everyone who mattered, and she had never in her life been told so many times how "amazing" and "strong" she was. She'd even told her cheering squad, carefully explaining that it didn't mean Jonas was gay.

Melinda explained to Pauline that Jonas—Joan—was like a new person. He was willing to go out more, and he laughed and smiled more than he ever had. He spent less time alone. He cooked, though not well. He wanted to learn new things. Could she imagine a man who did things with you not because he had to but because he *wanted* to?

"It sounds like what you're saying," Pauline said snippily, "is that we should hope all our husbands get a sex change."

Melinda tried again: Did she remember what it was like to raise a child when it was very young? How you could teach them one thing, like how to use a flour sifter, and it kept them entertained for hours? How every day they learned something new, and just learning it delighted them?

It was sort of, a little bit, like that.

"Well, I still don't think I'd want Roland getting his thing chopped off."

Vulgar, Melinda thought. Her sister was so vulgar.

"The thing that is still on my mind," Melinda began, a little too quick and businesslike, it felt, "is that my daughter is not speaking to us, exactly."

The therapist nodded, leaned back in her chair. "That's normal, under the circumstances."

"Well, it does not feel normal to *me*," Melinda said. She had dressed up more for this visit, thinking a more powerful presence would exact better advice from this woman. She had what she called high hair, the kind of hair that she required her girls to wear for competition. It looked good on the field. It made people remember you.

"I talk to my daughter every day," Melinda said proudly.

"Every day," the therapist repeated. "That is quite a schedule."

Melinda did not expect this woman to understand or come from a place where daughters were their mothers' best friends, boys their fathers'. She did not want to talk about why that might be a problem, in the therapist's eyes.

"How does Jonas feel about your daughter's rejection?"

"He is shy about it," Melinda said. She explained how it wasn't Jonas, exactly, who had told her, how Jonas really didn't like to talk about it to anyone. She told the therapist about Kevin, and how she didn't think Jonas had ever really cared for him, though of course they wished Jessica well. "I think he wants to just be a woman, a new person, and that's that. Sometimes I think—"

Melinda looked at the clock, noticed she had seven minutes left.

"Sometimes I think maybe he is practicing, with us."

The therapist shook her head, not comprehending. Feeling her eyes begin to sting, Melinda decided quickly to ration the rest of her time to Jessica. "My daughter used to have this amazing memory. Not for things like history and formulas, for math or school—she was honor roll and all, but that wasn't the amazing part. It was for little details. Like, if you were remembering so-and-so's wedding, she could tell you exactly what you wore, what everybody wore. It was this *talent* she had.

"So now, she's married to this reverend, and she wears sweatpants to the grocery store and goes out without her hair done and lies on her side all day and gives herself injections in the butt. And she won't talk to me for more than a second now when I call. Says she has to go in this short way.

"I accepted *all of that,*" she said, her voice breaking. "I accepted it because she was happy."

The therapist nodded but said nothing. Melinda wanted to say that she was happy now, too, but the words did not come.

Melinda had pictured therapy, before Jonas started going, as a place where you could go and get your embarrassing questions answered. You could say, for example, why did my father drink and whore around, or, why did my uncle abuse me? And the therapist would have an answer. You could say, what does life mean? And he would know what you needed to hear. If you told him your worst and weirdest dreams, he would tell you what they meant. Make you feel better, normal. Why else would it cost so much?

Driving home, air-conditioning cooling her bare arms and blowing back her high hair, Melinda knew what she wished she had asked:

How old do you have to be to understand how love works?

Jonas began therapy after suffering a panic attack at work, more than a year before. He had been a trucker, hauling lumber to Chesapeake Paper Co., and one day he pulled over and decided he was having a heart attack. He knelt in the weeds on Route 30 and clutched his chest until the feeling passed, then drove himself and his whole rig to the hospital. When the test results came up clear, the specialist at Tidewater Memorial had referred him to therapy.

And that was that. Melinda wondered if Jonas would have ever made this decision without the therapist leading him there. Another woman, she thought, might be angry with the therapist, angry with Jonas for having a fake heart attack when he was supposed to be working and for taking an early retirement and having something as inconvenient as the mind of a woman inside the body of a man. Surely she would be angry.

Maybe, Melinda thought, turning onto her favorite back road shortcut, they should have a get-together. Not at their house but someone else's. So that Jessie and Kevin could see how they were accepted by other, normal, reasonably Christian people. It would be sort of like a debutante's coming out, with Jonas in his modest, school-marmish drag so that Kevin and Jessie could see that it wasn't about blue eye shadow and fishnets and six-inch heels. So they could see that it wasn't about sex.

Melinda sped up on the straightaway, where she always tried to get the car up to sixty. There was a dip in the road. If you were going fast enough, you lost your stomach in the most pleasant way.

Jonas's voice was steadily growing softer and higher. He spoke in a half whisper and had become almost neat in his habits, folding his clothes and wiping crumbs from the countertops. It was almost like he knew that he was too big to be a woman and was trying somehow to contain himself, to leave less of his bigness and coarseness behind. Melinda found that she bossed him more, telling him what their plans were for the weekend, what movie she'd like to see. He acquiesced, generally. Doing the laundry, she noticed that even his sweat had a sweeter smell, more feminine. He was plucking his eyebrows now, and using a depilatory on his arms and legs and face. Melinda bought him a special astringent to shrink his pores, and a cold cream that cost twenty dollars a jar.

It had been nearly a month since she'd told Jessica, and she still had not talked to either of them for more than a minute. She'll come around, Jonas said. Just wait.

But aren't you sad? Melinda asked. Don't you miss her?

Of course I do. You can't make people talk to you.

Meanwhile Jonas had joined a support group in Richmond, and Melinda was tired of waiting. The group met two nights a week next to a tattoo parlor on the Southside, and Jonas would be gone, on those Tuesdays and Thursdays, from four in the afternoon until nine or ten at night. "Sometimes we get a beer afterwards," he explained.

On the Southside? Melinda asked. She had a big picture of that. There was a separate support group for partners, Jonas said, but Melinda told him she needed to think about next year's routines, at least for now.

So she stood outside in the backyard in her shorts and T-shirt and did jumps and kicks, listened to her boom box as the sun sank lower and lower behind the water tower. She played old favorites from C & C Music Factory and Janet Jackson and Salt-N-Pepa, jotted notes down on a pad. Doodled her own name in big curvy letters.

When the grass grew too high, making her legs itch, she mowed it. At first she was annoyed that Jonas had neglected the task, but she found that she liked the challenge of starting the motor, liked the feel of pushing and pulling a great weight, of cutting.

And the more she thought about it, the more she liked the term *partner*. It sounded more democratic, more freeing, than *wife*.

They planned the party for a Friday at Pauline's house. It would be like a tea, with tablecloths spread on the picnic table and ladylike finger sandwiches and jelly jars full of zinnias, and hats and calf-grazing dresses. Melinda worried that Roland might make a scene—he was *fine* with Jonas, Pauline reported, okay with it at least, but he tended to drink too much at family gatherings, and Kevin and Jessie were teetotaling Baptists. Please, said Melinda. Limit him.

I will try, Pauline said.

It was a delicate balancing act because without Budweiser, Roland was surly. And Jessica made only a halfhearted commitment to show up, but she could not promise that Kevin would make it.

"Please, honey," Melinda said. "It would mean so much to Jonas."

Jessica had sighed. She was not the type to make snippy remarks—*Is that what you're calling him still?*—but only to judge, silently, to judge and judge. "Okay, Mama, we'll see."

Melinda felt sure, despite her sister's skepticism, that her daughter and son-in-law would come. One time on a radio show she'd heard that a positive attitude and a belief in luck in fact produced positive results. People who felt sure that good things would happen, the argument went, subconsciously made those good things happen. She'd called in for transcripts and had them copied for all the girls on her squad.

When she shared the story with Jessica, around the time of her baby troubles, Jessica had said that maybe it was only that positive people felt more positive because they were better at things to begin with, hence "luckier" and more likely to be successful.

Well, maybe, Melinda allowed. It was hard to argue with that girl.

On a Thursday night, with nothing but reruns on television, Melinda got out her boxes of wedding photos—first Jessica's, then her own—and sat down on the bed with them.

Jessica had worn one of those modern, strapless dresses for her church wedding, and she had been tan and beautiful, with a blond updo that showed off her long, graceful neck. The photos taken inside the church were dark—Kevin's church had narrow, dark stained glass windows in blood colors, burgundy and red and navy and ochre—but you could feel happiness coming off Jessica like its own kind of light.

Melinda was shocked by how much she had changed; three years later, a dropout from nursing school, she had put on twenty pounds at least, and she was doughy-pale and tired-looking, waiting for the radiance of motherhood. When Melinda chided her, gently, for missing out on her education and her career, Jessica had said that being a reverend's wife was its own kind of job. She felt called, she said, to tend the flock.

Melinda had had two weddings—first to Charles, Jessica's father, and then, of course, to Jonas. She felt a little embarrassed now that she had worn white, poufy dresses to both weddings, and chagrined that she looked better in the first one.

Picking up a loose photograph from the box—for these, rather than the album-pasted ones, were always the ones that drew her—she traced her finger lightly over Jonas's smiling, posed features. Jessica was there in her pink junior-bridesmaid dress, hugging herself to Melinda's white, corseted side. She looked happy, distracted, a little scared. She barely knew Jonas at that point, was just becoming interested in her own little circle of friends and small dramas. She had been in Melinda's first wedding, too, as a fetus, and from then on Melinda had always thought of Jessica's presence in all important parts of her life as inevitable and sure.

What was Jonas thinking? Melinda wondered, looking closer at his face. Was he feeling uncomfortable in his too-formal tuxedo? In his role as husband?

And what was he talking about, now, over beers or church-basement punch and cookies? Was he talking about her? About sex?

Melinda then did what she always did when she looked at wedding pictures. She rooted to the back of her closet and pulled out her wedding dress: big, white, iridescently beaded. She slipped the plastic over the hanger, laid the dress smooth and shining over the bedspread.

She pulled her T-shirt over her head, stepped out of her shorts. Then, considering her unflattering brief panties and yellowed jog bra, she took those off too and stood before the oval, full-length mirror, tilting it back for a better angle before looking.

You are not so bad, she thought.

She was tan all over, thanks to tan-through bikinis and a membership to the tanning salon in Central Garage. She had long legs, and good, sturdy muscles there from cheering jumps and a squat routine she performed every night. Her breasts sagged, but not too much. She was only fat in the stomach and upper arms, but maybe, she thought, mowing the lawn would help that. She had begun to feel a tightness in her abdomen afterward and a soreness in her arms.

Still naked, Melinda washed her hands in the bathroom, then picked up the dress as if it were something holy. She unzipped it down the back—there was a row of pearls there to disguise the zipper—then held her breath and stepped in. The tulle rustled pleasantly against her legs, the nipped waist squeezed pleasantly over her thighs, the modest puffed sleeves felt familiar and right on her shoulders, the sweetheart neckline framed her cleavage like always. Reaching back to zip up, she found the zipper stuck halfway. She sucked in but could get it no higher than a third of the way up her back.

She turned around and examined the back of her dress in the mirror. A roll of tan fat swelled above the white fabric. The seams pulled against the zipper; she could see the white threads straining.

Melinda sucked and pulled, adjusted and shifted, for almost half an hour, inching the zipper upward. By the time she had the dress on all the way, she was sweating and weeping, and she found that she could not unzip herself.

Sobbing now, pressing tissue after tissue to her eyes so as not to stain her dress, she lay on the bed until she was calm. She let Jonas find her that way, hungry, breathing shallowly, and ashamed.

"Sweetie," he said, dropping his purse. "What happened?"

But Melinda would not answer, only rolled over so he could carefully and laboriously unzip her. It took as long as it had taken her to get into the dress, and Melinda thought that no regular man could have been as gentle. She was reminded of pre-meet dressings, watching her girls groom each other with practiced, nervous hands, or the tender way they consoled one another after each rare defeat.

When finally she was free, they marveled at the map of pink indentations the dress's seams had pressed into her body. For a little while, she let Jonas trace them, with just his fingertip running over her stomach, up her sides, along her breasts. When he went to kiss her there, his mouth parted, pink tongue out, she sat up and said she wanted some French fries.

"I probably could have gotten out myself," she said later, in the car, eating straight from the Wendy's bag.

"I know you could, honey."

It took until six o'clock, when the guests had started leaving, for Melinda to admit to herself that Jessica was not coming to the party.

"I really thought she would come, Sissy," she said to Pauline.

Pauline put down the garbage bag she was using to collect trash from around her yard, came over, and put an arm around Melinda's waist. Even though she lived an hour away, in Tidewater, she'd come to state cheering championships every year since Melinda had started coaching. She always said she booked her catering clients around it before they even held the regional meets, so sure was she of Melinda's success.

"She'll come around."

"It was a lovely party, though," Melinda said. "She missed something real nice."

"She did," Pauline said lightly. "We'll have another one."

It *had* been nice, Melinda thought. Pauline's kids had come with their kids, who did not seem fazed by Jonas. Roland had kept a respectful distance. Neighbors brought wine and beer and snacks, and almost everyone at the party had chatted politely if briefly with Jonas, who had picked out his own sand-colored silk suit from Hecht's and stood shyly on the sidelines. For the occasion, Melinda had given him a gold-and-pearl bracelet to wear that he had once given her. It just fit over his bony man's wrist.

"You know, I think hardly anyone called Jonas Joan," Melinda said. "And he was too shy to tell them. I wonder if some people even thought about the strangeness of a woman—someone supposed to be a woman—going by the name Jonas.

"I forget myself," she continued. "To me he will always be Jonas, I guess."

Together, they watched him wander around the backyard with a cup of lemonade in his hand. He was too tall to really pass as a woman, but mostly people did not ask, or even stare for very long. Once someone had even asked if he was Melinda's mother.

Ha, she had said. This old broad's my *partner.*

It grew easier, she found, every time.

"When do the surgeries start?" Pauline asked.

"Soon," Melinda said. She had sliced herself another piece of cake, almost all icing. "Before the holidays."

"You know," Pauline said, "if I were a hell-bent Baptist minister, I think I'd try and stop somebody from going through with it.

"I mean, if you are tending to your sheep, or whatever," Pauline went on, "if you think it's so sinful and all, you'd try to keep them from damning themselves. Isn't that a minister's job?"

"Kevin—," Melinda began, then stopped. She had been drinking wine and didn't want to say too much. "Well, Kevin probably doesn't want to be seen with us. We're not really members of his congregation anyway."

"What an ass," Pauline said. "Sorry."

Melinda shook her head. "It's okay. Jonas says that he's not sure he'll get the full package, so to speak. Maybe that will make some kind of difference."

"Maybe just boobs," Pauline said thoughtfully. "Tell him to definitely get boobs."

Melinda laughed a big, cheerleader's laugh. "Why?"

"To give you something to play with, that's why, silly."

Melinda told her to shut her mouth, and Pauline goaded her into showing her the new routines she was trying, and that was how they spent the rest of the evening.

On the way home, they listened to Melinda's cheerleading mix. Jonas drove because Melinda had had too much to drink, and she looked out the window as the darkening pine woods thickened into deciduous forest and the land grew hilly and pastured.

"Why do you think Kevin hasn't tried to stop you?" she asked quietly. She was thinking of interventions she had seen on television dramas. "Or even Jessie. Why haven't they come over?"

Jonas was quiet for a while. Melinda thought he must be searching for an answer.

"He has, I guess."

Melinda sat up, sobered, and asked what he meant. She turned down the volume all the way, looked at Jonas.

"He sends these . . . notes, I guess you could say," Jonas said. Most of his makeup had melted off, and he looked like a strangely hairless man in a woman's suit. Melinda felt a little sorry for him. "Bible notes."

"Bible notes?"

"They're passages, I guess, from the Bible."

"Do they say anything else? Letters from him? Or Jessie? Prayers?"

Jonas shook his head sadly.

"Well, what are the passages? What do they say?" Melinda felt herself growing hysterical, her face heated and red.

"I don't remember," Jonas said. "I tear them up."

If this were a movie, Melinda thought, at least the type of movie they show on cable television during the day, she and Jonas would get all dressed up in their Sunday best—hats and all—and go to Kevin's church. They would stand nervously in the back while he gave an inspired-sounding, fiery sermon, maybe something about loving thy neighbor or honoring thy mother and father, and there would be no room for them to sit. People would turn and stare, and finally Jessica would notice, would think about it awhile, would stand up, teary-eyed, and lead them to their rightful place at the front of the church, and Kevin would extend his reverent hand to them, or something, and all would be forgotten. And then Jessica would get pregnant.

And then the two devoted grannies would play with the child on a sunlit lawn.

Except as they passed the redbrick church—Jonas stubbornly refused the shortcut—Melinda and Jonas both noticed three plywood cutouts of stock cars lined up out front like a hideous modern manger, with Jesus's car in the pole position.

Melinda thought next year she would strongly encourage her girls to go to the Methodist church.

The following Saturday, they had tickets to the Fabergé egg exhibit at the Virginia Museum of Fine Arts. Melinda had gotten the tickets a long time ago, before Joan was even in the picture. She had planned to go to the exhibit with Jessica, in fact, even though Jessica told her that those eggs were vain and false, the product of a corrupt society.

But will you go? Melinda had asked, impatiently.

Yes, I'll go, Jessica had said, acquiescing.

It was a Big Event, for Richmond, and Melinda felt just a little bit guilty, standing in the long, hot line that snaked out of the museum and halfway down Grove Avenue, that she had not called Jessica to be sure she wanted to give up her ticket. All of Richmond's oldest old ladies, their daughters, granddaughters, deaf husbands, and nurses were there, the old ladies in their best scarves and suits and brooches and orthopedic shoes.

Jonas stood nervously beside her in his sand suit, one hand clutching the purse at his side. Melinda was wearing jaunty black capris, a silk tunic, and high hair.

"I wish Jessica could have come," she said. She looked again at their tickets. They still had thirty minutes before their admission slot. "Want me to go get us a brochure to look at?"

"Sure," Jonas whispered. He was still funny about talking in public, though Melinda told him his voice sounded natural.

At the front of the line, she saw an old friend from her old, old job, processing medical bills in Mechanicsville. "Melinda!" the woman cried. "It's Rhea!"

"Oh my goodness," Melinda said, clutching the programs to her chest. "Hello."

"You are looking better than ever," Rhea said, making a show of checking her out. "I read about you in the paper sometimes. You must be so proud."

"Thank you," Melinda said. "The girls do all the work. This your daughter?"

"Oh no, this is Emily, my granddaughter. You flatter me." She nudged the girl forward, and the girl mumbled hello. "Your daughter's here too?"

"Oh, no," Melinda said. "She couldn't come."

"How is she?"

"She's fine, fine," Melinda said brightly. "Married to a minister! Trying to start a family!"

Something in her voice, or the way she was standing, must have sounded sad to Rhea. "Come up and stand with us! Come cut the line!"

"Thank you, Rhea," Melinda said. "But I am here with a friend."

Inside the exhibit, everything was dark and cool, to preserve the eggs. Pinpoint lights illuminated their glass cases, and all around the ladies stood, quiet and rapt, transported, Melinda thought, to the world of miniatures that had been their childhoods, a world of finely made dollhouse furniture, hand-sewn doll clothes, tea sets painted with the tiniest of brushes.

Look, someone would whisper. Look-at-that.

Hush, the other would say back, but not unkindly.

Melinda thought it was the quietest art exhibit she had ever been to. She held Jonas's hand so as not to lose him in the dark and the hush.

She was surprised at the variety. Some of the eggs were pale,

Easter-colored, while others were lacquered in rich and royal blues and yellows and black. Some were tiny, like a baby's fist, and some were as big as a state championship trophy. Many of them, in fact, looked like trophies, and Melinda set her mind on deciding which one she would want, if she could have any of them.

She let go of Jonas's hand and began to wander. Her favorites, she decided, were not the giant serpent-and-clock eggs, on their grand pedestals, but the smaller surprise eggs. The surprise eggs were the ones with things inside them: a toy elephant or peasants dancing, or a rose. She wished they could demonstrate the workings of the eggs and toys somehow. The descriptive placards promised that everything still worked. She was sure it was a sight to see.

Almost by gravity, it seemed, she was pulled to a glass case at the rear of one of the narrow galleries, where a half-dozen ladies, including Jonas, stood gape-mouthed. Inside was an egg made of etched crystal and gold, opened at a bottom hinge to reveal the surprise inside: a mechanical peacock perched on an ornate, golden tree. She could not help but think how Jessica would have loved the exhibit in spite of herself.

"Made for the dowager empress Marie Fedorovna," a querulous voice read slowly. "It says the engineer hired by Eugene Fabergé worked on the peacock alone for three years."

"Isn't that something," and, "My," people whispered as they filed past.

Melinda and Jonas stood the longest, not touching or talking, just looking. What Melinda liked best, she decided, was the idea of the surprise inside the egg, something special and hidden and fine, something to make you catch your breath.

Buckets of Rain

For J. C.

Jeremy's dad was stone-cold sober when he pulled into the drive. Jeremy was holding a basketball, trying to look casual, but in truth he had been waiting for an hour, idly and unproductively bouncing the ball on the packed yellow dirt. His dad was taking him to see Bob Dylan at Wolf Trap, but only, Jeremy's mom said, if she could inspect him and his truck first.

"*Mom,*" Jeremy called inside the darkened house. It was a hot day so all the lights were off, and it looked like nobody was home except that the front door was propped wide open. He was hoping she would not make a big production of it, but see that John's truck was clean and most probably beerless, and John was sober, and wave them on.

"He's here."

Cheryl took her time. She had been reading a magazine on the back porch. Jeremy dreaded meetings between his parents, mostly because he saw, in their sharp glances and small comments, how each of them had changed for the worse since their divorce. Barefoot, in too-short shorts and a tank top, Cheryl minced over the crabgrass and gravel and peered into the cab of John's truck.

John did not even say "Jesus, Cher," like usual, but obligingly opened up the mounted steel toolboxes in back. They had been divorced for ten years, since Jeremy was four. Even after all that time, he had a hard time recognizing what was sarcasm and what was necessity.

They stopped at the 7-Eleven in Doswell. Jeremy got a bag of chips and a Coke and John got a six-pack of Budweiser and a foam cooler and a bag of ice. Jeremy waited inside the truck while John settled the cans, then shook the ice on top. The cooler rested neatly in the space between them, and they were on the road.

"Shit," John said, popping open the first can. "Your mother gets more uptight by the year."

"She just worries," Jeremy said. He always had the feeling that the parent who was being criticized was watching. He could see them watching, small and helpless, from inside his own eyes, imagined them hearing his voice as if it were their own.

"You're right, you're right," John said into his beer. He was being surprisingly easygoing about Cheryl. Jeremy supposed this was because of his love for Bob Dylan, and also because he thought it was Jeremy's first concert, momentous and special.

Jeremy had in fact been going to concerts for the past two years, sneaking out of the house after Cheryl went to bed to wait at the closed-down fruit stand on Route 30 for friends his parents didn't even know he had. That was how he had seen Sick of It All and Bad Brains and Faith No More. Mostly they drove to Twisters in Richmond, but sometimes they went to shows as far away as D.C., where invariably they got lost and nervous but never asked directions. It was a good feeling, to come home with no one noticing he'd been gone. Jeremy thought John might be proud of him if he knew, but of course he couldn't tell.

"I met your ma at a concert," John said.

An old story. "I know," Jeremy muttered. "You told me." He didn't want to hear it again; each of his parents told it so differently.

"Grand Funk Railroad," John said.

"I know."

"She was beautiful. Big and beautiful, blond hair she could sit on."

"So you said."

That was one thing about John. He had a softer side to him than Cheryl.

The good and normal part of Jeremy's life, he figured, started when his mom began AA. The time before that was hard to remember—Jeremy had been only seven when she quit drinking—but from stories and pictures he counted eight different houses and apartments, none of which they owned, and memories of that time were chaotic and loud, populated by too many men.

When she started they went to meetings every night, driving all over the county and even to Richmond, to smoky church basements and community centers and once, for a time, a Chuck E. Cheese in Mechanicsville. Now Cheryl went to two meetings a week—an AA group at the American Legion Hall on Sundays, and an Al-Anon women's group at a Methodist church on Wednesdays. They owned their house and two acres and a Labrador retriever, and Cheryl had a newish station wagon plastered with inspirational bumper stickers and a job managing the doctor's office in Aylett. When Jeremy turned fifteen he was going to get a job running roller coasters or taking tickets at Kings Dominion, and Cheryl was going to match what he saved for a used car. He even had it picked out: a Malibu that had been on the lot at TJ Motors for the past two years.

John, as his mom said, was just A. Working her twelfth step, she tried to make him see the power and good of the program and even convinced him to go to a meeting or two, but it didn't last long. Sometimes Cheryl hosted the AA group at the American Legion; the story she most often liked to tell new members was about Jeremy's first day in kindergarten, how she was too messed up to know that it was a half day, and that Jeremy had been driven home with peed pants by the cafeteria workers' bus, which took people home after the second lunch. I was halfway through a fifth of José Cuervo, she always told the crowd, and here was my kid coming home from his first day of school with wet britches on a bus full of sixty-year-old ladies.

Jeremy always felt like he was supposed to look up from his comic book and wave sheepishly at that part, and he was grateful when he turned twelve and his mom let him stay home by himself. The stories she told about his dad and her, saved for Al-Anon, were even worse.

Staying home from AA was what hooked him up with the crowd that drove him to the hardcore shows, where he sweated so much from dancing that his mom one time thought he was sick the next day, and where he got to look at girls who wore eyeliner and fishnets.

Because he hated the smell and the taste, and because drunk people made him sick, Jeremy did not drink on those rides to Richmond or D.C. He got high maybe twice a month, so that his friends wouldn't think he was uptight, but only on weed and even then just a little. A skateboarding friend of his took acid every day last month and wound up in a psychiatric institution after trying to breakdance on cardboard he dragged onto Route 600. A semi had gone into a ditch avoiding him. Jeremy only knew about it from the letter his friend sent on yellow legal paper; he was coming home, he said, as soon as his mom's insurance ran out.

Even before they got to Vienna, traffic was slowed almost to a stop, and the interstate roadside suddenly filled up with small blue signs for fast food—McDonald's, Burger King, Hardee's. Jeremy's stomach began to growl. One problem with his dad was the extreme lengths of time he could endure without more to eat than chips or beef jerky. "I'm hungry," Jeremy said, craning his neck to see around the traffic. It did not seem ever to end.

John said to just wait. They would have a real supper after the show. He knew a great little diner in Fredericksburg, open all night. Best steak and eggs off 95. John fiddled with the knob on the radio until he found the classic rock station. Creedence poured out, loud, and he turned it way down. He had been going over the course of Dylan's career for Jeremy's benefit. Jeremy knew a fair amount about Dylan from reading rock books he checked out at the library, but he let his dad tell him anyway. He liked it when his dad told stories just for him.

"Now, back in the sixties," John was saying, "everybody wanted a piece of Dylan. John Lennon, he thought Dylan was *God.*"

Jeremy nodded.

"Seriously," John said. "He worshipped him. They brought some tracks from *Sgt. Pepper's,* John and Paul did, played them for him, and Dylan just wandered off. Shit *bored* him.

"But then," John went on, "in concerts people used to boo him. Used to throw stuff if he didn't play what they wanted. They wanted the folk singer. He was doing something new, always, moving *beyond.*

"Just like they doubted him," John said, "when he found Jesus."

Though John did not go to church, he loved Jesus like an old friend you think about but never see. He had been converted back in the seventies by his evangelical boss at the cabinet shop; anytime Jeremy went over there, after school or in the summer, they would be listening to classic rock and Christian preaching tapes, alternating between the two. Cheryl said getting born again was John's only insurance against being fired by that Jesus freak. The cabinet boss didn't really look like a Jesus freak, Jeremy told her. He wore a long beard and jeans and a black leather vest. That's because you don't know what a Jesus freak looks like, she'd said. You don't even know where that name comes from.

Cheryl said Jesus appealed to John because of the forgiveness part, the little you had to do in return for it.

"I saw him," John was saying, "on tour in 'seventy-eight. I went up to Columbus and I waited for him outside his hotel. I saw him come out, and I said, 'You are my brother.' "

This was a story John often liked to tell. According to his account, it happened before Dylan had come out with his born-againness. John said he could feel it, he sensed it. He was born again near the same time, though he had no stories of being touched by Jesus, or feeling Jesus's presence.

By now John was on his last beer, so they stopped at a gas station and picked up another six-pack and a bag of chips and a wrinkled stick of beef jerky for Jeremy. "Don't ruin your appetite," John said. Jeremy laughed a little to himself, shook his head. John never seemed to get that Jeremy was almost always hungry.

John reached into the brown paper bag and pulled out a Coke for Jeremy. He was not the type to offer his underage kid a beer, but he wasn't the type to say *don't tell your mother* either. He was the type to keep popping beer cans at the rate, by Jeremy's calculation, of about four an hour.

John checked his watch; it was about time, he said.

"Let's roll," Jeremy said, trying for the easy slang his dad always used. He had a list in his mind of all the rare Dylan songs he hoped they would hear: "Moonshiner," "Seven Curses," "Wallflower." He knew that John did too.

"Isis," "Need a Woman," "Let Me Die in My Footsteps." "Long Ago, Far Away."

Jeremy had been listening to Dylan all his life, via his parents, but the first time he really *heard* him was one night when he played "If You See Her, Say Hello" on Cheryl's record player. She was on a date with a man she'd met at a meeting, and there was a severe thunderstorm warning on the radio station he was listening to and he got tired of the emergency alert system coming on over and over again, the old man from Sandston listing the counties that needed to take cover in the same slow, drawly voice. Jeremy opened up the record cabinet and found *Blood on the Tracks* at the front of the shelf. It said *C. Graham,* Cheryl's maiden name, in slanted black marker on the upper right-hand corner. Cheryl said that splitting up the music was when she and John had their biggest fights, so after that she made sure to keep her name on everything. Though she bought no more records after the divorce, Cheryl was meticulous about her collection.

Jeremy carefully unsheathed it and placed it below the needle. All the lights were off in the house and he played the same song over and over, lying on the braided rug with his head near the speakers. Peanut, the Labrador, lay beside him. Outside it poured, rain overflowing the gutters and coming in the windows through the screen, the sweet, dark smell of wet dirt and dog. Every time Dylan sang *I've never gotten used to it, I just learned to turn it off,* Jeremy got a big feeling in his chest, like his heart would break.

When Cheryl got home flushed and smiling and saw the stereo on, she asked him what he'd been listening to. Nothing, Jeremy said, not wanting to think about how the song was shared with her or any other grown-up.

It began to cloud up before the opening act went on, and by the time Dylan took the stage, at seven, the air was a cooling gray mist. They had been sitting on the low stone seats for an hour, and Jeremy's butt was starting to hurt. He stood up to stretch and see the stage better, then sat back down.

"Here he comes," John said. "Here he comes."

Dylan mumbled something Jeremy couldn't understand, then started in on "New Morning."

"You shoulda seen him with the Band," John said. "You shoulda seen him with Springsteen, or on one of his tours with Cash."

Jeremy loved Johnny Cash. Sometimes, when John disappointed him, backed out on a plan or showed up to the house too drunk for Cheryl to let him in, Jeremy would imagine that John was not his real dad. He pictured some more illustrious union than the brief one that had joined his parents: maybe Cheryl with Jackson Browne, Cheryl with Willie Nelson. He pictured her in the glamorous embroidered coat she still had hanging in the closet, and cowboy boots. He liked the idea of Johnny Cash as his long-lost dad, reuniting with Cheryl and him after a concert at a truck stop: all of them clean and sober, drinking coffee from heavy white mugs. He thought Cheryl would probably like that idea too. "Maybe they'll tour again," he said hopefully.

"Doubt it," John said. He held a frosted plastic cup of beer in one hand. "Those days are over."

After his third song, Dylan was not looking like a very strong contender for replacement dad. He was wearing a loud Hawaiian shirt and big, dark sunglasses. He had forgotten the words to "Fourth Time Around" and waved the band off after a few seconds, gesturing for them to go on to the next song.

The band played "Lay Lady Lay." Dylan sounded hoarse and his skin was pale. Maybe he was sick. His right hand beat at the guitar strings, but his left hand didn't seem to be moving around very much. Afterward he said, "Thank you very much. Thank you. That's a very romantic song for all of you people out there."

At the beginning of the next song Dylan stood still, strumming the same chord over and over for maybe two minutes. Occasionally he blew into his harmonica.

He sang, *We sit here stranded, we're all doing our best to deny it. Lights, lights, from the—*

Dylan turned around and shouted something to his guitar player. The band kept playing, but he was already walking offstage. The drummer gave up the beat and the music came to a halt.

Cheryl was coming up on an honest five-year chip since her last lapse, but there were days, still, when she did not get out of bed even to brush her teeth. There were men she liked too much and too fast, like the bald feed store man who convinced her to buy the chicks that then got eaten by foxes, or the gym coach from Mechanicsville who turned out to be married. Jeremy was the main person who remembered to use the vacuum, and that was not so often. Their house smelled of dog, and the fridge was often lacking the normal things a fridge should have. She let Jeremy drink coffee, which other parents said would stunt his growth. They shared a twelve-cup pot every morning.

Once, briefly, John and Cheryl had reunited. This happened when

Jeremy was eight, but he remembered it as if it were yesterday. It was around the same time that John tried out the AA meetings. Jeremy remembered John asking him, playfully, if he would mind if he took Cheryl out on a date. Jeremy had taken him seriously. "I guess not," he said. Cheryl arranged for him to stay with a neighbor while they went to see a movie, and they'd picked him up around midnight, giggling but not drunk. John carried him in his pajamas across the wet lawn and both of them had tucked him in. John stayed the night and two nights more, but then he left and didn't come back again, even to see Jeremy, for another month.

"Sobriety scares him," Cheryl had said, smoking a cigarette at the breakfast table on the morning after her first night alone again. She had dark places under her eyes like inky thumbprints, and her T-shirt was on inside out. "You need to know that, hon. If you're used to drinking ten beers by noon, you're gonna get a little freaked out by your sober self. Regular life, real life, is gonna be scary."

"Dad doesn't drink ten beers in the morning," Jeremy had mumbled.

She cocked her head at him, gave him a knowing, grown-up look. "It's sad, really," she said, and Jeremy wasn't sure if she was talking about John or about him.

The stage was still empty while everyone waited for Dylan, and the mist was now a light drizzle. People milled around in plastic orange ponchos, standing with their hands on their hips. Most of the people at this concert were old, with old-hippie hair worn tied back or loose. There were old bikers, old shirtless people who looked sort of like John, and a lot of normal-looking old people in khaki pants and golf shirts. All of them waiting. No one came over the PA to make an excuse or say when things would resume. There wasn't even filler music being played.

John stood up, stretching his arms above his head, exposing his tan, hairy paunch, then swung them back down vigorously. He bounced a little on his feet like he was about to do something athletic, like jump in a pool or go for a jog.

"I think I'll stretch my legs, see what's happening," he said. "You stay here."

It was still plenty warm out, but the accretion of rain on his clothes had given Jeremy a chill, and he was hungry. When Dad gets back, he thought, I'm gonna tell him we should leave and go to that diner. He wondered what Cheryl was doing, and if there would be any new kids at school next year, and when his friend Matt would come home from the mental institution. He thought about his car for a while, and how long TJ Motors could hold on to it without selling it, and when he could next go by there. He was wondering how old he would be when he finally got laid—the most he'd done, so far, was put his hand up his friend Amy's shirt—when Dylan took the stage.

"Technical—," he began, then stopped as if that were all there was to be said. He had a little hat on now, on top of his bushy hair. The rain was letting up. "This is my foreign language song right here."

Jeremy watched the rest of the concert alone. Every now and then he looked around for John. Probably he was sitting nearby with his eye on Jeremy but in a good spot, sound- and sightwise, so he wouldn't want to move. There was no reason to be worried, Jeremy thought.

Dylan was sucking. Forgetting some of the words to "Blowin' in the Wind" and "Maggie's Farm," mumbling the chorus to "Rainy Day Women."

Jeremy wished the concert would end. He thought about changing into dry clothes, about his room and his Walkman and the new Black Flag tape he'd mail-ordered on a friend's recommendation, heard that music banging around in his head, thought about calling his friend Amy on the telephone. He thought about steak and eggs. He wondered if John had had to mail-order most of the music he liked when he was a kid. Probably not, Jeremy thought; he'd grown up in Baltimore. And back then everybody liked the same music and everybody got laid and the music was all good. Then there was finding Jesus, and having a kid, and you didn't even have to *change*—

But here was payback, right here: wasted, old Bob Dylan in a weird little monkey hat. Jeremy craned his neck to look for John again. Was he cringing at this?

He was surely wasted now too.

Here are some alcoholic-dad things John didn't do: he didn't miss birthdays, and he didn't make Jeremy hang out with strange women. He never hit Cheryl, as far as Jeremy knew. He never hit Jeremy. He had never gone to jail for any length of time. He didn't complain about the money he gave Cheryl, though if she asked for extra he always asked what it was for. He knew what grade Jeremy was in, and how old he was, and he knew when Jeremy made honor roll, though that had been some time ago. If Jeremy played a team sport, John probably would have come to the games.

He lived ten miles from them in a built-out double-wide with a deck and a screen porch and lots of scrubby land all around him. He had a little camouflage-painted fishing boat, which he took Jeremy out in. Every summer they fished the Mattaponi for crappie and bass, sitting silent on beer- and soda-filled coolers, always fewer times than they'd planned.

Careful to mark his spot in his memory, Jeremy got up and walked around to look for John. But what if he came back, looking for him? Jeremy turned around and asked a woman nearby if she'd mind looking out for his dad.

"What's he look like, hon?" the woman asked. She bounced a fat toddler on her knee.

"Um," Jeremy said. "Beard. Jeans and cowboy boots. He has a Harley tattoo on his arm."

"*That* should be easy to spot," the woman said.

Her kid started fussing, and Jeremy just stood there, waiting. "Alright, hon," she said. "I'll keep an eye out."

Jeremy walked the full perimeter of the concert stage, up close and far back. No John. People were leaving by now, despite the forty-dollar tickets, walking back to their cars with their blankets and coolers and whiny kids.

Like a bad cover band, Jeremy heard someone say. He thought about all those times in Europe when Dylan had to take getting booed. Maybe, Jeremy thought, he was tired of singing "Blowin' in the Wind" to a bunch of guys in khaki pants. He wished he'd yell something at the crowd.

"This is my fashion song," Dylan said, before launching into "Leopard-Skin Pill-Box Hat." His voice crunched and strained like tires on a gravel drive.

No John. Not by the concession stand, with its strewn beer cups, not by the bathrooms, where he even waited to see if John would come out. He couldn't have left without me, Jeremy thought. That would be nuts.

He couldn't call Cheryl, so he decided to go back to his spot to wait. That was probably where John was, waiting with that woman and her kid. He was probably teasing the kid now, making faces at it and pinching its toes.

But when Jeremy made it back to the spot, the woman was packing her diaper bag, and John was nowhere to be seen.

"You find him?" she asked.

Jeremy shook his head.

"Well," she said, hoisting the toddler to her hip. "Good luck."

Sometimes Jeremy had dreams about his parents in which he was killing one or both of them while the other watched. Sometimes these dreams were bloody, with axes and knives and guns, tendons and bone, and sometimes the dying was clean and matter-of-fact. They never struggled much or seemed surprised.

It had begun to rain again, first soft and faint, like before, then hard, cold pellets that stung Jeremy's skin. He hugged his knees to his chest. Dylan had gotten better at the end, playing "It Ain't Me, Babe" and "Highway 61 Revisited." After two encore songs, the show was over, and everyone made for the parking lot.

Now I'll have to find him, Jeremy thought, and he stood up tall and straight so John could see him better. His stomach growled. He hoped they'd stop at Taco Bell on the way home. Thinking of Taco Bell, with its dirty counters and food he badly wanted but regretted later, just made him hungry and mad.

What's the deal? he'd ask John.

Or maybe he'd just say, *Thanks*.

Security guards were starting, near the stage, to shoo people toward the parking lot. Everywhere there was trash: cups, tickets, napkins, ketchup-smeared hot dog wrappers, crushed beer cans. Head down, tired, Jeremy walked with everybody else like things were normal. Probably John was planning to meet him at the truck.

Jeremy found his father lying on his side behind some bushes on the way to the parking lot. At first, he thought something had happened to him—a fight, a heart attack—but kneeling panicked beside him and rolling him over, he realized that he was just passed out. There were some deflated balloons beside him. His clothes were all wet.

Jeremy shook his dad by one shoulder.

"Hey," he said. "It's me."

John groaned as the rain hit his face straight on. White spittle crusted the corners of his mouth. He smelled bad.

"Dad, wake *up*." Jeremy shook him harder, squeezing his hand around John's shoulder. He squeezed until he thought maybe he made a bruise.

"Okay," John said, not opening his eyes. He sat up unsteadily, blinked them open once. "Okay, Jerm. *Okay.*"

"We have to go home now," Jeremy said in a loud voice. "The security guards will find you, and you'll get arrested."

"Arrested," John slurred. "For what?"

"Stand up, dammit," Jeremy commanded him. He hoisted John up by one elbow. One boot slipped out from under him, then John righted himself. "We have to go to the truck. Drunk in public," he added.

"I just had—"

"Shut up, Dad," Jeremy said. "Please?"

Jeremy was taller than his dad now—John was short, and Cheryl's people were all tall—and so it was possible, but not to say easy, to hook his arm around John's back and, grabbing him under his arm, sort of drag him along. Halfway there John made an angry show of walking himself unsteadily to the truck.

Jeremy had to open the door for him. Feeling the stares of other people, he thought better of propping John up at the wheel and instead pushed him across the vinyl seat to the passenger side.

"Hey," John said, but that was all.

Jeremy settled himself at the wheel, softly swinging the driver's side door shut behind him. "Let me have the keys, Dad," he said. Rain pelted the windshield, making a wet, warped sheet over Jeremy's field of vision. He could see the blue of security uniforms, the orange of traffic wands.

He repeated: "The keys, Dad."

Slowly, John dug into his pocket and brought out his keys. Jeremy had to reach for them and take them out of John's hand, but he didn't resist. Jeremy knew what they all were for: the truck, his work at the cabinet shop, his house, the boat, various padlocks. There was even a key to Jeremy's house.

"Okay," Jeremy said to himself. He put the keys in the ignition but didn't start it.

There was a knock on the window. Jeremy rolled it down a crack.

"Y'all gotta go now," the security guard said. "We gotta clear the lot."

"Yes sir," Jeremy said. He was wishing the guard would ask for his license so that he wouldn't have to drive.

"Buckle up."

At the end of last summer, John had begun teaching Jeremy to drive. He'd taken him to the new developments being built on the other side of Route 30, turning in off the main road and then switching places with Jeremy. He'd taught him to drive stick, just as he'd been taught to drive stick by his West Virginia grandfather. While Jeremy stalled out and ground gears, John told stories of visiting his grandfather, how the car was the only place he was able to drink, so he loved to take John and his brothers out driving. He'd suck Virginia Gentleman straight out of the bottle in the backseat while John careened all over the one-lane roads they favored. John's grandma paid him a nickel apiece for any not-empty liquor bottles he could find. He knew where they all were hidden, but he'd only turn them in if he was hard up, he said.

All of this while Jeremy practically destroyed his transmission. "Careful," he might say, or, "That's third," but he never got impatient or mad.

Jeremy pulled up the seat, adjusted the rearview mirror, slowly pushed in the clutch, and turned the key over. He jerked the truck into first and lurched forward. It was not until he was turning onto the road that he realized he needed lights and windshield wipers. The lights he found easily enough, but the windshield wipers were another thing.

"Where are the wipers, Dad?" Jeremy asked.

John's head was tipped back; he was snoring softly.

Jeremy swore under his breath and tried all the levers until he found the wipers. Seeing the road now, he shifted into second, then third gear. He figured the rest of the cars leaving the concert were probably headed for I-95, so he followed them. His stomach growled as they passed a cluster of fast-food restaurants, but he didn't dare stop. It was raining steadily.

Approaching the on-ramp, Jeremy wasn't sure if he should risk it. He had never driven on an interstate before. But he was in a line of cars all doing the same thing, and the rain wasn't that bad. He shifted jerkily into fourth, accelerated.

Merging, Jeremy hugged the shoulder too closely and threw up a spray of rocks. He turned his neck to look behind him, hesitated, barely made it out behind a tractor-trailer.

John startled. "What," he said. "Careful."

Jeremy could not believe John knew that he was driving them home. He smelled worse in the confines of the truck, a sweat and beer and shit smell.

"I don't have a license," he said. "I'm not *old enough* to drive." The rain picked up again. It pounded the thin metal roof. "I think you stepped in something, Dad."

"Mmm-hmmm," John said, his eyes closed. He leaned against the door.

Jeremy pictured crashes involving a crushed passenger side, or rolling over so that his dad lay pinned to the earth.

Here's the thing about alcoholics: they always know what to say, the true or not-true thing that keeps you from hating them.

"You're the best thing in my life, you know," John said. "Best thing in mine or your mother's."

The rain was coming down so hard now that it pooled over the wipers, cascading down from the roof in great sheets. In front of them, the long line of cars all braked at once, a red, bleary snake.

Jeremy braked too, and the truck skidded left. He held the steering wheel fast and straight until the tires gripped the road again and he could right them back into their lane. He just wanted to make it to a rest area so he could let John sleep it off, or they could call Cheryl. Vainly, he imagined Cheryl coming to pick them all up. Leaving the truck behind and stopping for coffee at a Waffle House. All three of them sobering up to a new life together.

The blue rest area signs approached. Jeremy put his blinkers on, held his breath as he exited. The road was slick and coursing with water. He forgot to downshift as he made it up the hill, and they stalled out. It took two tries to get the truck started again. Jeremy kept his eyes on the rearview mirror. A line was forming, the front car close to his bumper, but no one honked. The car shuddered up the hill in second gear.

Jeremy thought it was a miracle when they made it to a parking spot. He set the brake and cut the engine.

He sat for a minute, feeling the adrenaline drain out of his arms and legs, then dug around on the sandy truck floor for quarters. He found enough for a snack and sodas, but the rain was unrelenting. If he even opened the door he'd be soaked. It had to stop soon, he thought. When it did, he'd make a dash to the shelter.

Waiting, Jeremy remembered a story Cheryl told of watching a friend of a friend die of an embolism. This was before Jeremy was born. Cheryl had been partying with these people and it was late and they brought out needle kits and started shooting up. Cheryl never shot up, not once, that was where she drew the line. The friend of a friend hadn't noticed the air bubble until he was already pushing the needle. Oh shit, he'd said, and everybody at the party had watched the bubble travel up his arm till it made it to his heart, and he died.

That was enough to knock Cheryl off the drugs, though the alcohol took another eight years.

What was funny, Cheryl said, was how the things you encountered on account of drugs were sometimes what kept you on them.

Not funny ha-ha, she'd qualified, as if it needed qualifying. Funny queer.

Life is queer, she said.

John shifted in his seat, making a pillow of his forearm.

Finally the hard rain broke, and Jeremy took the keys and ran to the shelter's snack machines. He bought a Coke and popped it open, drank until his eyes watered. There was a coffee machine too. He put in fifty more cents and a little foam cup dropped down. Coffee squirted into it. He retrieved it, enjoying the warmth on his palms, then set it down next to his feet. With his last sixty cents, he bought a package of butter cookies. He tore the package open with his teeth.

One by one they melted, sweet and tender and uncomplicated, in his mouth. He thought of the smell of beer coolers and trout and river water at dusk. He bent to pick up the coffee, took a sip. It was bitter and burned-tasting, metallic. A faint, purple sheen of oil glistened on its surface.

Then there was thunder, and the sky broke open again. He could see the truck being pelted with rain, the shape of his dad inside it. He stood waiting, John's coffee cooling in his hands. The rainwater trickled into the shelter's cement floor, dark rivulets, but it did not touch his feet.

Homecoming

When Marcus's mother and her boyfriend and just about everybody they knew were put in jail for possession and conspiracy to distribute cocaine, Marcus went to live with his aunt for a while. Marcus was sixteen, a hurdler and sprinter on the track team at Boys and Girls, a solid B student. A good boy, everyone said. Even as a baby, his mama liked to say, he wasn't any trouble. He cried so little that she would forget all about him.

His aunt Tiff was twenty-two and good-hearted, but no one could say that she was good. Ever since Marcus could remember, Tiff was always deciding between boyfriends, and the May when Marcus moved into her apartment was no exception. He came by gypsy cab on a Friday, humping his three duffel bags of clothes up the four narrow flights, Tiff chatting all the while about this one versus that one. It was an eighty-degree day, ten degrees warmer on the stairwell. Tiff walked backward on the stairs, hands free, as Marcus hauled the last bag off the landing. Marcus had left a bunch more stuff at the apartment. What would happen to it? What about his mama's stuff, and the furniture? Nobody had told him anything.

You know, Tiff said, I bet I can get you into a club.

Inside the stale-aired apartment, Marcus looked around for somewhere to sit, but the couch was piled with clothes and balled-up sheets. There were old Styrofoam take-out containers stacked on the coffee table, roaches scurrying in daylight. The windows were grimy and yellow, the screens all busted out. Marcus kept a clean room at home, did the dishes every night. Inside his duffels, every shirt and pair of pants was rolled up in a special way to prevent wrinkles.

Eyeing Tiff's couch, he stacked his luggage neatly and made a seat for himself.

Papo took Mama to a lot of clubs, he said. Look how that turned out.

Tiff perched next to him and draped one long, lotion-scented arm across his shoulders. Don't worry, she said. You and me are gonna have a good time, and Briana will be home before you know it. You ever get high?

At Tiff's place, it was hard for Marcus to study or keep to his runner's schedule, and he failed two of his final exams. When they were finally put out after a big fight between Tiff and her boyfriend and another girl, it was arranged for Marcus to go down South on a Greyhound, to Virginia, where he would live with his father's mother.

"Be good," his mama said over the jail phone, the seriousness in her voice a formality more than a real warning. "Be sweet to your granny and stay out of trouble."

What trouble was there to be had in a little town—not even a town—in Virginia? In his mind he saw cows and fields, weedy ditches, long dirt driveways to nowhere. But he promised her. The way he figured it, he was an expert at staying out of trouble.

It was early September when Marcus arrived. School was already in session, but the air still had that sticky, sweet feeling Marcus remembered from summers a long time ago when he was a little boy. Granny lived in a white house crouched at the very back of a long dirt road. The trees that hid it were bigger now, but it had the same cinder-block steps, the same creaky porch boards. There was one bedroom, where his granny slept, and a sunporch with a foldout couch for Marcus.

Marcus spent the first few days getting reacquainted with Granny, a small, stooped woman with curly gray hair and dry, gray-brown skin. Like Marcus and his dad, she didn't talk except when she needed to. She told him the rules: No going out except on Friday or Saturday, eleven thirty curfew. No girls to the house unless she was there. He could have a job if he wanted but only on weekends and one or two afternoons a week. Keep his room clean, do homework first thing. Church on Sundays.

"Same rules I gave your father," Granny said. "Maybe they'll work this time."

Marcus's father had been in jail since Marcus was eight. He'd come out twice, both times cut short by his probation officer. You can't fight it, he'd told Marcus on those brief and painful visits.

"I blame the city for what happened to Jerome," she said quietly, after a minute. Marcus knew by "city" she was talking about his mother, Briana. She was like the city: loud and flashy and trash-talking, pretty when she took the trouble. Granny seemed to be seeing Briana before her eyes, but then she blinked heavily and looked at Marcus. "It'll be good for you here," she said.

At first it was relaxing, like a vacation. He liked the order of Granny's house, always having clean towels in the bathroom, dinner served to him at a regular time, nobody just popping by for no good reason. He cleaned up every night after supper and Granny said, "Thank you, son." He especially liked looking through old pictures she kept in two shoe boxes. They were of Jerome and Granny and a bunch of relatives he'd never met, and in no particular order. There were pictures from a cousin's wedding and from a family reunion at a park in Washington, D.C. Marcus sat on the scratchy plaid couch and shuffled through the box, looking for a picture of himself. He'd find a baby and ask, "Is that me?" and Granny would look at it and say, "No, that's so-and-so." The closest he ever got to himself were the pictures of his dad when he was Marcus's age—same eyes, same chin.

But it didn't take long for Marcus to get around to missing Brooklyn. On weeknights his granny would be in bed by eight, and since the television in the living room got such poor reception Marcus would go to his room. The windows in Granny's house had no curtains or blinds, so when it was dark he got a creepy feeling, like he was being watched. There were no yellow streetlights, no sirens or car stereos, nobody calling out to anybody else outside. Just unfamiliar sounds rising and filling up the air until it sounded like it would burst from loudness: Frogs? Crickets? He couldn't tell. He'd make up his bed and lie down in it and put on his headphones and close his eyes and think about home.

The funny thing was, what he remembered was not the daily quality of his life, ordinary things like his screeching, one-stop subway ride to school, or the shiny white walls of his small room in the Brevoort Houses, or the weedy courtyard where homeless dudes sat all day with their dicks in their hands. He didn't think about the loud, profane hoochies at Boys and Girls, or how on Saturday mornings there would be glass and needles and vials and condoms all over the track. He didn't remember getting patted down by security guards at school. Instead he pictured the old mansions on Stuyvesant Avenue, with their wavy glass windows and their dark, redbrick exteriors. He remembered the prettiest girls on the track team, with their elegant long leg muscles. He remembered the nicest, youngest teachers, the time the coach said he had a real shot at the state championships. He remembered his one and only field trip to the Museum of Modern Art, all the crazy shit inside, and when the subway would careen out of darkness onto the Manhattan Bridge and you could see everything—the Brooklyn Bridge, the Statue of Liberty, the Chrysler Building, everything.

None of the kids he met at King William High School had ever been to New York City, so Marcus could have told them the Empire State Building was made out of MoonPies and 50 Cent was his uncle and they would have believed him. These were kids, black and white, who hung out at *gas stations* for fun. They looked at his clothes, the spotless Enyce and Fubu and Rocawear and Nike that Papo bought him, and heard the word Brooklyn and figured *he* was the reason he was down here. They figured he had done something, and the rumors started up within a week: that he was a dealer, that he saw a drug murder, that he robbed a jewelry store, that he was part Puerto Rican.

"Rumors, man," was all Marcus would say, shaking his head and smiling, when people asked.

Marcus was in the tenth grade. He signed up for harder classes than he would have bothered with at Boys and Girls: chemistry, English, Algebra II, Technology I, and world history. He figured with not much to distract him, he might as well see what he could do. The track team practiced only twice a week; he signed up for that. He looked in the paper for a weekend job, something to keep him out of Granny's way on Saturdays and out of church on Sundays. He wanted a cell phone—Granny didn't have long distance service—so he could call his friend Khalil and tell him how boring everything was. He wanted a car, because you needed one here to have a girlfriend.

That was how he found Skinny. The ad in the paper said: *Odd jobs for local mechanic. $8/hour. Plus you fix it, you can drive it home.*

That sounded good to Marcus.

Skinny lived on the Mattaponi Indian Reservation, just down the road from Granny. Secretly nervous about the reservation—he pictured teepees and feather headdresses, stony silences—Marcus had her drop him off even though she said it was walking distance. Quickly he discovered that the reservation was no different from anywhere else he'd seen in King William: trees, fields, squat little houses and trailers. All you saw when you pulled up to Skinny's place were cars—old, busted-up foreign cars on blocks: Volkswagens and Saabs and Mercedes and MGs. You could tell they had all been exceptional cars at one time, the kind of cars rich people drove, and Marcus went about picking one out—a dark-blue diesel Mercedes that needed work—before he'd even found the house. As he got closer, he noticed that not one of the cars was fixed up, not even on its way to being fixed up.

Well, he thought. At least the man knows when to ask for help.

Skinny's house was not a regular house, Marcus could tell that much, and Skinny was not skinny but giant and fat. His house was two or three small houses, like shacks but newer, holding on tight to the side of a cliff above the river. He came out of one of the shacks with a beer in his hand and two dogs and another guy with sunglasses and a beard. He did not seem surprised to see Marcus—they'd set up the appointment over the phone—and didn't look twice at Marcus's baggy jeans or clean white T-shirt.

"Can't get a permit to lay a foundation," he explained, waving his hand in the direction of the shacks. He and Marcus didn't even sit down. With effort Skinny propped a boot on the bumper of a trashed Saab, his great gut spilling over his belt, and Marcus stood with his hands in his jeans and answered no to all of Skinny's questions about experience. He didn't ask where Marcus was from, or what grade he was in, or where he went to school.

The sunglasses man stood drinking a beer and laughing, and Skinny spoke to him instead of Marcus.

"Well, Bruce, he was the only one to answer the damn ad. What do you want this job for, anyway?"

Marcus said he wanted to buy a cell phone.

"Good a reason as any, I suppose. When can you work?"

"After school, I guess, on Mondays and Wednesdays and Fridays. I can work any time on the weekends."

Skinny thought for a minute. "What time does school let out? Hell, never mind, better make it weekends starting at nine o'clock for now."

"He's too drunk by three o'clock to work," Bruce explained.

The first time Marcus ran sprints at track practice, the coach called him over. Her name was Mrs. Stephens, wife of Jay Stephens, the football coach. She yelled for the other runners, mostly girls and skinny guys, none of them even very fast, to do a mile of laps. "Wait here, honey," she told Marcus, and then she got on her cell phone. Before long Jay Stephens was chewing on an unlit cigar and leaning on the back of his giant pickup, pulled close to the track.

"Go ahead," Mrs. Stephens said. "Run a forty for us."

When Marcus ran, there was nothing in his head. All he thought about was his body, the way it felt pushing the ground away from him. When he had first started running he ran so fast he sometimes tripped over his own legs. It had been the speed he liked best, everything a blur. He'd run down Atlantic Avenue, under the Long Island Rail Road, just until the first thrilling burst of speed left him and then he'd stop, leaning over and panting hard. Now he liked the control, the way he knew just where his foot would go down to push against the track, the way the force and effort of running traveled up the muscles of his legs and into his abdomen and shoulders and arms, ending in his hands. His fingers curled loosely around this ball of energy, and when he was done he shook them out, releasing it. He trotted back and lifted his chin at the coach, hardly out of breath.

"You ever play football?" Jay Stephens asked.

Marcus shook his head.

"Well, you're gonna play football for us," he said. He nodded at the track. "S'alright, but it ain't football, not here anyway. You'll see. Practice is every day at four"—he pointed with his cigar toward the football field—"over there."

He didn't give Marcus a chance to say yes or no, just hopped back in his truck and drove off, a cell phone to his ear.

Marcus started to stretch for the next round of heats. "I like to run," he told Mrs. Stephens when she asked him, nervously, what he was doing. "The road I live on is too rough."

The coach paid for everything—the uniform and pads and cleats and helmet, all brand-new and in the school colors, black and gold, with a C on the helmet for Cavaliers. Granny made a fuss over them when Marcus showed them off, but asked if he might want to think about quitting his job or taking an easier course load. You don't have to do everything all at once, she said.

"I'll be okay," Marcus said. He didn't say so, but it was good to have something to take his mind off his mama, whose letters were growing more and more bitter. She'd never been in jail before, and she was used to being taken care of in style. She had a closet full of Rocawear herself, which she bet, in letters, her sister had taken and ruined. *And to top it off Papo forgot about me,* she wrote. *I got nothin in my comisary.* Marcus had put off his cell phone plans; he figured he could send some money up to Briana and just talk on a phone card for now.

It took him a few practices to decipher the rules of football; or, more like it, it took a few practices for Coach Stephens to realize that Marcus had barely even watched football before. He sat Marcus down in the locker room and explained it, drew diagrams on a yellow legal pad. They were full of circles and Xs and arrows, and Marcus nodded like he understood. "You'll get it," Coach said. "Just do what we tell you to and you'll be okay."

The first time he was tackled, in practice, was like nothing Marcus had ever experienced. His breath knocked from him, it was like he was flying, like every bit of feeling in his body was concentrated into the place where he had been hit. This is what I've been running from? Marcus thought, standing up. This was nothing; it was better than nothing. It felt *good.* He wanted to be hit again and again and again.

"Wait till they hit you for real, in a game," the coach warned. "These kids are a little scared of you."

"Yeah?" Marcus said. That part felt good too.

"Football!" Skinny cried when he told him about it one Saturday. "I didn't take you for the jock type. You any good?"

"I run fast," Marcus said. They were doing what they always did when Marcus came to work: shooting the shit. Normally they talked about fixing up Skinny's place, or which car to work on next, or the NBA. They had the hood of a green MG open to reveal its engine, a door propped open to Skinny's house, country music blaring. They were fixing it up for Skinny's son; it was going to be a belated graduation present. Marcus's job was to fetch tools and beers and cigarettes for Skinny, run errands to the Food Lion and the 7-Eleven when Skinny was too loaded. Marcus would point out that he didn't have a license and only barely knew how to drive, but Skinny always waved him off. Can't take something you don't have away from you, he'd say. *He* was one ticket away, he told Marcus, from losing his license for good.

"I was on the track team at Boys and Girls," Marcus offered.

"Boys and Girls? What's that, some kinda private school shit?"

Marcus laughed. "Naw," he said. "It's a big public high school in Bed-Stuy. It's got, like, five thousand kids. It has a good track team," he added.

"Bed-Stuy, huh?" Skinny leaned under the hood. "That where Biggie Smalls is from?"

"That's the place," Marcus said. That was the thing about Skinny: he knew more than you'd give him credit for just looking at him. "Track up there is like football down here."

"So, what're you doing down here then? Come to play football?"

And so for the first time Marcus told him the whole story, about his mama and Papo and the police raid. Everybody in his family who could be responsible for him had another five years before they could even think about parole. By then, Marcus said, he'd be all grown up. When he said it, it was the first time he realized that it was true. He'd be a man the next time he saw his dad outside of jail, maybe even his mama.

Skinny shook his head. "That's rough, man. Goddamn police."

Skinny had had his own brushes with the law over the years. He'd been a junkie, and he'd been to jail a few times for that, plus DWI charges every now and again. Now he was clean except for the pain-killers he abused for his hepatitis, and all the beer and sometimes weed. He had an ex-wife and two kids he never saw.

"They shouldn't have got messed up with all that," Marcus said. It felt strange, saying it. He'd never passed judgment out loud on his family before. "I mean, we had this two-bedroom apartment, we had plenty to eat. They had more without the drugs than my granny has living down here."

It wasn't true, but it was something he told himself. Before the drugs Marcus and Briana lived for a year in a shelter, commuting all the way to Bed-Stuy from the Bronx so Marcus could stay in his school. It took the whole year of riding trains and being late every day to get them off the waiting list and into Brevoort.

"People do all kinds of things," Skinny said. "You can't know why."

Wheels weren't the only way, after all, to get a girlfriend in King William County. Football was just as good. Being the newest player on the varsity squad was even better than that, and Marcus soon found that he had the pick of the best-looking girls at school. He chose Charlene, a short freshman with thick legs and a pretty, round face. She waited for him at the end of practice, and they walked home together. She lived less than a mile from his house, and there were dense woods in between where they could sneak off and have sex. Charlene was so sweet, she wouldn't even let him dirty his Enyce jacket by spreading it on the ground under them. "Use mine instead," she would say, offering her dingy down coat.

Marcus wrote mostly about her in letters to Khalil:

Man, it doesn't take much down here to live large. You remember me: skinny dude who ran track? Well guess what. I've got a fine girl (look at her picture) and a job fixing old Porsches and I'm already like some kind of football star and we haven't even had a real game yet. And the girl, let me tell you. We done it in the woods, in her little bedroom with her teddy bears on the bed, even in a car and I don't have a car yet! She's even smart, not some hoochie, she takes Algebra I and helps me with my Algebra II. Did I mention that she is 14 and never even had none before me?

For real, you should move down here. All the girls are like Charlene.

This last part was not true—there were plenty of dogs—but it sounded good.

The first game he played was in early October, an away game. Marcus was hit brutally at the end of most of his carries. After the game was over, he thought he'd never walk normally again, and he felt that way for days.

"You need to gain some weight, some muscle," the coach said. "Take some supplements, drink some energy shakes." He wrote out some suggestions on a note card, even offered to drive Marcus into Mechanicsville to the GNC.

Instead Marcus went with Skinny in his truck, and Skinny even gave Marcus an advance on his paycheck so he could buy the supplements in bulk. Marcus hardly ever made trips outside of King William, and it felt good to be going fifty, sixty, miles an hour on a divided highway. "Broadus's Flats," Skinny said, pointing to the wide harvested fields that stretched before them. They said little more than that until they got to the store, where Skinny made a big show of talking to the salesclerks, comparing nutritional information, and joking about Marcus's training. "Our big hope for the championships," Skinny said. "You're looking at the next T.O. right here."

They spent an hour inside the store, and it didn't occur to Marcus until later, on the way home, that Skinny had done all of that talking and label reading to show off, that he was proud of him. His own son was older than Marcus, in college, but he didn't come around much. At home Skinny had a framed picture of him at high school graduation. He was wearing a long shiny robe and smiling. Marcus tried to remember the last time someone took his picture at home, and he couldn't.

Marcus was ten the last time his dad had been paroled. He was in the fifth grade, and his dad had picked him up early from school. Marcus didn't know that he was coming—the teacher came and got him at lunch, and he'd copied his homework without thought of doing it and packed his backpack and walked into the early afternoon with his dad. It was April and chilly.

They had gone to Coney Island on the F train. Marcus remembered that his dad couldn't keep still on the train. He kept pacing back and forth, reading and rereading the map, tracing his finger along the routes of the A, C, and F trains. When they got to Coney Island, there was a stiff cold breeze off the ocean. They sat with their backs to the wind and ate four Nathan's hot dogs each.

"Man," his dad said, shaking his head. "I missed this."

At the time Marcus didn't think about how rarely, if ever, they'd come to Coney Island. Maybe his dad came out by himself. Or maybe he had come a lot as a child. Probably he just missed the idea of Coney Island. The fact that he *could* come, the same way Marcus would later miss the Museum of Modern Art.

"You sure must be glad to be home," Marcus said. The hot dogs made him feel warm, excited. He started asking questions all at once about when Jerome would be coming by to see his mama, and when he would be moving back in.

Jerome held his hand up, palm facing Marcus. "Son," he said. "Marcus. You know it ain't like that."

And he explained the part about how he'd probably be back in jail pretty soon, for one damn thing or another. After that they rode the Cyclone, Marcus trying to understand the whole time why it was that his dad would be going back, why parole worked like that. It was hard to think with all that up and down, the Cyclone's short fierce run, the way it felt like it was trying to shake him off on every turn. There was no line, so Jerome gave the operator a ten and they rode it again and again, for as long as the money lasted and a little longer.

Marcus waited for his granny to go to sleep before fixing his Pro Performance mocha-flavored protein drink. She said good night and kissed his cheek, and he heard her door shut softly, her dresser open and close. After a half hour, when he heard her snoring, he poured milk into a tall, wide-mouthed Mason jar and stirred in two scoops of grayish powder. He stood at the counter and drank it slowly, steadily, looking past the uncurtained windows into the blank, black night. The taste was chalky and sweet, and he closed his eyes and imagined that new cells—stronger ones—were gathering up in his arms, his stomach, his back, and his legs.

Over the sound of his own swallowing, he heard a low rustling. He looked more closely through the window, past his own reflection at the oak branches closest to the house. There on the lowest branches were the black shapes of the biggest birds he had ever seen. He thought they might be owls, but they were silent and pointy-headed, black-feathered. He didn't think owls looked like that.

Baby Boy,

I am writing you from jail, hoping things are going better for you than they are for me. My hearing came and went. It got postponed. I dont know why but I think its something to do with Papo's case. Damn state lawyer hasnt been here once.

I been thinking alot—all I have time to do—and I been thinking about how when you were a baby me and your daddy liked to take you to Prospect Park to the zoo. I had a nice stroller for you, a big blue one I got almost new. We would wheel you around to look at the polar bears swimming in their pool. The sides of the pool was glass so we could sit your stroller in front of it and you could watch them diving under water, rolling around like it was a show. You loved them bears with their dirty white fur.

You know your daddy and me we loved you and we still do and we want to make things up to you. Its not right having two parents in jail but thats the way it is for now I guess. You know that I picked Papo for you dont you? I picked him so I would have somebody to take care of you, to buy you what you needed and help you get where you needed to go in life. He was so smart and strong and he took care of us. I never loved him. I guess I made the wrong choice but I made it for you.

I want you to be good, but anything you can do for me, for us, would be good too. I think if I can get a real lawyer I can beat this and we can move. I think we should move to Philly.

Love,

Mama

By the end of the month, Marcus had put on five pounds and saved two hundred dollars, but it wasn't enough. The Cavaliers had lost an away game and a home game, and Marcus was benched for much of the time over worries about his knee, which he'd twisted at a game they won in Mathews County. "We got you for two more years, might as well save you for then, when you're bigger," Coach Stephens said, but sitting sidelined and costumed, Marcus felt as useless as a cheerleader, and he knew it was because he hadn't put on enough muscle. He could see, too, that Stephens was disappointed, chewing on his unlit cigar and frowning at the field. Marcus felt bad every time he looked at his shiny new helmet, his expensive pads and cleats. Then there were the letters from his mama pleading for money, protection, a lawyer. Marcus knew you couldn't get a lawyer for two hundred dollars. Charlene wasn't speaking to him, even though he'd spent forty dollars on a trip to the mall with her and Skinny. They were shopping for a birthday present for Skinny's daughter, and he hadn't counted on buying Charlene a present too. He still wanted the cell phone, and the new girl he'd been seeing wanted him to have a cell phone too, plus a hundred other things he didn't have.

Tasha Davis was a cheerleader, varsity, seventeen, twin to Wally Davis, the team's quarterback and captain. Their mama owned a popular restaurant on Route 30 and they lived in a brick split-level house with a neat green lawn and a lawn jockey painted white. School days, if Wally could be persuaded, Tasha would pick Marcus up in her mama's old Camry. Tasha always drove and teased Marcus, calling him "BK all day" and "city boy."

Those two are wild, Granny told Marcus. I remember them from when they was little.

Nah, Marcus said.

Used to drive their mama to distraction in that restaurant of hers. A nice woman, but she spoils 'em.

People change, don't they?

No, they don't.

After losing the home game on the last Friday before Halloween, none of his teammates felt like partying. Tasha was waiting for Marcus in her car.

"Where's Wally?" Marcus said. Normally they shared the car.

"He's mad," Tasha said. "He went home."

Tasha showed Marcus her bottle of Boone's, and they drove on a dark, snaking road Marcus had never been down. Benched again, Marcus was hardly even tired, and what little about the game he remembered disappeared when he saw where Tasha wanted to put the car: in a little gravel spot behind an old burned-down church. After a few sips of wine poured into a Dixie cup, Tasha let Marcus hold her against him in the front seat of the Camry, and he didn't give a thought to Charlene. Maybe it was because Tasha was so different: tall, thin, put-together. Haughty, his granny said. But in the car she was sweet, telling Marcus how she liked him because he wasn't ignorant. Because he'd seen stuff outside of this damn county. She said she hoped she would get in early admission to Grambling State so she wouldn't have to be separated from Wally.

"You don't look like twins," Marcus told her. It was a good excuse, he figured, for looking at her and touching her. "I thought you was cousins at first."

"We do too!" Tasha said. "We've got the same lips, same color and shape of eyes. Same hair if he let his grow."

"He's so big," Marcus said. He pinched Tasha's tiny waist. "You tiny, girl."

Tasha squirmed and laughed, pushing his hand away. "That ain't *natural,* you know."

"What?" Marcus tried to kiss her neck.

"Wally being big," she said, pulling away and widening her eyes in surprise. "You can't say you don't know, BK."

"Don't know what?"

Tasha leaned in close to Marcus's ear. "He *dopes.*" She whispered it breathily, then laughed a hard laugh and took a drink. "He puts a needle in his ass. Sometimes I do it for him."

Marcus didn't say anything for a while. He didn't want Tasha to think he was stupid. Then he said, "I thought he was big."

"You could get a scholarship like him, you know," Tasha said. "With your sad story and your speed, you could get all kinds of college money. You just gotta get playing time. What you do to bulk up?" Tasha said.

Marcus was quiet, then admitted that he lifted every day and drank the powder drinks he'd bought from GNC.

Tasha wrapped her long fingers around his bicep, squeezed. "I'll tell him to come talk to you."

The drugs came in a plain manila envelope on a chilly, cloudy day. Wally's dealer, a white kid with mirrored sunglasses, met Marcus in a hardware store parking lot in Ashland and took his two hundred dollars in a handshake. Inside were a clear glass bottle, three syringes, some antiseptic swabs, and a narrow bottle of pills. Marcus drove home in Skinny's truck, checking his rearview mirror the whole way. He dropped off the truck, threw the keys into the floorboard, and walked off the reservation with the envelope under his arm like a school assignment.

At home, he stashed the drugs in his dresser, then under his mattress. He told Granny he wasn't hungry but made a shake in front of her and took it back to his room. He leaned back in his bed and drank slowly, watching the darkening windows for those big black birds. It was chilly, air seeping in from every crack. He pulled on a sweatshirt and shook a woolen blanket over his legs.

After a while Granny knocked and pushed the door open. She had a pile of blankets in her arms.

"You warm enough?"

"Sure," Marcus said.

"Time to cover up these windows soon," she said.

Marcus asked what she meant.

"With plastic," she said. "I put plastic sheeting up in the winter to keep the cold out and the warm in. What's that you're drinking?" she said.

"It's a shake the coach said to drink," Marcus said. He could feel the milk drying in a mustache. "For nutrition."

"I thought only old people drank those drinks," she said, looking around for laundry to collect. "You'll do it for me then? You'll get the plastic and staple it up?"

Marcus said sure. He asked her about the birds he'd seen—what were they? Owls?

"Buzzards," Granny said, shaking her head. "Not owls, buzzards. We've got a buzzard problem in this county, but they won't hurt you if you don't bother them." She looked around at Marcus's careful pile of schoolbooks, the CDs stacked on his dresser. "You do keep a neat room," she added skeptically, as if that were proof he wouldn't go messing with buzzards.

Marcus stood to close the door behind her.

The raid happened on a Saturday, early, while everyone but Marcus was asleep. Marcus was running at Boys and Girls. When he thought of that morning now, he remembered things in separate fields of sensation: the way the sun looked coming up over the Albany Houses, the sound of the LIRR rushing by, his feet slapping the track. He had on new shoes that Briana had bought for him, black and red Nikes, and he remembered their stiffness on his feet. There was a rock in one of his shoes, a tiny pebble near his left heel, and he remembered its pressure, and stopping to remove it. No one was at the track; it wasn't even seven o'clock. No one was on the street, and the only cars he remembered were livery cabs and yellow cabs on their way down Atlantic Avenue, back to wherever it was that cab drivers lived.

He had run for about an hour. His lungs burned a little, and he had a fine beading of sweat all over his body. His hamstrings tightened as he walked slowly home, drinking water. He thought he'd stretch when he got home, maybe take a nap or do some homework: a five-page personal essay on any topic.

The cops were parked outside, sirens off, when he came inside. It wasn't unusual to see cops outside his building, but he had a nervous feeling as he walked up the stairs, and a dread thud in his chest when he saw his own apartment door open to the hall. Then he heard Briana crying and saw Papo in his shorts and no shirt, hands cuffed behind his back. The coffee table had been tipped over, a basket of laundry that Marcus had done the night before was upended, underwear strewn from one side of the small living room to the other. Sit on the couch, a black cop said to Marcus. He sat. There were no cushions on the couch, so it was uncomfortably low and hard, and he was close to the floor, where almost everything they owned had been tossed. Marcus could see past the living room to the kitchen, where the fridge and freezer doors stood open, their contents spilled onto the floor. All the drawers had been dumped. In the hallway, mounds of clothes and shoes were piled outside of both rooms.

The mistake, Marcus learned later, had been Briana's. That was why she was crying. She had a package she was supposed to stash at her cousin's. She'd been drunk the night before, too lazy to go out and get it done before Papo came by. It had been raining; she put it in the freezer.

Papo had a tattoo on his neck from when he lived in Los Angeles, and a lady cop was asking him about it in an angry, teasing way. His head was thrown back, and he kept saying in a low voice, *Shut up, Bri, don't say nothin'*, and, *I want my lawyer.* When she saw Marcus she wailed louder.

And Papo, louder: *Come on, Bri. Keep it tight.*

It took almost the whole day for them to release Marcus into his aunt's custody. They must have asked him a thousand questions. The only one he knew how to answer was, where was he? Running, he said. Running the track at Boys and Girls. Even that question, the only one with a simple and truthful answer, they asked over and over again.

The waiting, that's what Marcus remembered when he thought about that day. Waiting on a wooden chair in a cold, yellow room. When he turned over his own contraband in his hands, when he swabbed the place he'd chosen, when he drew the medicine into the needle.

He thought about waiting, not knowing what was happening. He thought about the last time he saw his mama, her messy hair falling out the elastic, no makeup, a crust of sleep in her eyes. Through the prison shirt he could tell she wasn't wearing a bra.

Be good, she said, then pressed her fingertips into her eyelids and groaned. It's me that's bad. You always been so good.

At practice he did high knees, butt kicks, crazy legs. He power-skipped across the field faster than anyone, did power slides, quick feet, carioca. He jumped, hitting his knees against his chest so hard it hurt. If the coach said to do five reps, he did eight. After practice he ran cross-country in the scruffy little patch of woods behind the school. "Don't overdo it," Coach Stephens said. "We don't want some hunter shooting your ugly ass."

He was like a TV coach—they were all ugly, stupid, sorry sons of bitches at practice. He drilled them on scenarios and plays, and if they didn't say their answers loud enough, if they didn't shout them like Marines, he mocked them, got in their faces. But before games he slapped their backs and told them they were the best, and they all bowed their heads to say the Lord's Prayer.

In the school's sweat-humid gym he bench-pressed 160 pounds, curled twenty- and thirty-pound weights, did incline sit-ups and leg curls and lat pull-downs. Sometimes at work Skinny would catch him doing squats and shake his big, bearded head. Then he would threaten to make Marcus drink a six-pack of beer, ruin all that work, but instead he fed him hamburgers, lean steaks, soups cooked from scratch. He kept a mug in his freezer and a gallon of milk in the fridge for whenever Marcus came by.

Marcus gained a few more pounds, then leveled off. "You need to buy the whole package," Wally told him one day on the drive home from practice. "The, the . . . testosterone pills, the T-four-hundred, it works together with the other."

Wally seemed to always be forgetting what he was about to say. He would snap his finger in the air or thump his head until it came to him, or say "you know" and "the thing." Marcus once asked Tasha if he'd always been like that and she said, what, you think it's the drugs? Wally's just got a lot on his mind.

"How much is that?" Marcus asked.

"One-fifty."

Marcus shook his head. He'd just sent some money to Briana; he'd bought some groceries for his granny and finally paid his textbook fees. You didn't have to pay textbook fees at Boys and Girls, just like you didn't have to say "free lunch" at the cashier in the cafeteria. There wasn't a cashier. Lunch was just free. "I don't have it."

"I could loan you—"

"No," Marcus said.

"You know, if you had some, you know, connections, there's hardly any competition around here."

It took Marcus a moment to understand what he was saying. They turned onto Marcus's road and Wally stopped the car. By now the road was deeply rutted, and Wally wouldn't drive his mama's Camry down it. Marcus made ready to get out. The tops of the pine trees swayed in the wind. Marcus zipped his jacket. "No, I don't know nobody."

"You sure?" Wally asked. " 'Cause I know you came down here pretty quick. You just have to get the stuff, that's all. Anything. Some weed, some coke. You could sell crack. Crack for crackers."

"I'm sure, man," Marcus said. He got out and leaned in to thank Wally for the ride.

"My sister, she's hard to please for long," Wally said. " 'Specially if you're broke."

Homecoming was late this year; Tasha was on the committee that picked the song and the theme. She told Marcus he'd need a patriotic vest and tie for his suit. The theme was "Red, White, and Blue"; the song was "Courtesy of the Red, White, and Blue" by Toby Keith. Tasha had fought hard for "Air Force Ones" by Nelly. She told the other cheerleaders that it too was patriotic, too, but they didn't buy it. She gave in, picked a red dress, strapless, with shimmery white insets in the skirt. She thought Marcus would be pleased by this theme; it was in memory of 9/11. The year before, she said, the memory had been too fresh, so it was time they did something. That year the song was "Country Grammar."

Marcus thought it was funny how serious everyone here got about 9/11. There were FDNY and NYPD T-shirts and caps for sale at the gas stations, plus "These Colors Don't Run" and "Never Forget" bumper stickers. He didn't tell Tasha how nobody he knew at home thought much about it; at Boys and Girls, they'd talked and laughed as usual during the moments of silence, and never paused to say the pledge or sing any anthems.

Marcus didn't have a suit, but he didn't tell Tasha about that either. He needed one anyway, he figured, for his mother's trial, but he needed so many other things too: the cell phone, free weights for his room at Granny's, plastic sheeting for the windows, more money to send to Briana. The Mercedes wasn't done yet—she still ran rough, and her body was a patchwork of primer spots. Skinny said hell, drive his kid's MG—it was almost completely restored, Skinny's best work in years. The MG wasn't exactly what Marcus had pictured himself driving to pick up Tasha, but the paint job was so shiny he could see his reflection in it. He squinted at himself in his long T-shirt and coat, pictured a sharp gray suit in its place. Marcus would be seventeen in March; he was almost a man.

He and Wally got the Ecstasy in D.C. from a club-owner friend of Wally's dealer. Wally picked Marcus as partner, he said, as a marketing maneuver, that and loyalty to his sister. They would tell the kids in King William that it was from New York, let Marcus do most of the selling. Waiting outside Passions II in his mother's Camry, just off a busy avenue in the northeast part of the city, Wally tapped his fingers against his knees and wobbled his legs, nearly shaking with nervousness. Marcus knew it was also his experience in cities that made him partner. The neighborhoods they'd driven through to get there didn't look much like the worst neighborhoods Marcus had been to in Brooklyn, with their towering brown-colored projects and elevated railroads and truck depots ringed with high, razor wire fences. Everything was low and crouching, ground-oriented instead of sky-oriented. The buildings were two-story frame houses that leaned into one another or crumbled into empty lots. Next to their car, a seagull picked at a McDonald's bag.

"Man, what is it about seagulls and the ghetto?" Marcus said. "Those must be some lost-ass birds."

Wally didn't say anything, so Marcus went on: "Maybe they're looking for some bootleg DVDs."

When Wally didn't laugh Marcus knew he must be really nervous. He had a lot at stake: the scholarship, for one, plus his mama'd probably kill him if she found out he even drove the car to D.C. She thought he and Marcus were going to Tysons Corner to shop for the homecoming dance. Marcus thought about what he had at stake. Not much, he guessed—a job running errands for an ex-junkie. His granny would sure be mad, but his mama and daddy couldn't say much, could they? He envied Wally, with his big muscles and his nice house and all he had to lose.

When the metal door opened and a man in dreads waved them inside, Marcus nodded at Wally to reassure him. They didn't say anything as they got out. Wally had to close his car door twice to make it stick.

The nightclub was cavernous and empty. On a landing a DJ was setting up his equipment. The perimeter of the room was set with dirty couches. There were smeared, hand-printed mirrors along one wall. Marcus and Wally sat at the bar and waited for Wally's dealer's friend. Wally's dealer had said to put the money in a FedEx envelope. Wally took the envelope from his backpack and set it on the bar, then changed his mind and put it back.

Marcus was expecting someone who looked like Papo, or the men who used to sit in their trucks on Nostrand Avenue with a thick chain and a ring on almost every finger. Instead they were approached by a muscular man of about forty wearing a lavender dress shirt. He smiled broadly at them. "You must be Marcus and Wally. I'm Tony." He sat down next to Wally and asked the man in dreadlocks to bring them three Cokes. Marcus saw Wally's hands shake as he handed him the envelope.

Tony looked in the envelope for a long moment. He nodded to the dreadlocked man.

"I hear you boys are football players," he said, standing. His voice was friendly and calm.

"Yeah," Wally said, straightening up like he was a recruiter.

"I played," he said thoughtfully. "But that was a long time ago. I had a coach that would bust your ass. They still doin' that?"

"Sure," Wally said.

"I hated that motherfucker."

Tony bounced his fist lightly on the bar, like he'd cleared something up. "Well, thanks for stopping by, boys. You're always welcome here. Don't forget your radio."

On the bar a few feet down from them had appeared a small black nylon bag; it might have held a CD player. Wally picked it up as they went out.

Fifty-fifty, that was how they would split it.

Everybody had a part to play. Wally had to secure the connection, pass the word around school. He started by giving a couple of pills to Percy Wills, a big redneck everybody knew smoked weed after practice, and L. T. Betts, a stoner kid who hung around the field waiting for his girlfriend to be done with color guard. "Be more at homecoming," Wally said. "But not for everybody and not from me. I got these from Marcus Conway. He says he got some more, but only for those that can keep they mouths shut. Forty a pill, have yourself a good ol' time like they do in New York."

Marcus had to look sharp, keep his clothes clean, run the ball. He had to buy new clothes for the dance, get an all-blue corsage for Tasha, wash the MG on loan from Skinny. Granny didn't want him driving it at first; she frowned into its paint job, saying no young man needed such a shiny car, but she gave in after he told her he could keep it until Sunday, to drive her to church.

The game was on Friday, the dance was Saturday. Before the game and without Granny's knowing, Skinny cooked dinner for Marcus, Tasha, Wally, and Wally's girlfriend, Shay: barbecue, coleslaw, and potato salad and sweet tea for the girls, homemade energy bars and milk for the players. Granny had made it clear that after the borrowed car and the dates, Marcus was to *stay home some,* to drive her to Tappahannock for shopping and to her Ladies' Circle but other than that to *stay home* and do his homework. But even she wasn't hard enough to spoil homecoming season. She'd seen his father through it, after all, twenty-some years before.

Jerome had been a football player, too, though he didn't get to play as much as Marcus. But as the season advanced, as Marcus ran yard after yard, Jerome just got better and better. The way Granny told it, racism was the only thing that kept Jerome Conway from the pros.

He'd been on offense too, and fast, Granny said. "Like lightning," she'd say, shaking her head as if at a driver going too fast down her road. Marcus hadn't grown up hearing any of these stories; he knew his dad played, but it was never anything he made a big deal over.

Skinny, he was another story. He'd been at King William about ten years before Jerome, and he claimed he'd never played a single sport, not in any organized way. Marcus thought he must have regretted it; how else to explain the homemade granola bars, the time it must have taken to clear his table and four mismatched chairs of paper and tools and parts catalogs? The barbecue sauce he'd made for their dinner was a homemade, secret recipe. Marcus didn't think he'd ever had homemade barbecue sauce. It smelled delicious.

"Aw, man, just a taste," Wally said as his sister laughed and licked her fingers in front of him. It was almost time for them to go. Skinny was brown-bagging the plentiful leftovers for after the game. "After you've kicked King and Queen's ass good," he said. "Not before."

Marcus hadn't said much at dinner, but he wasn't sweating the game. King and Queen would be an easy defeat—both their good players were hurt, and they'd beaten them bad in September. With all of them crowded into Skinny's small dining room and Skinny bustling around them like someone's mom in dark glasses and low-slung Wranglers, Marcus felt anxious, the way he'd felt when his coach came over to his apartment at the Brevoort Houses and Briana had just gotten up from a nap. Did he have to smoke in this tiny-ass house? Marcus coughed dramatically and waved his hand back and forth in front of his face. The room suddenly felt too small, crazy-small, and he thought how Tasha and Wally must see it. A run-down shack with a fat Indian drinking himself to death. A coffin. Marcus craned his neck to read the time on the stove's clock.

"This'd be a chill place for an after-party tomorrow night," Wally said. He stood and walked to the room's only window, onto the field across from Skinny's. It was true; the reservation was empty and open, inviting. "Shit," he said. "What's that?"

Skinny had been drinking—a lot, Marcus could tell. He was slurring his words, and he stumbled as he moved to stand next to Wally. "Goddamn it," he said, grabbing a broom and rushing outside. The little house shook as he opened the front door and stomped onto the front steps, waving his broom.

"What the hell?" Tasha asked.

"Buzzards," Skinny announced. He seemed soberer, more awake. "Can't keep 'em off my property."

"They hunting something?" Wally asked.

"Buzzards are scavengers," Skinny said. "They like dead meat. Rotting meat."

Everybody looked at the barbecue. "No, not that," Skinny said. "Something must have died down there, on the riverbank." Marcus didn't admit that his house had buzzards too.

"So," Wally said. "Cops come around here, like at night?"

Marcus interrupted. "We can't—"

"No, it's all right," Skinny said. "I don't think I remember them coming by lately. It's pretty far from the Fas Mart, pretty far off Route Thirty. I suppose if you wanted to come here and drink some beer there wouldn't be any harm in it. I can't be responsible, but I can try to keep an eye on things."

Marcus was shaking his head even as Tasha and Shay and Wally were grinning and planning and thanking Skinny. In his excitement, Skinny spilled a full can of Budweiser across the cluttered little dinette.

But then Marcus started thinking about Tasha in her cheering uniform, Tasha after the game, and about borrowing the MG and finally about the game, about the advances he'd make, and suddenly he forgot to be worried.

Marcus had been nervous and absentminded at the pregame warm-ups, and the coach yelled at him to get it together. Sorry, sorry, he'd mumbled too low for the coach to hear.

Maybe you don't want to win? the coach asked. Maybe you just wanna *hang out* for the month of December, huh? Do some Christmas shopping?

The game started badly, with the Chargers quickly shutting down the Cavs' offense and getting the ball back in under a minute. They looked bigger on the field than Marcus remembered. They were a team of mainly black boys, while the Cavs were about half and half. They had a reputation for playing dirty, but Marcus had chalked that up to racism. Now, looking at them across the line of scrimmage, he wondered. It seemed like they were all looking at him, marking him. He squatted down, touched his finger to the dry, chilly grass. They were at their own thirty-yard line, and Marcus could see Stephens standing with his arms crossed.

The Chargers blitzed on first down. Wally overthrew a pass to Martin James, who had always been short on speed. On second down, they managed to advance only two yards.

On the sideline, Stephens shook his head in disgust. He signaled for Wally to hand off to Marcus.

The ball was light in Marcus's hands, slippery almost. One of the Chargers' linebackers was already around the Cavs' line. Marcus ran straight at the sideline, straight at Stephens, the linebacker on his tail. Then he pulled up, spun, and felt the linebacker drop off behind. He ran, expecting the hit from the safety, knowing he'd make first down. The hit was low, and he came down heavily on his chest.

When he stood up, he saw that everybody in the stands was on their feet, glad for some good news. Nobody much had come out for track meets at Boys and Girls, only a few parents and relatives for some of the older, star runners, the ones with college scholarships and plans. Briana had never gone to one, and nobody had said much about college, but Marcus always thought that would happen later, in eleventh or twelfth grade. He looked for Tasha, saw her pom-poms in the air. He swore he could see Skinny's big gut shaking with his clapping.

The Cavs drove down the field, and Wally's touchdown pass connected. The Chargers responded with a touchdown of their own, but missed the extra point. At halftime the score was 7–6. Stephens wasn't happy. Are we going to lose our own damn homecoming game to a bunch of boys who can barely count to fourth down? he said.

Wally's passes had been straight and true—a girl could catch them, Marcus thought—but he hung his head with the rest of them. Then they prayed and Wally asked if he could say something.

"Assuming the good Lord sees right to let us win," he said, standing up in the middle of them. His shoulders were massive in their pads. "Assuming that the Lord is with us, I just want to be there to do His will. I want to do right by y'all, to put the ball in the air and get it down the field.

"We're gonna have the ball back when we go out there, and I want you to slam 'em. I want you to come down hard on 'em, I want to see 'em spittin' out mud."

He went on for a while longer.

Marcus was silent. He'd been slapped on the back by a few players and told he was doing right by the coach. He just wanted the ball again. He could hear the band playing "We Will Rock You" on the field.

It was colder after halftime, the sky blacker behind the floodlights. They charged forward on the kickoff. A white kid named Jim Shelton caught it at his belly and managed to get it to the Cavs' forty-yard line.

They set up for a running play and Marcus felt all eyes on him as the other team hunkered down. Marcus carried the ball into the Chargers' territory. No one had laid a hand on him. He felt like he could outrun anybody on the field.

The Chargers blitzed, and the Cavs ran a draw. As several Chargers rushed from the outside, Marcus again took the handoff from Wally, and ran straight up the middle, juking a linebacker and winding up in the end zone. He watched the Cavs' side of the stadium come out of their seats. He saw the cheerleaders' feet leave the ground.

On his next carry the linebackers ran his face mask into the turf. The Chargers had failed to get anything on their last possession and they were gunning for him. It took a long time for someone to take his weight off Marcus's helmet. Cleats sank into his leg.

He retched once. Then he stood up, looked at Wally, and hollered. Wally hollered back. The pain was superficial, a condition of his strength. The strong were going to get knocked down; they were going to have people coming at them from all sides. They had to be ready, they had to be looking for the hit. That was what Briana should have known when she put the cocaine behind the frozen pizzas. That was what Papo should have known when he trusted Briana—what he did know, now that he'd shaken her. That's what Jerome should have known when he came out only to go back in weak and tired after a couple of weeks of drinking and looking people up, for robbing the same bodega he always robbed.

Marcus saw that now. The bruising he felt was just on top. Underneath, where it mattered, he was muscle and heart.

The Cavaliers won the game by two touchdowns. Marcus had carried the ball eleven times. Tasha jumped into his arms when the game was over, and Skinny and Granny were standing together at the fence, smiling at him.

Marcus slept late on Saturday, read twenty history pages without committing a word to memory, and finally showered at around four. He soaped his body tenderly, massaging all the sore parts until the hot water ran out. He still had to pick up Tasha's corsage and put gas in the car. He had to organize his thoughts, play back every moment in the game before it disappeared. First he remembered them in order of importance, starting with his touchdown after halftime; then he remembered them in chronological order. When he'd done that three or four times he turned his thoughts to the dance. There was money to be made.

He'd thought that they could keep the pills in the car to keep from dealing inside, but Wally said no, that wouldn't work. You could only come into the dance once; when you left, you left for good. Marcus wasn't eager to deal the drugs out in the open like that, but Wally said not to worry. They kept the gym lights dim. There'd be so many people that no one would even notice. Plus, didn't kids at Marcus's school start dealing when they were, like, eleven? Didn't they deal in the bathrooms?

Marcus told him the story of a third grader he'd known way back when who sold dime bags in summer school. He remembered the runner he knew in fifth grade who wore a diamond in each ear and attacked the principal at lunch, the ninth graders who dealt in gym class. Wally listened with a pleased and unsurprised look. Marcus didn't mention that he knew all these stories because the kids had gotten caught.

Tasha would be putting up the decorations. She would be wearing that tight velvet tracksuit of hers and standing on a chair, her hair done already, calling out orders to the other girls. It made Marcus smile to think about her. He wondered if she was thinking about tonight too—if she'd be ready to go all the way. He wondered if she felt nervous about that, or about the drugs. Probably not, Marcus thought. Things came easy to Tasha. She'd already talked on and on about being crowned homecoming king and queen. The way she figured it, her toughest competition would be Wally, and Wally's Shay was too shy to be queen. Tasha was the most beautiful senior girl who was also smart and classy, and Marcus didn't really look like a sophomore, not anymore. Just have yourself a good time, Marcus told Tasha. Don't be thinking about that.

No, she said, looking at him. Not like a sophomore at all.

Doing his errands, though, Marcus thought she might be right.

He was congratulated by three different people at the florist's, and asked when championships were when he gassed up the MG. How many more games would they have to win to make the championships? He was asked that question a half-dozen times; everybody knew the answer. Two more games.

Granny fed him a sandwich and took his picture alone and with the car; Tasha's mom took about fifty pictures on the stairs, in front of the house, on the lawn, beside the car. Marcus wanted to drive Tasha and Wally to Granny's house so they could take more pictures over there, but Tasha said no, there was no time, their reservations at Outback Steakhouse were at seven and they were already late. She'd love to see you, though, Marcus said, looking at Tasha. She was gorgeous—tall, slim and curvy both, her hair done up high and glossy, sparkly eye makeup. He thought he'd never seen such a beautiful girl before, and he worried about never getting a copy of the photo to send back home. We can't be late, Tasha said, hurrying him to the car. We'll see her after.

Your mama can get double prints?

Tasha laughed. What? You think we're never gonna look this good again?

Music was pouring out of the gym. Marcus said he didn't know country music could get so loud. Don't worry, Tasha said. I rigged it so they play one song for them, one song for us.

And what do you mean by them and us? Wally teased. She rolled her eyes.

Red, white, and blue streamers brushed Marcus's face as they entered the gym through the double doorways. Tasha took his hand and showed him the balloons, the banners, the tablecloths, the punch. Taped over the exit doors was a giant painting of the Twin Towers at night. Someone had painted hundreds of square yellow windows in each of the towers. They looked like giant tenements. Underneath, in cursive, were the words *Never Forget*.

"See?" she said, leading him to the wall of collapsed bleachers. "All the girls painted a poster with the different player numbers." She pointed out the neatest, most elegant poster—number 22, done in sparkling gold paint. "I painted yours."

Marcus nodded. Everybody was looking at them. He scoped out an empty table in the corner and took his seat. His knees bounced a little; he hid them under the table and told himself to be cool.

Wally walked off to get them some punch and say a few words to some people. He'd told Marcus to expect about ten customers. If each bought two hits, that was eight hundred dollars—four for Marcus, four for Wally. That wasn't so bad, but it just paid for dinner and Marcus's suit and Tasha's corsage and gas, with only a little left over. If they did better, well, that would be good. He had forty pills.

From where he sat, Marcus could see his history teacher and the home ec teacher, the fat principal and his wife. The youth minister was there, plus the cheerleading coach and her sister. Seven chaperones, as far as he could tell. They were all busy talking, lingering by the punch bowl. Marcus had heard rumors about spiking the punch bowl; apparently, this was something that had happened in the past.

Marcus could see Charlene standing with another boy, a junior he recognized from track practice. He was also in Marcus's technology class; he was stupid and lazy, couldn't decipher an electrical circuit to save his life. What was Charlene doing with that guy? Trayvon, that was his name. She wore a lacy, strapless white dress that was too long for her. It trailed the floor when she walked. Her hair was sprayed up into a fan on the back of her head and Marcus could see tiny, sparkling rhinestones stuck to its surface, catching the light. She cut her eyes at Marcus.

"What you looking at, baby?" Tasha stood before him, smiling broadly. She held out a cup of red punch.

Marcus shook his head and focused on the plastic cup in his hand. The ice cubes were white and blue; where they melted the punch was starting to turn an oily-looking purple.

Tasha leaned in close to him. "Don't be nervous," she whispered. "We'll relax later."

Marcus put his hands on both sides of her narrow waist and drew her nearer. "Will we?"

"We will."

His first customer was L.T. It was strange to see him dressed up in a suit. The tweed jacket and pants didn't match, and his hair had been slicked back with gel. He wore a narrow-collared white shirt and a skinny black tie. He sat down next to Marcus. "That shit was awesome," he said.

Marcus nodded, leaned forward, and looked around. The adults were all the way on the other side of the room, probably talking about church or Costco or whatever it was they talked about. They were near the bathrooms, though. It would be better, Marcus figured, to hand over the pills right here.

"Seriously," L.T. said. His eyes were on his girlfriend, who was dancing in a circle of other girls. She was a plump girl in a short red dress. "Brittany and I never did it like that before. I mean, she was wild, man."

Marcus held up his hand. "I don't need to know all that. How much you want?"

L.T. shook his hand, passing him eighty dollars. "That was an awesome game last night."

Marcus set two pills down on the table, under a napkin. "Thanks," he said.

"You know Brandon and Shaun 'n' them?"

Marcus nodded, though he didn't. Wally came over, fresh from the dance floor. He wiped his face with a handkerchief and sat down, turned to L.T. "You got friends who want some?"

L.T. nodded.

"Send just one over. Tell them to be cool, act like they're coming to talk to Marcus about football. Shake his hand, pat his back, shit like that."

He looked at the clock; it was nine thirty. "He's done at ten thirty."

For the next hour, Marcus was congratulated by every stoner, redneck, doper, and druggie-preppie at the school. He danced only once with Tasha, a slow dance. Her back felt warm and strong under his hands; he could feel her breasts as she leaned against his chest. She laid her head on his shoulder and whispered the dirtiest things he'd ever heard from a girl into his ears. Then he walked back to his chair and waited for ten thirty to come.

Some people he told to take just one; others he dealt to silently, accepting their praise stone-faced and serious. Wally kept coming by, even though he'd said he wanted to stay out of the dealing part. He told a few people to meet them out at the reservation by Skinny's. He said they'd play better music; there'd be beer there too. Between customers, Marcus said he didn't think that was such a good idea, but Wally told him not to be so uptight; it'd be fine.

The first person to lose her cool was Wally's girlfriend. Giggling, she spilled punch on Wally's lapel and tried to lick it off. She spilled some more into her own cleavage and tried to sit on his lap, then Marcus's. When that didn't work she settled for Tasha's lap. She leaned her head back into Tasha's neck and moaned a little.

"You are so fucking stupid, Wally," Tasha said.

Shay looked plastered. The strapless bodice of her dress was askew. Her hair had fallen out of its careful arrangement. Her lipstick was worn away from kissing on Wally, so that only the dark liner remained. Normally she was cute.

"Borderline retarded," Tasha said, bouncing her knee. Shay squealed. "Get her out of here."

"I can't," Wally said, nodding toward the exit doors. The principal was dancing with his wife to "Unforgettable." "We can all go when they get up onstage to do the awards," Wally said. "We'll slip out."

"*Fuck* that, Wally," Tasha said. "I spent two hundred dollars on my dress, not to mention my hair and nails. I am *not* leaving early."

"Here," Wally said, shaking out a napkin and throwing it over his sister's head. "You're the goddamn queen already."

Tasha snatched the napkin off her head. "Don't make Marcus beat the shit out of you."

Wally started to laugh, his broad shoulders convulsing under fine charcoal pinstriping. The song ended and the principal and his wife bowed while the students clapped. Wally was still laughing when the next song started and everybody ran onto the floor.

"Oh Lord," Tasha said. "Look."

Two of the cheerleaders, Megan Trice and Stacey Adams, were grinding each other to the opening, censored-for-radio bars of "Back That Ass Up." It had been a cheerleading favorite, though no one would let the cheerleaders perform the routine they choreographed. Near the stage, a freshman was wiggling out of her dress.

"Hey," Shay said, sitting up and frowning. "Why'd you think you and Marcus will be king and queen? Wally played good last night too."

"You better hope they don't pick you, you dumb slut," Tasha muttered.

"*Tash,*" Wally said.

"You better hope they don't pick you too," Tasha said. "If I was you I'd be over at the ballot box right now, voting for my non-fucked-up sister."

Before the night was over, two couples were thrown out—one for making out in the hallway to the bathroom, the other for trying to have sex under an uncollapsed portion of the bleachers. The home ec teacher found both of them and marched them outside, but seemed to suspect nothing. Marcus didn't know either couple well enough to be sure they wouldn't snitch, but they hadn't looked embarrassed as they walked out.

"Don't worry," Wally said. "You think they'll care about missing the rest of this boring-ass dance? They're about to wear each other out."

In a little while, Marcus was the king and Tasha was the queen.

The crowns were plastic, and the comb that held his in place bit uncomfortably into Marcus's carefully groomed head. Wally had sneaked off with Shay; they were probably in the back of the Camry by now. From the stage Marcus could see the yellow and black disposable camera he'd brought along sitting unused on the table.

Newly crowned, Tasha wouldn't hear of going off by herself with Marcus. And she couldn't just leave her brother, could she? She didn't want him to drive anyway; she'd take Shay in the Camry, and Wally could ride with Marcus. Wally had just taken a hit, and he wanted to go to the reservation with everybody else. Come on, Tasha said, let's have some fun.

Marcus was relieved that the night had gone off without more problems. He and Wally each had more than six hundred dollars. He could send some of that to Briana, use the rest to buy his next round of steroids. When the season was over he'd spend time lifting and running, and by next year he'd get scouted. In the car as they made their way onto the little gravel road, Wally was talking about what was next.

"I mean, this could be a regular weekend thing," he said, "if we get some more stuff. We could get some pills, some coke, maybe some heroin."

Marcus thought about Skinny, what he'd said about being a junkie. "I don't want to deal heroin," he said quietly.

"Okay," Wally said. "We got to give the people what they want, though. Am I right?"

Both hands steady on the wheel, Marcus repeated himself.

The reservation had no streetlights. They parked alongside a field and stumbled out of the MG. Two football fields away they could see Skinny's little shacks, one light shining through the fencing. Marcus looked up; the sky was creamy with stars, more stars than he'd ever seen in his life. He thought about how he didn't know any of their names. He couldn't even find the Big Dipper.

"Whatcha looking for?" Tasha asked. Her eyes were shining; she smiled and looked up at him. He hoped that she hadn't taken a hit.

"It's right there," Tasha said, pointing. She took his head in her hands and pointed him in the right direction. He could feel her long, red nails grazing the skin on his face. "The Big Dipper. Right?"

Shay fell back into the long dead grass of the field. Wally pretended to tackle her. Far away, then closer, they could hear the whoops and hollers of rednecks advancing across the field in their trucks. Marcus looked up at the stars, a whole bewildering sky full of them.

Above Skinny's house, dark shapes were circling and swooping low, grazing the treetops. The field was filling up with people now, but nobody else seemed to notice the stars or the birds. After a while, Marcus forgot about them too.

By the time Marcus gets around to winterizing his granny's house, it is December, and it is the last good thing he does for her. He approaches the task methodically, measuring and cutting the heavy plastic sheeting and laying it flat on the frozen ground outside each window. He starts with Granny's bedroom window. He climbs a rickety wooden ladder leaned against the windowsill, hoists up the plastic, and rests his borrowed staple gun on the sill.

She is at church. Through the casement panes he can see her little iron bedstead, the smoothed sheets and quilts just so, the pillowcases taut and ironed. He can see her framed picture of Jesus on the wall, his face thin and sorrowful inside the cheap ornate frame. There is her nightstand with its windup clock, her hooked rug, her white wooden dresser. Her closet door is open and he can see her rack of dresses, limp and accusing.

It took just days for Marcus to get caught. One of the football players' girlfriends went too far at the bonfire with another guy, and the football player snitched. Marcus was dragged into the principal's office during Algebra II the Wednesday after homecoming. By the end of the school day, when he should have been practicing, getting ready for the championships, he was at the police station in Aylett. All alone—no mention of Wally, who was in that very same Algebra II class. He hadn't even looked up.

The principal had gone on about fresh starts and taking people's goodwill for granted. He'd shaken his head over the championships. He said Marcus might never get another opportunity like that again, but it didn't sound like it meant much to him. Think about all those people you hurt, he said as he handed over the expulsion hearing paperwork he'd already prepared. Think about all they were trying to do for you.

Marcus had looked at the thin stack of papers the principal handed across but did not take them. Wally. Where the fuck was *Wally?* Sitting in Algebra II, right where he was when Marcus left, hunched over his notebook like those x's and y's held some kind of secret. Marcus puffed out a long sigh and leaned back in his chair, slouching to one side to show that those papers didn't matter any more to him than they did to the principal. He lifted his chin and narrowed his eyes like he'd seen kids do at Boys and Girls, the kids who waited with their mothers or grandmothers in a line of chairs outside the office, the kids going out on long-term suspensions, expulsions. He didn't say a thing.

And the principal had cleared his throat and set the papers down, very gently, at the edge of his desk, so that an inch or so of paper hung off the edge and Marcus could snatch them up without touching anything. Marcus kept his eyes slitted until they burned, shifted back farther in his seat. The chair scraped the tile floor and the principal flinched. You're not a bad kid, he tried, looking over Marcus's shoulder to the door. Marcus blinked twice and the burning stopped. He took the papers.

Think about all those people you hurt. Marcus didn't think he'd hurt anyone except Granny, and even she seemed unsurprised at how things turned out. What he'd done hadn't touched Wally or his scholarship, and Tasha would find another boyfriend easy, some college boy most likely. Marcus tried to call them after he was home again, but he just kept getting their mother's voice on the machine. He'd called and called until finally Tasha picked up. *Don't call here,* she said. *Please.* He hung up without saying a word to her.

Marcus thinks a lot about Skinny. Skinny was the one who bailed him out; he finished and sold the Mercedes himself to cover the cost. Skinny said he'd have sold the MG too if they needed. Naw, Marcus told him, that's your son's car. Skinny said the boy didn't want the car. He wanted something else, something newer. He had this look on his face that made Marcus hurt inside. Just keep it, Marcus said.

Marcus has a state-appointed attorney, a woman he met in person once, when she brought him the plea agreement. If he didn't take it he'd be looking at a felony sentencing in an adult court. Did Marcus know what a felony meant? the attorney asked in her brisk way. He did, he said. No military service, no voting. Those weren't things he'd counted on or looked forward to.

No, she corrected him. It meant time in prison. Years. And there were two of them. Sale of a schedule I controlled substance. Five years. Within a school zone. One more year. She looked down at her yellow legal pad. Marcus could go to circuit court and risk six years in an adult jail or take sixteen months in a juvenile facility in Richmond, and on his eighteenth birthday, he would be free. The attorney said they have a high school at the juvenile hall. You can take the classes you need to graduate, or you can get released from compulsory attendance and just study for your GED.

Would Marcus's mother or father be there to read over the plea agreement? I brought it home and they read it, he said. They said go ahead and sign it.

She moved to sit next to him while he read over the statement of facts, an outline, hour by hour, of the night of the homecoming dance. He read it so slowly she asked him if he wanted her to read it aloud. Asked it delicately, like he couldn't read well. He said *no ma'am,* polite like he was taught to be, though he was thinking something else. He picked up the pen and she showed him where to sign.

Would there be a track to run on at the juvenile facility? She wasn't sure but told him she'd check. So far she hasn't checked.

He lifts up the plastic and fits it over the window. He staples the corners first, smoothing out the gaps and wrinkles. He holds the staple gun against the worn window frame and presses hard. It makes a loud, echoing *wa-pow.*

When he is done with Granny's bedroom window, he does the kitchen, the living room, and the bathroom. He trims the extra plastic with a razor so it doesn't look sloppy. He's saved his room, with all its windows, for last.

There is his foldout bed, his little desk with all his half-written letters on top: to Khalil, to Briana. To Jerome, who told him the truth a long time ago: no sense in fighting it. There are his schoolbooks in the corner. His Walkman on the dresser. His closet filled with clothes.

It's cold. Marcus blows on his bare hands, zips his jacket, and wonders who will look after his things. He fits the plastic neat and tight over the old windows. *Wa-pow, wa-pow.* If you don't pull the plastic tight across the window, cold air will get in.

When he's done he presses his face up close to the plastic. You can't see anything except the vague dark shapes of furniture and doorways. He goes inside, where he tells himself it is already warmer. In his room he lies on the little couch and puts his headphones on but doesn't turn on the music. He looks up at the windows, which stretch around three sides of his room. From the inside he can see a little better, but there isn't much to see after all. If he'd stayed in Brooklyn he could be practicing for spring meets, running on a track that this time of year was almost empty. If he'd won some meets, who knows, maybe he could have thought about scholarships, college. Football had been a mistake from the start. He wasn't a good strategist, like Wally, anticipating plays, looking ahead. Nobody he knew was like that. They were runners like him. Sprinters looking back from the finish line.

Tonight Skinny is making dinner for Marcus while Granny visits a church friend. He has to sneak out to see anyone. He's going to be good for his last weeks with her; she is making sure of it. *Good:* it's a word she still hangs on to. It means nothing to Marcus now. It's a lie, something you tell little kids about but you know they'll figure out the truth later, like Santa Claus and college. Nobody's good, Marcus thinks, but some people are tolerable.

The wind pushes the plastic against the windows, releases it, and pushes it again like breathing. Down the road Skinny's been cooking for days in his tiny kitchen, making chestnut stuffing and cranberry sauce and sweet potato pie. He's calling this an early Christmas dinner, like Christmas can be moved from one date to another. He's frying a turkey in an oil drum and he's got pictures, two whole rolls he took at the homecoming game. A lot of the shots are blurry and dark, but he and Marcus are going to look at every one of them, they're going to take their time, and when Marcus goes home again he'll have his own set to keep.

Election Day

A hard frost coats the crabgrass, stiffening each blade with a fine, frozen dusting that sparkles in the clear early light. Down the sloping lawn it approaches the mill but stops short where the shadow lies. Under the cedars and boxwoods there are frost-free spaces too, damp circles of darkness around the trunks and roots where the sparse growth was protected. The flower beds need to be cleaned for the winter; the stalks have hardened and browned but they are marvelously unfamiliar under the frost, covered like the boxwoods and holly leaves and lawn as if by snow or sugar. Cutie stands by her kitchen window and watches, notices how even the pale silver gravel in the driveway has been touched by the frost. When she was a little girl she liked the sound of the raised, frostbitten dirt crunching under her patent leather shoes; she remembers stomping down every bit.

It's election day, and Cutie is waiting to be driven to the polling place. She has a warm mug of coffee that she must lift to her lips with both hands; they shake violently, so that each task, even eating or drinking, is a chore to be tackled alone or else abandoned. She is wearing a deep-blue suit and has gotten her hair done in Tappahannock, slept last night on a satin pillow so as not to muss it. Her good blue coat is draped over the chair by the doorway, her maroon leather gloves smoothed and ready on the dinette table, next to her purse. It's Loretta who will drive her, in Cutie's own car, which waits in the carport. From where she stands she will see Loretta when she pulls up, slowly, in her Chrysler.

And it isn't long before she does, carefully parking the car and then huffing up the steps to open the door without a knock. Cutie has grown used to Loretta's brusque ways, and she supposes Loretta has grown used to hers. Sometimes when she sees her, like now, she cannot speak or be pleasant but must immediately busy herself with something, act as if Loretta is bothering her. Like now, she has been looking forward to Loretta's arrival, has been enjoying standing alone and expectant beside the window with the slight pressure of cold air emanating from the panes into the air before her face. But she cannot show this, must instead be impatient, rinsing her mug in the sink as if that is what Loretta's absence this morning has prevented her from doing. Sometimes Cutie thinks that it is only her age and its attending indignities that make her behave so, but when she is honest with herself she remembers that she has been delicate in her moods all her life.

"All ready, Mrs. Young?" Loretta asks. She moves to take the mug from Cutie's trembling hands, but Cutie shrugs her off by the merest movement of her back and head. Though she cannot tie a pair of shoes or drink one-handed from a cup her body language is clear.

The mug trembles and drops to the rust-stained porcelain sink, where it does not break but falls over on its side. Cutie must use both hands to turn off the tap. She turns to Loretta and says, "My coat is there."

Loretta lifts and holds out Cutie's coat. She is dressed and coiffed too, her hair combed stiffly out from her face, a gold-colored brooch pinned to her purplish coat, and Cutie can smell a faint gardenia perfume as she eases her arms into the sleeves. Cutie takes up her purse and gloves, lets Loretta help her down the steps; they do not lock the door behind them but move slowly toward the car. The frost is already beginning to dull and melt beneath the sun, leaving only the dying grass, but the dirt still crunches beneath Cutie's shoes, a satisfying, crisp sound.

"My car's already warm," Loretta says.

Cutie shakes her head. Loretta's car is nicer than her own, but that is a barrier she does not want to cross. Besides, it is only right to use Cutie's mileage, Cutie's gas, on errands meant for her.

"All right," Loretta sighs. "Wait here."

Cutie paces in the drive, crunching earth with her shoes, while Loretta starts and revs the engine. Smoke, the color of frost, pours out of the tailpipe. Loretta backs up without looking for Cutie, who must trot to get out of the way.

The polling station is in King and Queen Courthouse, only a few miles from Cutie's house. Loretta has turned the heater on high so that warm, dry air blows against their skin. This part of the county, near the courthouse, has remained virtually unchanged for many years. There are no new stores or even gas stations, no subdivisions full of trashy plastic houses like the ones across the river. Back in the summer Cutie's family silver was stolen, almost every bit of it, by teenagers from one of those subdivisions, no concept of home or what it means to live somewhere you don't lock the doors. The houses they pass have been there for years, little tenant farmer houses sitting behind fields, little shacks in the woods. Cutie has owned and sold some of them herself and it pleases her to see them there, the same as always. It's because of the schools, Cutie's son tells her, that's why we can't attract any Richmond people, even Mechanicsville people. Good, Cutie says. I don't want any strangers coming to live near me.

How well do you know these people that *are* here? he asks.

I know them, Cutie says, thinking of the men who trim her box-woods and nap under her porch, their brown glass bottles tender and glinting in the grass. I know them like my kin, she says, and she does— she feels she knows them better than she knows Horace's wife and daughter or even Horace, all of them so particular and strange, with their dinners out and their new, gadgety things, their winter vacations to places where they know no one.

The road winds pleasantly, with dips and hills. The cloudless sky is a pale, porcelain blue. They pass Cutie's own bare fields, a squat little cinder-block house she used to rent to a black family before they left for some other place. In the center of the next field is an old untended cemetery, the gravestones obscured by dry weeds and fallen tree limbs.

"It's a pretty land," Cutie says approvingly. "I've been here and there, but I always say home is best."

"Hmmf," Loretta says. "I can't say I wouldn't take somewhere warmer."

"But this is your home," Cutie insists, thinking of that family that left. Where did they go? She couldn't remember, and it hardly mattered. "You can't take something else over your home."

"Haven't been too many places, that's true," Loretta says slowly. "But I suppose that could change."

"I remember when husbands used to go behind the curtain with their wives," Cutie says, changing the subject.

"My husband never did that," Loretta says. "But I remember it too."

"They told them who to vote for," Cutie says. "My husband never did either."

"I don't imagine so," Loretta says, cutting off the conversation there. "You have your identification?"

"I do." It is only a gubernatorial and local election, but Cutie votes every year. Even the year her son was born she voted on election day, a week after the delivery, for Harry Truman.

The parking lot is nearly empty, and so they do not have to choose between a regular or handicapped space, which always embarrasses Cutie. Inside, she is preoccupied with the slow echo of her own shoes as she makes her way across the marble floor to the card tables where ladies older than herself wait with wide paper registers. Their cotton-white heads droop like flowers above the cheap tables; they wear sweaters tied around their shoulders. The two choices for governor are both fools anyway, and dishonest besides. Cutie saw the Republican's teenage daughter chewing gum on television; the Democrat will raise her taxes. But she knows that whether you voted, though not for whom, is a matter of public record, and she has a private horror of being discovered to have missed an election. She will write in her own name, as she often does.

Loretta and Cutie are the first voters; they stand ready to present their licenses but there is some problem with the books. Neither of their names can be found. One moment, says one of the registrars, and they carry off the books.

"I need to talk to you this afternoon," Loretta says in a low voice as they wait. She's fidgeting with her driver's license and Cutie is suddenly worried.

"What about?" she snaps.

"My notice," Loretta says. "I want to give my month's notice today." Cutie sucks in a short, stabbing breath.

"I'll make sure to give you time to find someone else," Loretta says quickly.

"No," Cutie says, her voice weak and petulant as a child's. She can't possibly find someone like Loretta. Loretta is quiet and neat and competent; she has a driver's license and doesn't let anyone in the house. There is no one like that, she's sure, in the county, and she is overcome by an image of the parade of shiftless women who will try to take Loretta's place. She whispers, "If it's the money—"

Loretta shakes her head, looking down at her license. "I need my time, Mrs. Young," she says. "I'm not a spring chicken."

In the tiny laminated photograph she has longer hair, brushed full and shiny down to her shoulders, and a faint smile. It has never occurred to Cutie that Loretta was ever any younger than she is now.

"You've left me in a place," Cutie says finally. "You've left me in a real place."

"Nobody's left anybody yet," Loretta says. "We can talk about it later."

The registrars return with delighted faces; they have fixed the problem. They direct Cutie to the felt-curtained booth on the right. Her ballot is clamped beneath the voting machine, and she must ask, before the curtain closes, for the special paper ballot with the write-in space. The registrars are not flummoxed this time; it is common, Cutie understands, for the stubborn-minded people around here to write in.

"You may sit at our table," the registrar says kindly, but Cutie says she will be fine in the booth. She likes the dark privacy there, no one to see her hands shake as she practices her name first in the air before committing it to paper. Cora Tyler Young, she writes finally in the space for governor.

But her name on the ballot, it looks wrong. It is a stranger's name, the hands that wrote it, shaking and spotted, a stranger's hands. She thinks of her age—eighty-four—and sees the long silent ride home, past those shacks and fields Loretta doesn't care for, the arduous trip back up the stairs to the house she has lived in since she married. Throwing your vote away, that's what her husband would have told her. What has it come to, all that time, the effortful waking and working and sleeping of a lifetime? One name on a ballot, and what does it even matter? In her mind she is still a little girl, shiny shoes buckled onto her feet, stomping the frozen earth flat and familiar again.

Mattaponi Queen

The *Mattaponi Queen* had been Mitchell White's wedding present to his second wife, a woman so pretty it made him uncomfortably happy just to look at her, but now that he was done with women he was free to sell it. Joanne had given up material things when she broke the marriage contract and ran off with her yoga instructor to live in a geodesic dome outside Charlottesville. But it was a present, Mitchell told her. I gave it to you.

Joanne had never liked the boat, not even when things were good between them. She had complained about the noise from the time he coasted it up to the public boat landing where she stood with a scarf over her eyes and he'd leapt from its bow onto the pier as surely and gracefully as somebody in a movie. She hadn't liked it even after Mitchell had spent all that summer fine-tuning its retrofitted diesel engine so it wasn't so loud. They were married for four years and never in that time did she give Mitchell a present he could hold in his hands.

Her practice, she said, didn't leave her time for things like boats. She put a warm, moist hand on his arm and smiled as she said it. What drove Mitchell crazy was how, once she left him, it was Joanne who acted like she was forgiving him. And that she didn't want the boat, which he halfway restored with his own two hands, which he didn't *have* to give back to her—that was enough to put him off women for good.

"What you get for marrying a woman so much prettier than you," his brother, Gary, said after some of the sting was gone, while Mitchell paged through glossy powerboat catalogs in Gary's kitchen. Gary had been a wild man in his youth, sleeping on people's floors or in cars almost every night of his twenties and for a lot of his thirties, but now that he was forty he was settled down in a house-painting business. Married to a cheerful, fat, redheaded writer of self-published romance novels. Her name was Darlene. They had a house in a subdivision, a rancher cluttered with decorative geese and chickens, and Mitchell liked to stop by in the evenings on his way home from work, especially if his daughter was out at some extracurricular activity or another. Darlene kept country music playing softly, George Jones or Willie Nelson or Loretta Lynn, while she cooked dinner and Gary and Mitchell watched cable news.

"Sell it, buy yourself a new bass boat or a motorcycle," Gary said. "It'd be a good tour boat. Pleasure cruises, like the old days. They could point when they pass your place: there's a damn romantic fool."

Mitchell shook his head, and Darlene chimed in sympathetically, "Any other woman would've loved it. Any other one."

The *Queen* sat on a trailer for most of Mitchell and Gary's childhood, her squat hull nosing out of their grandfather's barn, and served as a dark, cobwebby stage for the usual wars and competitions of brothers close in age. Who could jump farthest from the bow. Who could climb fastest up her rusty, just-for-show smokestacks, kicking wildly to knock the other off. They played hide-and-seek, pirate games, prisoner of war. One Fourth of July Gary hid in the pilothouse and shot bottle rockets at Mitchell. The next weekend, Mitchell smuggled blacksnakes inside to startle his brother. They talked about navigating her to Yorktown, setting up sleeper bunks and a kitchen, running away. At some point, their interest turned to other vehicles—cars and motorcycles, boats that were actually seaworthy—but Mitchell always remembered the *Queen* as a place for laying a certain kind of claim.

When Mitchell got the idea to fix her up, he asked if Gary minded, fully prepared to argue or pay his way into full ownership. A string of cancers had knocked down just about all their family, and the *Queen* had been passed down to them, the only ones who ever really appreciated her. Gary had laughed and said, go ahead. A boat is a hole to pour money into, you know. A boat like that is a deep hole.

Gary had always been better than Mitchell at conserving and allocating his resources of energy and ambition, from the time when they were teenagers and used to hunt relics as a way to pay for trips and concerts, repairs to their cars. The fields and woods around their grandfather's house were teeming with valuable junk they could cart off to dealers and trade for a stack of fresh bills: silver gravy spoons, rusted rifle stocks, Civil War belt buckles, bullets, coins, knife blades. Gary was a patient hunter, listening for a certain pitch and steadiness to the metal detector's beeping before striking the earth with his pick. Mitchell got overexcited by any faint beep or promising dirt clod or ringing of metal, clawing his way past deep roots and rock beds, making a mess. Their grandmother forbade him to dig anywhere near her yard, but she let Gary do as he pleased. He stuck with hunting long after Mitchell gave up, financing a roller-coaster life for himself well into his thirties. He took winter trips to Aruba and Key West, was hauled repeatedly out of national parks and into jail. It was from this life that he'd fallen into his new one, the life he made with Darlene. He gave up drinking. He paid his bills. He took his medicine regularly.

Mitchell's next idea was to give the boat to his daughter, Annabel, but she didn't want it either. And though Annabel was generally more careful with his feelings than Joanne—a trait remarkable, he understood gratefully, in teenage girls—he could see that its connection to Joanne spoiled whatever appeal it might have had.

I hope you don't expect me to act *sad* about it, Annabel had said after Joanne moved out.

No, he had said. He didn't expect that.

Good, she said.

He tried piloting the *Queen* himself some evenings and weekends but felt silly—she was tall and slow and matronly, and he felt exposed and judged by all the small, agile speedboats that raced around him, water-skiers in tow. When she broke down in low tide and he had to accept a difficult tow to his own half-rotten pier, he resolved to sell her.

It took him a month of advertisements in the local papers to find a suitable buyer, a woman named Loretta who lived in St. Stephens Church and was a nurse. She had no intention of running any tours, nothing like that. She crossed her arms like she was in a dealership, though they were just standing awkwardly together on the pier down the steep hill from Mitchell's house, where the *Queen* was docked. Mitchell held a can of beer in his hand. He showed her all the weak parts of the boat, the wood that needed replacing, painting. Told her about the faulty starter, the gas leak. She was mostly interested in the wheelhouse and smokestacks, the parts that were just for show, like hitching posts next to parking meters in some tourist towns. He obliged her, turning the stiff paddle wheel in the water, pulling the lever that lifted the cap from the black chimney. The *Queen* had been a gambling boat, he told her, built as a miniature replica of a famous Welsh stern-wheel riverboat in the 1920s. She took vacationers on pleasure cruises between Walkerton and Urbanna. They ate oysters and played cards in the little three-quarters-enclosed room on deck. They celebrated weddings and birthdays and good business deals.

Loretta shook her head knowingly while he told her these facts. Everything in this town, she said, used to be something more interesting than what it was now. She told him she could only pay in installments, her mouth in a twist like she was sure that would sour the deal.

Mitchell said that was fine.

And she would need to make the repairs besides. She was no handywoman. Could Mitchell recommend someone to do that while she paid the boat off?

Mitchell knew a few people with time and expertise, mechanics and hobbyists he'd met at antique shows. He was about to get a piece of paper to write down some names when a speedboat raced by, creating a wake. The familiar hollow sound of water slapping the *Queen*'s hull stabbed at his heart, and he thought of keeping her awhile longer.

He could do even better than that, he told Loretta. For a modest fee he would do the repairs himself.

Mitchell had especially liked to look at Joanne from afar. She had long strawberry blond hair and creamy skin and a tiny pointed nose like Sissy Spacek's. At a distance, in profile, she had the sweet and unworried look of a high school cheerleader. As the single parent of a teenage daughter from his first, disastrous marriage, Mitchell had never expected things to go beyond looking at her from afar, and once he had her he hadn't known, exactly, what to do with her. She didn't have a job, though she volunteered at the animal shelter in Tappahannock and talked about getting a job at the vet's. She was an indifferent stepmother to Annabel, a halfhearted housekeeper and cook, and she complained bitterly about their distance from everything. The Food Lion was too dirty and poorly stocked for her; she had to drive all the way to Mechanicsville to go to Kroger. ("Well, la-di-dah," Annabel said to her dad. "Kroger.") She always found a way to miss Annabel's softball games and made fun of things in the county that Annabel and Mitchell used to make fun of but now, listening to her, were shamed from mentioning. "She acts like she's from somewhere good," Mitchell once heard Annabel say to a friend. "But she's just from *Powhatan*."

Joanne had a condition that made her menstrual periods excruciatingly painful and kept her from having children. For a week out of every month, she lay curled up in their bed or on the floor next to it. She was mistrustful of medicine stronger than Tylenol and so made things harder than they had to be. Mitchell installed new, plush carpet in the bedroom, for when she would lie on the floor, and generally spent time away, at Gary's house or on the river or at work, when Joanne was sick. Annabel took up set building for the school's drama club and joined the Academic Challenge team, and so she was away a lot too.

Joanne started taking yoga to help with her condition. She began a class at the King William Recreational Center but was soon going three times a week in the west end of Richmond, an hour's drive each way. Mitchell complained about the gas she used up, the cost of it all, but then Joanne pointed out that his welding business was doing fine and this might really cure her.

Now she lived in a little cluster of three white, plastic-topped domes with her instructor. The geodesic dome was nature's perfect shelter, she told Mitchell, like he might change his mind about the eighty-year-old saltbox he'd owned and lived in for a decade now. Maybe she was cured, but maybe not. He pictured her inside the dome like a nut in a giant shell game.

Mitchell grew up on the Mattaponi, just up the river in Aylett. As a boy he swung from the same rope that still hangs from the arching branch of a red oak tree. Summertimes he swam in blue jeans, saw water moccasin heads shining and coursing toward him steadily as he made himself as still as a stick. He felt his toes nipped by snapping turtles, caught baby painted turtles, clawing like kittens in his bare palms, then let them go. The mud beneath his toes when he let himself sink beneath the pollen-dusted surface was an ancient mud, the leaves that his feet churned were thick and rubbery. Tired from swimming, he rested muddy and bird-chested on the bank and traced fossilized leaf patterns in sandstone with fingers amazed by their own good fortune. In winter he lay in bed listening to the river pulling apart its frozen surface with a wailing sound. His father set each year's Christmas tree out on it once it was frozen solid; it sank when the ice melted and became a nesting place for fish. He caught yellow perch starting in late February, then moved on to shad, catfish, and striped bass. In spring he watched as young osprey learned to fly and hunt. He and Gary had their own metal johnboat that, overturned, was a shelter for snakes and lizards. Once he found a black, heavy shark's tooth buried in the mud.

In school they learned about it, how the Mat joined the Ta in Spotsylvania to become the Matta, the Po and the Ni connected in Caroline to become the Poni. In Caroline County near Bowling Green they became the Mattaponi, which coursed through forest and farmland, past Aylett and Walkerton, dividing King William and King and Queen until emptying into the York at West Point. They made sand models of its topography, tested its pH, grew its algae in Mason jars.

He'd lived away from the river only one time in his life, when he was married to Annabel's mother and renting a little house in the east end of Richmond. When all was said and done, when he couldn't help her any longer, she had packed up every scrap and left for Florida, and the river, the town, had been a refuge for him. Neighbors fed him and Annabel, gossiped about them, told Annabel she was pretty. He bought a boat and taught her to fish. He showed her all the river places he'd gone as a boy, tried to reconstruct his own childhood for her. All the while he had the feeling it was impossible, like trying to tell someone else your dreams; he was reminded of how the person you were telling waited for clarity but did not expect it.

Now they wanted to dam it up, to make a reservoir feeding the new white plastic developments in Newport News and Hampton Roads, the old, mean brick ones too. The retirees in Williamsburg needed more water; the NASA scientists in Poquoson and their smart children and their patient wives needed water too, for sprinkler systems and soccer fields and koi ponds.

Mitchell saw all this approaching like a snakehead. It would come or not come; there wasn't much he could do to attract or deter it. The reservoir was hardly any different from the loud, new speedboats or the fat teenagers and their Jet Skis' high, lazy whine, which filled the river every sunny weekend. He said as much to Annabel, who was working on a school project about endangered rivers. She was petitioning the EPA, the governor, writing emails past her bedtime at the cluttered little computer desk they kept in the hallway.

"You've gotta do something, Dad," Annabel said. "Don't you?"

Mitchell replied that he did not know that you did, in fact, though he admired her for trying.

Unlike Annabel's mother, Joanne left a lot of her things behind. There was a dresser full of jeans and sweaters and scarves, a collection of antique dolls with blinking eyes and matted hair, several small furniture restoration projects started and abandoned. Mitchell was always finding her things: a sock in the wash, a grocery list in the truck's floorboard, a gold earring back scratching against the bottom of his nightstand drawer. He imagined that Annabel found things of hers too, though she never mentioned it.

Annabel had Alateen meetings every Wednesday at a church in Tappahannock; she rarely missed them and Mitchell wondered what she told the people there. When his brother's wife first recommended Alateen, he was too relieved to ask questions—there were some rough years there—but now that Annabel seemed to be doing better, he wondered why she could not talk to him instead. He grieved and raged at her mother's choices as much as she did, didn't he? Mitchell had even gone to Al-Anon for a time, as a measure of support, but he felt awkward and intrusive as the only male member of his group. A few times he had tried to entice her into other activities on Wednesday nights—dinners out, bowling, trips to the batting cages—but Annabel had only frowned as though he had forgotten and said, "That's my meeting night, Dad."

If Mitchell had known what he was doing he would never have married Joanne. He hadn't taken her leaving well—there'd been about two months when he'd cry without warning in front of Annabel, and he had been too absorbed in self-pity to notice much about her life for a while. Two divorces, that's what he kept thinking. *Two divorces.* His sister-in-law had taken over when it became clear he wasn't functioning; Darlene cleaned the house, cooked casseroles and lasagnas, and took Annabel shopping in Richmond. His guilty understanding of the harm he'd done Annabel was partly what caused him to write off women in general, a decision so new and strange—and yet so *correct*, he felt—that he found himself, normally a reserved man, telling Darlene about it over the phone one night when Gary was out.

She'd had a couple of bad marriages herself before she found Gary (how *he* computed as a romantic find Mitchell couldn't figure), but she counseled Mitchell not to give up. "There's still love to be had," she said.

"Maybe in books," Mitchell said, "but not even good ones. No offense."

"Not at all," Darlene said cheerfully. "You should read my books. They could help." So far she'd published two: *Home Fires* and *Hungry Valentine*. They both featured the same redheaded heroine, Darla, and were to become a series. In each novel Darla would be pursued by a different gallant country lover who did courtly things like photograph her plates of biscuits with a tripod-balanced camera and wash her truck inside and out and plant colorful beds of flowers in her yard. The lovers were plumbers, carpenters, electricians. They were shirtless landscapers and fair, gentle mechanics. They fixed things and paid attention. The novels sold at the local grocery and hardware stores and even managed to make some money.

"Maybe," Darlene said thoughtfully, "maybe I'll write a book about you."

"Bad idea," Mitchell said.

"A welder and a good father. That's something."

"A good welder and a father," Mitchell corrected her. "That's something else. Write a book about Gary. And don't put it anywhere I might accidentally read it."

Darlene burst out laughing. "I know him too well," she said. "There's nothing for my imagination."

Darlene's laugh was high and metallic and warm. It reminded Mitchell of nothing more than the color of her hair.

Annabel and Mitchell were sitting on the porch on the half-painted rockers Joanne had bought and abandoned. They were to be red; the backs had been done but everything else was a rough and pulpy pine. Joanne painted everything red, Annabel had once observed, and she was right. There were half-red things all over the place.

She did not want Mitchell coming to her Academic Challenge meets, which had started up again and took place, she said, not even in gymnasiums or auditoriums but in history and government class-rooms and yeast- and detergent-smelling cafeterias. There would be one tonight, and she didn't want him to go.

"Nobody's parents come," she explained. "Besides, I don't ever answer the questions."

"Why not?" Mitchell wanted to know. "You're smart."

"I don't know," she said.

"What do you do then?"

"I sit there, mostly," Annabel said. "I think they let me on the team because I was the only girl to try out. Actually, everybody who tried out is on the team."

Well, Mitchell thought. There could be worse boys to have after your daughter than a bunch that knew the periodic table and all the presidents in order. Annabel had taken to wearing makeup this year. Though she only wore a little lip gloss and eye shadow to school, around the house she seemed to prefer a theatrical look. Sometimes she gave herself Cleopatra eyes, with dark liner turned up at the corners. Other times she rouged her wide, pale cheeks until she resembled Snow White, the ice-skating version. Today she was in her trailer trash look, with startled, ice-blue lids and shiny pink lips. It was hard to know what you were supposed to do with a daughter, Mitchell thought, hard to know when to step in and say something.

The grass was short and dry in the September drought; water from a hose beaded up on the packed dirt, rolled away. Even the shaggy boxwoods were browning at their bottoms. It was low tide; Mitchell could smell the mud exposed by the receding waters. Through the maples he could see the dense fields of lily pads, the awkward yellow stalks supporting the dry floppy leaves. It had been weeks since Mitchell had been out on the water.

From the direction of the town he could hear a soft crunching of gravel. He watched and saw Loretta appear around the bend, slowly but purposefully walking toward his house. Sometimes she liked to sit on the pier next to the boat. He'd look down the hill and see her sitting there, hands folded in her lap, her broad back hunched tiredly. It would look like she was talking to the boat, which made Mitchell feel a little funny but he guessed he didn't mind.

He raised his hand until she saw it. "Hey, Loretta. How're you?"

"I'm okay," she said, still walking. She had on jeans and a short-sleeved sweater and Mitchell could see that she was sweating a little in the heat. The dry pine needles softly carpeted the street's edges. Her loafers made a shushing sound as she walked over them and into his yard. "I came to pay you my installment."

She made it to the porch and reached into her big, maroon-colored shoulder bag for her checkbook. She was direct and a good payer, but she was not a smiling woman. "I'm making this month out for double."

"Oh?"

"I'm paying double because I'd like to have the boat by Christmas," she said, neatly tearing the check and holding it out. "It's my Christmas present to me." When Mitchell didn't say anything she asked, "That all right with you?"

Mitchell stood up and came down the steps to take the check, scratching at his head. "I guess so," he said. "I'll have to speed up on the repairs though."

Loretta nodded like this was expected.

"Loretta, this is my daughter, Annabel. Annabel, can you get Mrs. Johnson some tea?"

Loretta raised her eyebrows at Annabel's garish eye makeup. "You goin' somewhere, honey?" she asked.

"Academic Challenge meet," Annabel said. She brought the tea, which Loretta accepted with a nod and a quick thank-you. She acted, Mitchell sometimes felt, like the boat was hers, like she was buying some family heirloom back from a pawnshop owner. She never commented on repairs or improvements except to nod, and she always got the payments over quickly, though she insisted on making them in person. Mitchell didn't know where she would keep the boat; she didn't live on the river.

"How's Mrs. Young?"

"Oh, I guess she's the same," Loretta said. She had turned away from him and was squinting at the steps down to the pier. The afternoon light was clear and golden; it dappled her brown skin and black hair, the loose weave of her sweater. Annabel had gone inside and now she burst through the screen door carrying her petition clipboard.

She gave Loretta the whole spiel.

"Sure, honey," Loretta said. She took her time reading the whole thing through, and then she signed it and handed it back. "I think I'll go sit by my boat," she said, and Mitchell felt a little sting in the words *my boat*. He had the money, every cent she'd paid him, sitting in a savings account. It would be easy to give it back.

Mitchell had trained himself into calling Gary every time he thought about calling Joanne. It worked because he didn't know Joanne's telephone number and because more than half the time Gary wasn't even home and Darlene would answer the phone in her loud, merry voice. Mitchell would hear her cooking or washing dishes or typing as she talked, and she would sound distracted but still happy to hear from him.

"I don't know that I can sell it after all," he told her one night. "I think I was wrong to."

"Sounds to me like you already sold it," Darlene said.

"It's on installment," he explained. "She hasn't paid it off yet."

"Still," Darlene said. "I bought something once on installment before I knew what a rip-off that could be. It was a couch and a chair and ottoman, in a pink and green plaid. This was after I was divorced; I figured I could have whatever damn color couch I wanted. I made the payments by the week, and sometimes with a credit card, but that furniture was mine."

"She doesn't even have anywhere to dock it," Mitchell said. "It still needs a lot of work."

"I would've been awful sad if the owner told me he was giving my money back, he'd decided the couch was his, even if he was doing me a favor," she said. "In fact, I would've been pissed."

"This is different," he said. "I'm no store owner."

"Seems the same to me. You said this woman works for Cutie Young?" Darlene knew everybody even though she'd only lived in the county for a few years.

"Yeah."

"Well, you better not cross her," she said. "Anybody works for Cutie Young is tough. Tougher than you, anyway."

"Hmmf," Mitchell said.

"I still have that ottoman. You better get the repairs done quick, then. Hire somebody. Get Gary to help you. Hon, you'd help your brother fix up that boat he's been mooning over, wouldn't you?"

Mitchell hadn't thought Gary was there, he said.

"He wasn't," Darlene said. "He just came in."

It was funny, Mitchell thought, how things changed without you knowing or being told.

"I'm working on your book," she said, like this would cheer him up. "I wrote a whole chapter."

"What?" Mitchell said. He could hear his brother laughing on the other end.

His plan had been to restore the *Queen* to her old glory, a floating wedding cake that would represent to Joanne a new life here, one capable of old-fashioned charm and surprise. He checked out books on riverboating in the Northern Neck, read oral histories of Walkerton, scanned Web sites on hull repair. But once he'd fixed the engine and patched the hull, he was too excited to wait. He launched the boat before he had a chance to see it as it was: old, not even repainted, even listing a little to one side.

You think Joanne's gonna go for that? Gary asked.

I do, Mitchell said. Annabel says it's shabby chic.

Good thing you already gave her the ring, said Gary. Good thing you bought a big 'un.

She'll love it, Mitchell said, more like he was convincing himself than Gary. She'll love it and I love her. Gary had been married a year by then; he had the annoying air of knowingness that emanated from newly happy people.

Mitchell and Joanne were married in September at the botanical garden in Richmond. It had been a hot, dry summer, but the plants all around them were green and lush. Their picture was in the paper; Joanne had insisted, even though it made him feel foolish. Annabel collected bride photographs in an album, but she liked the funny photographs: brides with pearl necklace–wearing dogs, brides with tuxedoed dogs, hoopskirted brides with their grandchildren in the wedding party. She skipped theirs.

Mitchell forced himself to start making the repairs to the *Queen*, and they came together quicker than he expected. She no longer listed, and he'd scraped off some of the peeling paint. He fixed a miss in the engine so that she ran steadily instead of coughing and chortling like a gas-starved Volkswagen. She wasn't pretty, not yet. Mitchell thought she was more like a teenager with her awkward angles and blemishes, but you could see through them to the graceful beauty she would become. He called the only person he thought might appreciate her, and she agreed to meet him at the pier after work.

Darlene stood at the end of the pier wearing a white sundress and holding an uncorked bottle of wine and two plastic wineglasses. Her round, tan shoulders were bare.

"I suppose it isn't time for christening her yet," Darlene said. "But that doesn't mean we can't toast her."

It was nearing high tide. They made it out into the deep, narrow channel at the center of the river. A fine gray mist of humidity hung above the water, blurring the low, deep-green tree line.

"This is my favorite time of day," Darlene said. She was standing next to him in the closeness of the pilothouse. A gentle breeze cooled their backs. "Crepuscular."

"What?"

"When I hear words I like, I write them down," she said. She repeated it slowly: "*Crepuscular*. It means animals that are active at twilight. Like deer and certain bats." She pointed at a swarm of careening black bats, hunting insects over the water.

"Gary and I used to catch them in our baseball caps, when we were kids. Then we let them go." He was sorry at once for mentioning his brother. Darlene squinted out at the river, smiling slightly.

He nodded at the wine bottle she'd rested at her feet. "I brought champagne on the boat when I showed her to Joanne. Good stuff, too. Dom Perignon."

He told her how Joanne just stood there with one arm wrapped around her waist like she was cold, the feigned interest she took in the osprey nest he'd scouted to show her. "And there was a bald eagle, flying. I pointed it out to her and she said it looked warlike.

"It used to be so rare to see them that you were supposed to call the game warden when you saw them. Now you can see them pretty regularly, if you look."

"I'm not a good bird-watcher," Darlene admitted. "No patience."

He made a turn at the little creek that drained the mill pond. It was shallow but navigable at high tide. The pines and oaks along this stretch were good for spotting osprey, eagles, and hawks. He wanted to show Darlene how easy it was to see them, how much richness the river offered. The *Queen* brushed against dense fields of lily pads on both sides. He slowed the engine, then felt a soft thudding against the boat's hull. He swore, shifted into reverse. The water grew pale with churned-up mud and they could smell it from inside the pilot-house. Blue smoke, the smell of diesel fuel.

"Shit," he said. "We're stuck."

"Is this like one of those I-ran-out-of-gas, teenage-boy things?" She caught his eye. "Just kidding."

"Okay," he said. "The tide's still rolling in. We just have to wait for it, then we can steer our way out of here."

Darlene lifted her hair off of her sweaty neck. Had she worn that dress on purpose? It was low-cut and sheer, but that could be what she wore all day. She was a romance writer, after all. "We should at least open the wine, sit out on deck," she said.

The wine was in a screw-top bottle, and she poured it—light pink—into the glasses. He offered the worn bench seat to Darlene and she sat delicately, smoothing the hem of her dress over her freckled knees. Mitchell gulped his wine, sat hunched on a turned-over bucket.

Now that the engine was silent, they could hear swamp cicadas and frogs filling the air with their electric humming. It was growing dark, but neither Mitchell nor Darlene said anything about calling for help or trying to get unstuck. She poured him another glass. They sipped their wine for a while.

"How'd your family wind up with this boat, anyway?" Darlene asked.

"My grandfather bought her at auction," Mitchell said. "He wanted to fix her up, make her a present for my grandmother, but he never did. My mother said he was too busy chasing women. After he died, his old mistress came around asking if she was named in the will. She meant to take the boat one way or another. She said it had been a present, that he named it *Mattaponi Queen* after her, and my mother had to run her off before my grandmother found out. This was a long time ago. So I guess she has a history of mistaken queens." He paused. "I guess I knew Joanne wasn't it, but I wanted her to be. I really wanted it, and I'm sorry for that."

"Everybody makes mistakes," Darlene said after a while. "But wanting something—that's nothing to be sorry about."

"When you have a kid it is."

"But what if you never wanted anything, if you just closed up shop and were lonely all the rest of your life? You think that would be any better?"

The frog-cicada song rose and fell, rose and fell. Mitchell felt absolved, weightless. He leaned close to her, studied her round, freckled face. Her eyelashes were pale gold; he could have counted them. "What if I wanted to kiss you?" He didn't wait for her to answer.

Darlene stood up, blinking hard like someone waking from an unexpected nap, and the boat rocked a little. She grasped the new railing's raw wood. The lily pads rested flat and smooth against the river's glassy black surface. "Look," she said. "We're free."

Waiting for Annabel in the parking lot of Tappahannock First Methodist Church, Mitchell watched the trees, then the sky, grow dark. The sunset had been beautiful, bright pink and orange, but now the sky had released all its color and faded to slate gray. The church was seventies-modern; it had no stained-glass window, no steeple. Somewhere inside was Annabel, listening and waiting her turn to talk. Or did she talk? Maybe she just sat there the way she did in Academic Challenge, knowing the answers but not saying them. The meetings lasted exactly an hour, like a therapist's appointment. They never went over.

His cell phone vibrated against his thigh; it was Gary. He winced, but he'd never been a call screener.

"Yeah?" he answered.

It was Darlene. "What manners," she said. "I was calling to tell you about your book."

Mitchell could tell from Darlene's voice that Gary was out. She never drank when he was home, but on his nights out, his meeting nights, she filled a tumbler with chardonnay and ice cubes. He could hear them knocking against the glass, against her teeth.

"I changed it," she said. "I got to thinking about all this Mattaponi River stuff, the reservoir, and I thought, why not write a book about that?"

"Nonfiction," Mitchell said. *"Reportage."*

"Sort of," she said. "So in my new version you are an Indian, and your daughter is like a modern-day Pocahontas except her love is the river. And you have to overcome your fear of public speaking to convince the governor to spare the river at a big town hall meeting in Richmond. And Darla is a reporter for the local paper who falls in love with you."

"That sounds brilliant," Mitchell said. "But not a bit like me, which is just fine."

"Oh no, it's you all right," Darlene said. "I describe you down to your shoes."

For a while they were silent. Mitchell found himself thinking about Darlene's round thighs, her surprisingly delicate ankles and wrists. Her *amber-freckled décolletage,* as he imagined she called it in those books of hers, those books he never read. The crickets and katydids and cicadas filled the empty space with their high whining. "Darlene," he said.

"Hmmm?"

"I wanted to kiss you on that boat."

"You did kiss me." Darlene was silent for a long moment. "You knew me all along, before you knew Joanne and before Gary and

I were together. He *chose* me. He didn't go looking for something better."

"I never—"

"I asked Gary about that *Mattaponi Queen* story you told me," she said.

"You told Gary I took you out?"

"He's my husband," she said, but her voice was gentle, pitying. "I told him the story about your grandfather and his mistress, and he said you were wrong. The boat was the *Queen,* he said. She was always the *Queen,* and you need to let her go."

Mitchell mumbled a quick good-bye, hit "end," and threw his phone into the truck's cup holder. Good God, he made a mess of things. His life was one big field of empty holes, dug-up patches with rusty old cans and torn-up roots and nothing else. He sat with his arms crossed, listening to the cicadas. They drowned out the other insects once they got going. His heart raced uncomfortably, and he remembered something Joanne used to say about breath when he was struggling to lift something. Let your breath do the work, she said. Like that helped.

Soon the meeting was over; from the burgundy church doors teen-age girls began to appear. They didn't look, he thought, like survivors of something bad. They didn't look like they carried a lot of sad-ness around. They were smiling and talking, self-consciously pushing their hair out of their faces. Annabel was walking with a girl with short bleached hair and cat-eye glasses, and he could hear a little of their conversation as they approached his truck.

"I just don't know if I can accept that idea," Annabel was saying.

"You know what they say," the girl said. She had a backpack slung over one shoulder. "Take what you like, leave the rest."

"A good meeting?" Mitchell said, his voice tight, as they pulled out of the parking lot.

Annabel frowned in concern. "What's wrong, Dad?"

"Nothing," he said. The sweetness of her, he thought: it was enough to make you cry. She'd go anywhere with him, just to be able to tell him things and have him listen. He brightened, hoped it didn't seem like he was faking. "Why not try the new place?"

The China Inn was a mistake from the beginning, squalid and fluorescently lit, smelling of fish, but Mitchell and Annabel had agreed a long time ago never to walk out of a restaurant. Once you were in the door, you were in it for the long haul, no matter what was on the menu. It used to drive Joanne nuts. The two waiters were solicitous, falling all over themselves to point out the orange-hued chef's specialties and staff favorites. Annabel ordered the Buddhist delight; Mitchell ordered the kung pao chicken. They had the best table, right by the window.

"So what idea are you having a hard time accepting?" Mitchell asked.

She tilted her head at him. He hardly ever asked about her meetings.

"Sorry. I wasn't trying to eavesdrop. Just looking for a little wisdom."

Annabel told him that the theme tonight had been self-acceptance, and they had a reading about how you were not what you did or what you made. You were just you; you were a miracle. If you sat in a room and did nothing for the rest of your life, that would be enough.

"I know it's just a metaphor, the room," she said, "but the idea seems creepy to me. It seems scary."

Truck after truck groaned by on 360, just a couple dozen yards away. The trucks were loaded with timber bound for West Point, pine trees that would be made into paper. It was fully dark now.

"You're enough for me," Mitchell said. "You don't have to be anything or do anything."

"But I *want* to be something," Annabel said, taking a bite of steaming tofu. "I just don't know what." She paused and considered her food. "This tastes like Mr. Pibb."

"Mine too," Mitchell said. "It is just it. It does not have to *be* anything."

"It does not have to *taste good*."

They were struggling so hard not to laugh out loud that they didn't notice Loretta come in. She'd come to pick up a large take-out order, bag after bag of food that the waiter set on the countertop. She noticed Mitchell and Annabel before they noticed her.

"Well, hey there," Mitchell said, composing himself. "How're you, Loretta?"

"I'm okay," she said, hefting the bags. "I've got my niece outside waiting. How's my boat coming?"

"It's coming fine," he said. He got up to hold the door for her, saw a woman waiting in a little silver car by the curb.

"Ready by Christmas?"

"Why do you need it so soon?" he asked. He wanted to ask, why do you want it at all? Instead he added, feebly, "It'll be cold then."

Loretta looked at him. There was something severe and teacherish about her, a distance she imposed. He was about to apologize when she laughed, shaking her head. "I don't know, I guess it's crazy. I know myself well enough to know I always get a little down at Christmas. You know what I mean?"

Mitchell nodded. He did.

"And right after Christmas, it's worse. I guess I just thought if I had a boat, I could look forward to spring better, and my father taught me a long time ago not to take old debt into a new year. So Christmas. You think you can manage it?"

Yes, he said. Surely by Christmas.

When he finished with the *Queen,* she was like something out of an old photograph. The white paint was glossy; the railings were straight. He'd fixed the broken paddles, replaced the old, scratched glass on the pilothouse, and polished all the brass hardware. He'd even gone over the peeling black lettering so that *Mattaponi Queen* was clear as day on both sides of the hull. The engine just hummed.

Loretta picked her up on the Saturday morning after Christmas. The weatherman called for rain, but the high white clouds looked more like snow, and the river had started to ice around its edges. She didn't say where she was taking it, where she would dock it, but she hugged Mitchell, and he could tell that it was no small thing to be hugged by her. She was wearing a long camel coat and she smelled like gardenias. She listened patiently to his instructions and warnings.

They made their way together down the steps, careful in case of ice. He held her leather-gloved hand in his bare one as she boarded the boat, and she took her time inspecting it as he waited on the pier. She started the engine on the first try. The boat came to life at once, vibrating slightly as blue-white plumes of smoke floated out over the water. She came back out on deck, smiling.

She thanked him, smoothed a shawl over her head and shoulders, and tied it in a loose knot to keep out the wind. The water was dark gray, the brown, leafy shore lacy with ice. How much longer would the river even accommodate boats like this? They said the reservoir would take five feet of the river's depth, but that wasn't something to take up with a woman who'd spent months paying off an old and outmoded thing like the *Mattaponi Queen*. She had lasted, though—the men who made her must have never imagined she'd be running today.

Instead Mitchell said, "Loretta, do you think women and men both need each other, or is it just men that need women?"

She smiled, creasing her brow and seeming to think about his question. "Only thing you truly need is somebody to love you when you're little," she said after a moment. "Anything more is a bonus."

He wondered why he couldn't have loved somebody like Loretta or Darlene, somebody sturdy and no-nonsense. He hoped that Annabel, with her sweet vague yearnings to *be something,* would at least be like that, would make somebody feel lucky and grateful they'd chosen her. He was fairly sure she would.

It was low tide. The pier jutted only twenty-five feet from shore, and the *Queen* had been tied up parallel to it, so that the bow closely faced several low-hanging branches jutting off the shore. For a moment, untied from her mooring, the *Queen* just idled. Mitchell could see Loretta inside the pilothouse, pivoting her head to determine the best way to back out and around the pier into deeper waters. He thought that he'd have to come help her, maybe ride as far as the town boat landing, but after a moment he could see from her calm, determined expression that she was comfortable figuring things out for herself. Soon the *Queen* was safely in the channel, and Loretta was waving good-bye. The tang of diesel fuel mixed with the smell of wood smoke coming from the chimneys up above.

It hurt as she pulled away; it was a physical feeling, like pressure, that happened inside his chest. A cold wind blew up off the water; he stuffed his hands inside his jacket and watched as the *Queen* slowly chugged westward. For some reason he thought of the old yoga tapes that Joanne used to play on their VCR. The instructor said the same things over and over again in a soothing voice, and Joanne would move silently through all the postures. *Melt the heart,* the instructor would say. *Svanasana. Let your breath do the work. Melt the heart.* The words came upon him like ghosts from a life he could barely remember, as if they were supposed to help him. As if they meant something.

Mitchell turned away before the *Queen* disappeared beneath the bridge connecting King William and King and Queen counties. Slowly he made his way up the steep steps toward home. He crossed the road but stopped before going up the porch steps; he thought he could hear her low rumble from where he stood in his yard. Though it was morning the sky was dark, and the windows in his house glowed yellow with lamplight. He stood there, weeds and topsoil frozen under his feet, and listened until he was sure she was gone. It was a while before he went down the steps again to look at the empty pier.

Shelter

All Nikki talks about, since they put the bus shelter in front of our house, is going back down South. Down South where it's warm, where it's quiet. The people are all so friendly down there; we'd plant a vegetable garden, have picnics, go to church again. Our children wouldn't sass us or have school problems.

I tell her our troubles are the same; where we live is just the stage they sit on. We've got a pale yellow townhouse in Shaw. We won the right to live here in a lottery and there are rules in the deed about reselling. Look at the nice new carpet, I tell her, go look at the kitchen appliances, the little washer-dryer combo sitting neat in the closet. She cried tears of joy on moving day, ran the washer-dryer like it was a roller coaster, planted flowers out front in July.

But then in August they put in the bus shelter, and there's been no quiet or peace ever since. It's a metal frame structure that sits halfway inside our small yard, slightly askew like somebody dropped it there by accident. It's maybe eight feet from our living room window. The flowers got trampled right away, and I've been picking up cigarette butts, candy wrappers, and brown bottles ever since. We've been broken into twice, had to call the cops on teenagers a dozen times for fighting. Things are a little better now that it's winter, nobody has the energy for fussing, but we still keep the blinds closed most of the time. I say look on the bright side: at least you know when the bus is coming. She'll go to the window and sigh or cuss me. She'll be looking out at the people sitting hunchbacked against the cold, black hoods cinched tight, salt spray and a crust of snow on the clear acrylic windstop. Misspelled profanities scratched on the posters.

She stands at the window, parts the blinds, and makes pronouncements about the riders.

Crack man, she mutters at a skinny couple in dirty coats. Crack man and his crack wife.

Crack people don't ride the bus, I say. They walk.

They do when it's ten degrees outside, she says.

No they don't, I say. Leave them be, I say, like she's bothering them. And it isn't ten degrees, that was the low.

That's another argument we have: the weather. Nikki says she never knew anything to cut through you like a D.C. wind. I say it's the same as down in Virginia, maybe a difference of five degrees.

You feel it more here, she says.

I look at my watch. Don't you have to go soon? I ask.

I thought you were driving me.

Now it's my turn to cuss. She won't ride the bus if she can help it, even though it would pick her up right outside and drop her off in front of her school, no more time in the cold than if I drive. She likes to take rides from me, like it proves how much I love her. Nikki doesn't have a license. She went three times to take the test when we lived down in Virginia, failed the driving part every time. Said she wasn't one to ignore a sure sign from God. I said maybe the sign meant she should practice her driving some, but Nikki's hardheaded. That was back when she thought D.C. was the place for her, back when she talked about public transportation like it was some kind of golden chariot.

All right, I say, and I stand up and look around for my shoes. It's my day off, and on my day off I like to relax and read the paper, but I don't want to fight with her. I like to read the financial pages, the real estate section, now that I'm a homeowner. Mr. Big Shot, Nikki calls me. Donald Trump the janitor. Custodian, I say quietly. Assistant custodial manager. It's a good stable job and she knows it: working for the public schools, health benefits and paid time off. It's how we entered this house lottery. Plus I can keep an eye on the kids' school;

I can watch out for bullies, keep them out of the wild classes. I'm friendly with the school secretary. She looks out for them too.

Nikki's taking adult ed classes at the community center. Medical Administrative Assistant and Medical Insurance Billing. Once she's done with her courses, she'll be eligible for a good job, too, and we can save for our next place, out in Riverdale or Laurel. At night I lie next to her in bed and tell her about it. Brick with dark red shutters, a little green yard in front. Trees lining the street. Kids riding bicycles. In my mind it's like a cartoon, the colors flat and bright. The heating vent will click on above our heads, dry hot air, and Nikki just lies there while I rub her broad, soft back. Outside there are distant sirens and shouting. When her breath tells me she's sleeping I'll get up again and go to the window and look out. It never gets really dark here, and on cloudy nights the sky reflects the city lights like a blanket held over a flashlight. From our upstairs windows I can see the blue glow of the MCI Center, yellow streetlights, little row houses like ours all scrunched together in the still, cold air. It amazes me to own a part of it, I've got to be honest.

We have to sit in the car until it's warmed up enough to drive. Nikki rubs her hands together and blows on them, and though the bus would already be warm I don't bother saying so.

"You'll be here when the kids get home," she says. Her classes are from noon until five on Mondays, my weekday off. I work Tuesday through Saturday.

"Yes," I say.

"Then make sure that Benny gets started right away on his homework. His teacher says he hasn't been doing it. I check what he shows me, but there's more he ain't showing."

"How about Pauline? She keeping up?" I ask, just to remind her we've got one that always does what she's told.

"Shoot," Nikki says.

I tell her I'll get on Benny. For all you can say about Nikki, she looks after the kids. In her writing class she wrote her final essay on the theme "What's most important to me." She wrote about our kids, listing reasons one, two, and three in perfect five-paragraph style: *they're mine, they represent me in this world, and nobody else will look after them if I don't.*

I rev the engine and we are enveloped in blue smoke. The sky above is pale washed-out blue like the lines on notebook paper, the cheap kind we can get at the corner store except Pauline won't use it. Martin Lawrence smiles flirtatiously from a new poster at the bus shelter, a damn fool in drag. No one is sitting on the bench.

Our first place together was down South, in King and Queen County, Virginia: a little cinder-block house we rented from an old lady. There was a cornfield in front of it, so that in the summertime you couldn't even see the road, and we had to warn the kids to stay out of there so they didn't get lost or bit by a snake or some rabid animal. We had a forsythia bush that grew nice long switches; they knew what not to do.

Anyway, I liked it fine. I liked the sweet fresh smell of corn growing, having a yard for the kids to play in. I liked being close to the river for trout fishing, being able to pee off my back step when I came home from work or before I went to bed. I grew up near there and so did Nikki, and for a while it seemed like our kids would too. But Nikki and me, we started thinking: this can't be it. Over the years we started to notice some things: the ratty old textbooks the kids used, falling apart at the spines; how cold and drafty our stove-heated house was in the winter, and how small it was and how frustrating it was, every month, to turn over a check to a landlady who didn't fix things when they broke. My construction job didn't provide health insurance, and Nikki only worked part-time at the brake shoe factory, so money was a struggle whenever somebody got sick. We started talking about "what if"—what if we moved to the city, got jobs there?

Nikki had a cousin who moved to D.C. to go to beauty school. They weren't really close, but I guess moving to the city and opening her own salon gave the cousin something to talk about, so she called Nikki. Called her every weekend, in fact. Told her about the city programs for home ownership, weekends dancing at nightclubs, how you didn't need a car. This was in the spring, when the corn plants looked like green ribbons in the ground.

Then Nikki got laid off, and she had nothing to do but sit at home and watch the corn grow. Nothing but hog feed anyway, she used to say when I defended it. But money was tight, and I have to admit I was curious. We made some phone calls, took some trips up 95. I applied into the city system, took my TB test, and got fingerprinted downtown. It didn't take much to get into a little place off Florida Avenue, and then we won the housing lottery and moved here. Bus stop or no, I can't see going back.

To appease her I've written letters, made phone calls. The city says the bus shelter is part of their plan for urban renewal, a public service for the residents of our historic neighborhood. I understand that, I told them, I just wonder why it has to be in front of a private residence? Why not move it down the street, to the corner?

You can't argue with the city is what I finally had to tell Nikki. They're as hardheaded as you are.

That bus don't bring nothing but trouble, she says.

She won't change her mind when it drops Love off, either, with her two duffels of scorched clothes and our address written on an envelope.

I'm sitting in my easy chair that faces the street, newspaper in my lap, when I see her. It takes me a minute to recognize her and I'm ashamed, looking at her standing confused and out of place on our stoop, holding up the envelope to match it with the numbers on our house. I pull on my jacket and go out to meet her, closing the door right behind me to seal in the heat.

"Love," I say in a soft voice. You have to be soft and slow with my sister—you can't go rushing at her with hugs and yelling. I walk up and reach out my hand.

"George," she says, not looking at me. She's always had a hard time meeting people's eyes. I can tell something has happened right away, but I know better than to hurry her with questions. I take the heavy bags gently, one from each hand, and she follows me inside.

Love is my baby sister, named Love by my father because he and my mama were old, by then, and she was a surprise. It was a name that fit her, my mama said later, or maybe she grew to fit the name. Her sweet child, she called her, gentle with animals and flowers and people's feelings. Before she died Mama made me promise to always take care of Love. She never got too specific—take care of her, that's all she said—and that's how Love wound up living in group homes, first in Tappahannock, then in Alexandria. It was the best thing, Nikki said after we were married. She'd have responsibilities, she'd feel more welcome around her own kind.

But now the group home has burned down, all the residents given bus fares out to their closest family. Someone was frying chicken on the stove, now the place is condemned—that's all I can get out of her. It takes me ten minutes to get her to sit down on the couch, and even then she won't take off her coat or even unbutton it.

"I tried calling you," Love keeps saying, and then she recites my phone number, closing her eyes as she says it. She talks into her chest, head down like she's swallowing the words. She takes out a bus map from her pocket and points to the route she took, highlighted by some Metrobus driver, or someone from the home. She tells me the buses she took to get here, as if she needs some kind of reassurance that she's in the right place.

"I must have left the Internet on," I tell her. I'd been checking out house values and mortgage rates. "The computer," I say, when she doesn't say anything back. "Never mind."

Love is bent over, retying the laces of her shoes, and I remember how long it took her to learn. I used to tease her, telling her she couldn't go to school until she knew how. When our father found out he switched me and made little cardboard shoes for her to practice with. He would sit with her for long stretches, and when she got discouraged he bought her shoes with buckles instead. Now she's an obsessive shoe tier, making triple knots in the dingy laces of her nurse-white sneakers. I wonder if she remembers those cardboard shoes, if she remembers anything at all from our childhood. It seems like she struggles so hard just to keep the basics straight: I picture her mind like a chalkboard that gets erased but never washed, little bits of yesterday, last month, last year, poking through.

"The kids'll be home soon," I say. "Benny and Pauline."

Love nods. She remembers them, good, I think, and then I'm embarrassed by the thought. We visit every month, don't we? A good brother bringing his sister her niece and nephew.

"We better get you settled," I tell her. "You can sleep in Pauline's room."

I make a move to get up, but Love doesn't follow. "Let's get you settled," I say again. "Let's see what you've got, unpack your bags."

She shakes her head, scooting the bags closer to her with her feet. I notice her ankles are fat and creased like an old woman's, though she isn't thirty.

Once I asked my mama, if Love is your sweet child, then what am I?

You're my one to brag on, she said. My one that's going places.

When the kids come home they overwhelm her with questions. Their aunt is still fascinating to them, a giant child living job-free, child-free, stress-free, in the world of adults. They loved the group home, never missed a visit. With its wide brick porch and balconied windows, they thought it was a mansion, their aunt a rich person with her glass dishes of cracked M&M's. Now they want to hear about the fire and the bus ride, and they want to smell Love's singed flannel nightgown.

"We were just there!" Benny keeps saying. "And now it's burned to the ground."

"It isn't burned to the ground," I say, and then I remember something. "Benny, go do your homework."

"No," he says, eyeing Pauline sitting practically in her aunt's lap. They are twins, in different classes in the third grade, and naturally competitive. Normally I'd pop him for being smart, but I see the kids have had a calming influence on Love. She has unbuttoned her coat and she's showing Pauline her notebooks, which it turns out take up most of one of her bags.

"Oooh," Pauline says, passing her hand over the pages, crinkly with Love's hard pressing. I don't look too closely, but it seems like she's written the same thing over and over. "You have nice script. My teacher won't let me write in script yet, but I'm practicing for next year."

"You do not know how to write in script," Benny says. "All you write is scribbles."

"Yes I do," Pauline says. "Get me a pen and I'll show you."

"I'm not your slave!" Benny says.

"Benny," I say. I'm thinking about how this is all going to work out. "Don't say slave."

"Why not?" he says.

"Just don't," I say.

"Yeah, but why not?" Pauline says. "Slave isn't a bad word. *Slavery* was a bad thing, but slave isn't a bad *word.*"

Benny looks at me smugly. That's how twins are: they'll turn on you, together, in a heartbeat.

I change the subject: "What's in the notebooks, Love?"

"Notes," she says, closing the one she holds open in her lap, a speckled composition book like the ones children use for homework. Her hand moves back and forth against the cover. "Notes to me."

Nikki, like I predicted, is not pleased when we all show up to pick her up from school. She gives Love a kiss and a pat and then sits stone-faced in the passenger seat all the way back home. She makes

Hamburger Helper and is all questions at the table, things I didn't think to ask earlier.

"So where are your medicines, Love?" she says. "Do you have the prescriptions? Your doctor's name?"

Love is hunched over her food, her eyes down. She eats in a clock-wise circle around her plate. She's past six o'clock and doesn't say anything. She's always acted nervous around Nikki.

"What about the people that run the home?" Nikki says. Her voice is gentle but she is looking at me meaningfully. "They must have given you a number to call."

"I had your number," Love says in her nervous voice. That means she says it softly, repeating it: *Ihadyournumber, Ihadyournumber.* She's shaking more now, a product of the long day or lack of medicine, I don't know.

"It's all right," I tell her. "That's enough, Nikki."

Nikki gets up to start clearing the table even though she's the only one finished. I follow her into the kitchen.

"What am I supposed to do, Nik? Throw her out?"

"I just don't see how you think," she says. "You don't think, Love needs her medicine. Or, what really happened? Or, who can I call? It's after working hours when I get home and you ain't done a thing to figure this out."

"She told me what happened," I say.

Nikki rolls her eyes.

"You think she's lying?"

"Where she gonna sleep?" Nikki says. "Who's gonna watch her?"

"She doesn't need to be watched," I tell her. "She'll sleep in Pauline's room."

"Pauline's room?" Nikki says. "I thought all this moving here was about giving the kids some space. You didn't want them having to share a bedroom, all that."

I tell her it's temporary, but she isn't having it. She's slamming the plates into the dishwasher, first I ever owned. Water from where she's rinsed them sloshes onto the floor. I sigh and walk to the front room to get my slippers. Outside, at the bus stop, I can hear a group of men laughing, telling jokes, and for a minute I feel jealous of them, free and easy as they are.

I scuff my damp sock feet into my slippers. The kids' homework is everywhere, and Love's two bags are still beside the sofa. I carry them up to Pauline's room, set them on her pink comforter. I unzip them and reach my hands in, not looking, feeling through her nylon drawers and whatever else for the sturdy plastic pill bottles. I come up with two: Risperdal and Nardil. I read the labels, shake the contents to hear how many are inside. Her doctor's name is on the side, too, and a number, so we can get refills and find out what else she takes. The kids' rooms are small, tucked side by side in our narrow house, but there's room on the floor for a pallet bed.

Like a sleepover, I tell Pauline as we're bringing up the sofa cushions. She's young enough to buy it, young enough not to worry about another person's strange breathing keeping her awake. She asks if she can be the one to sleep on the floor, like that's the lucky place. Sure, I say. I bet your aunt won't mind at all.

When we get it all set up, Pauline has an idea. She wants to put mints on the cushions like at a fancy hotel. Where you learning about fancy hotels, girl? I want to know.

Television, she says. Silly.

We get the room set up nice, turned-back covers and Hershey's kisses on the pillows, a soft blue night-light in the outlet. We call up Love and Nikki and they both take a long time coming up the stairs, heavy women that they are. Nikki walks like a tired person, rolling her hips and holding on to the railing. Love's walk shows her nervousness, her arms at her sides, torso bent forward a little. Aunt Love walks like my dolls, Pauline said once.

Love takes possession of her bags, and I start to explain about the open zippers but decide against it. I've always had a hard time figuring out what she's thinking. She starts rooting through them right away.

Before long she pulls out a lacy blue thing. It's so big and the color so electric and unnatural that it takes me a minute to recognize it as a bra, department store tags still hanging from the back. It has a burned smell, like everything about Love, but it doesn't look damaged. She thrusts it at Nikki, and at first we both stand there thinking it's a present.

"I can't put it on," Love says. "They bought it for me and it has too many hooks."

"Okay, I'll show you," Nikki says stiffly. Then the niceness inside her takes over her put-upon self and she says, "That's a sexy bra, girl."

"I told them blue," she says. "I said I wanted a blue one."

I was a bachelor for a long time before I met Nikki and we lived in the cinder-block house. I worked on Sheetrock crews, building new condos and four-thousand-square-foot houses all along 95. Steady work, a good paycheck on Fridays, the weekend to do whatever I wanted. I never wondered what life would be like in one of those houses, not once.

Then my daddy died, and then my mama, and it was just me and Love. I started going to church, looking for answers. I heard Nikki singing, she saw me there eligible in the pews. She asked me to a picnic, then to a movie. She made dinner for me and Love, fried chicken and gravy, biscuits to float away on.

I'm not saying she tricked me, that I'm some prize she won and changed the rules on. Nikki's a planner, but she thinks move by move. She wants to get the most out of every change, doesn't want to make sacrifices or wait, and she doesn't have a good handle on her own limitations. She's like a pretty smart person who's just learned to play chess. A frustrating opponent, my daddy would say.

But she bore my kids, she cares for them, and it isn't her fault that life is disappointing. And it isn't just for herself that she feels let down. She's got friends from school, single women with babies to feed and more babies on the way, who call her to cry about their trifling men or the rent, and Nikki takes it all hard.

She's a master at pep talks for other people. You're smart, I'll over-hear her saying, her favorite and best compliment. You just gotta get yourself your education, take care of your kids. You'll find your way. God will take care of you.

Then she comes in to me to say we gotta get out of here, these city people are crazy, they gonna wear us down till there's nothing left.

The bus stop has a rhythm, an ebb and flow like the rush hours they spend so much time describing on the news. There's the morning crowd, old ladies on their way to the supermarket with shopping bags tied to clacking pushcarts, mamas taking little kids to day care be-fore work, a few construction guys in coveralls. These people don't leave much behind, maybe a coffee cup or a napkin.

There's some more traffic at lunch, but the next big crowd, and the one to worry after, is the high school after-school crowd. Boys and girls come over from Dunbar, pushing each other and yelling, teasing, and calling names. Sometimes fighting, though mostly for show. Always throwing cans and wrappers, McDonald's bags. Our kids usually stay in afterschool until I get off work so we don't have to worry about them walking through the crowd, which can be large. The other times to look out for are Friday and Saturday nights, when you can count on noise from about eight until long past midnight. Night people leave behind all kinds of things.

The day after she moves in Love joins the rhythm of the bus stop, sitting out there like it's a park bench, not waiting for the bus, just waiting. She bundles up in her overcoat and takes a notebook and a pack of Newports with her. Nikki calls me at work to tell me about it. I'm scattering wood shavings on throw-up in a kindergarten room when she calls, and I'm pulled away in the middle like it's an emer-gency, my heart thumping, so I'm a little mad when I find out the reason.

"But she's just sitting there," Nikki says. "I don't know what to do."

"She's not getting on the bus?" I ask.

"The bus pulls up and she just sits there," Nikki says. "Then it drives on. What if she runs away? What's she doing there?"

"Why don't you ask her?"

"I already did."

"Then take her some hot chocolate, she loves that," I say. "And don't call me about it anymore."

"She's your sister," Nikki says. "I thought you'd want to know."

"I've got to work," I say.

The truth is that I don't want to know, not about where she sits all day or why, or how she puts her brassieres on or who buys them for her. I don't want to know if a man has ever touched her or what's really in those notebooks she carries. I remember the sight of her bloody panties in the hamper, how she never could take care of things in time, and I remember missing, as she grew the normal curves and smells of a grown person's body, the little girl's body that fit her, that took so little caring for.

On my way back to the throw-up room Benny's teacher stops me in the hallway. She's a tough woman, older; Pauline got the young white teacher who does art with them on Fridays. He needs to do his homework, she says, or he'll be in summer school. The tests are coming, the homework is what prepares them.

I apologize and ask her does she know Pauline? Pauline does her homework every night, and Benny sits right beside her at the table, doing something at least. Maybe he just isn't turning it in? And she says this isn't about Pauline, it's about Benny. We talk a little while more and she suggests giving me the homework in a folder, so I'll know what's due and can check it.

It's got to stop, Nikki says, meeting me at the door when I get home. This sitting at the bus. People are looking. She's gonna get hurt, mugged, kidnapped.

Then she starts in: down South we could look after her better. We wouldn't have to worry about her getting mugged. She liked that home in Tappahannock, with its screened porch and shady lawn. They ate crabs every Friday in the summer. Don't I think Love would feel better near where she grew up?

You're the one who brought her up here, I want to say, but I don't. I also don't say how much better things were at the home in Fairfax, where Love had friends, strange as they were, a mix of men and women, black and white, young and older. Addicts and alcoholics and regular plain crazy people. But the home isn't reopening; the owner says she's looking to open a new place but just for veterans, who are cleaner and don't leave chicken frying on the stove. She says it suspiciously, like Love was the one who fried the chicken, which she wasn't.

I take my shoes off—I'm the only one worried about protecting the damn carpet—and walk through the living room into the kitchen.

Love is on the telephone. Inside her notebooks Love has a few of her friends' numbers. She sits by the phone in the kitchen while the kids are doing homework and calls them. Hi! she says, twisting the phone cord around her like a teenager. I miss you!

Pauline and Benny are sitting at the table next to Love. I see that Pauline is wearing one of her aunt's medical alert bracelets, a worn copper chain with an engraved plate. It's too big for her hand and it clanks against the table as she turns the pages in her textbook. She used to ask to wear it at the home, after she petted the stray cats and persuaded Love's roommate to take out her teeth.

"Benny, my man," I say, holding up the thick homework folder. "I had a little talk with your teacher."

"Ha!" Pauline says. "I knew you had homework!"

"Shut up," he says.

"Don't say *shut up*," I say. I set the folder down in front of him. "You don't want to spend your summer in school, you got to do this work."

"Summer school!" Pauline says. "I'll be sleeping in and you'll be on your way to school!"

"You're too young to think about sleeping in," I tell her.

I think about how I used to tease Love about her knotted shoe-strings, put my hand on Benny's shoulder, and give him a pat. He rolls his eyes and takes out a single math sheet.

"All of it," I tell him.

He sighs and takes out the rest, a thick stack. I'm a little amazed at how much there is, in fact. "Lemme see that," I say. He hands it over.

I take it into the living room, where Nikki's sitting on the couch, reading through her medical terminology sheets. "Look at this," I say, flipping through the pages. "For an eight-year-old!"

"It's this city school system," Nikki says. "They know there's nothing for the kids outside their homes but trouble, so they keep them busy."

"I used to play outside from three fifteen until dark, every day," I tell her. "I don't remember this kind of homework."

"Me too," Nikki says. "Hopscotch, Red Rover, Double Dutch. Made-up games too. I used to love the afternoon."

"It's good for them, I guess. Homework. All Benny needs is some discipline. And who's to say all that homework isn't what's made Pauline so smart."

"I still say a child benefits from the outdoors," Nikki says, which is news to me. I'm flipping through the pages, fractions and spelling words and reading passages, when I come to a starred page that says *Extra Credit* on top. I call for Benny, and he comes dragging his feet. "Hey," I tell him, holding out the sheet. "Look at this."

"Yeah?" he says.

"It's extra credit," I say. "You can do this to get points to make up for the other work you missed."

"I saw it already," he said. "I told the teacher you wouldn't let me do it, 'cause it's past my bedtime."

I grab the sheet back. *"Watch and record the Geminids,"* I read. Pauline calls out from the kitchen to correct my pronunciation. It's not a big house.

"They don't happen till ten o'clock," he tells me.

"We can work that out," I say. "This once."

"Me too?" Pauline has come in; she won't be left out. Benny looks at us skeptically, unsure if staying up late to do homework is a good deal. He looks at his mother to try and guess the truth.

"I don't know," she says. "I'm tired already."

But my mind is made up. "These Geminids look interesting," I tell them. "We'll all go. And we'll benefit from the outdoors."

"You mean we gotta go outside?" Nikki says.

"No falling stars in the house, last I looked." I make a pantomime of looking and Pauline giggles—she likes my dumb jokes—and Nikki rolls her eyes.

What my mama said about being proud wasn't idle. I had a streak going for a while. From the time I was Pauline's age until I was in middle school I was always winning stuff, contests for writing and drawing. Spelling bees. I got to go to special classes for reading with kids one grade up. Looking back I suppose the school must have told my parents that I was destined for something bigger than hanging Sheetrock, though I wish they hadn't. I loved school then, loved being able to watch the clock myself and walk into the hallway without a word to anyone; everybody knew I was going to my special class. Didn't even need a note. The middle-morning hallways were so quiet and private; I'm reminded of them now sometimes when I'm at work, headed to fix something, and just the memory makes me happy.

Then Love came to school, and there was all that teasing. First about her name, then about everything else that made her different. I started getting into fights, stopped staying after school for my special clubs just so I could ride the bus with her. Then there were fights between my parents and the school about the classes they wanted to put Love in, with kids that drooled on themselves and couldn't make it to the bathroom even.

I think about this now, making "cool coffee," spoonfuls of hot coffee stirred into sweetened milk, for the kids, and regular coffee for the grown-ups. I wonder if my parents knew if that was what turned me away from school, made me look twice at those teachers and principals who patted me on the back with one hand and pushed Love away with the other. Or maybe it was my parents who changed their minds about school, and I was the one who followed. Either way, my mama never stopped telling me and everybody else that I was special and "going places," even after it was clear I wasn't going to college or anything like that. It embarrassed me but I wish it hadn't. Those houses I used to build were more beautiful than they had any right or need to be, and I know there's no talent bigger than raising a good family.

We sit in the living room, everyone with something in their laps—me with my newspaper in the easy chair, Love with her notebook and Nikki with her vocabulary flash cards on the sofa, the kids on the floor with their homework.

"Everybody's doing homework," I say. "No TV. I should take a picture and send it to the paper."

Nobody says anything. I can't focus on my newspaper. I'm worried about Love, with no real room for her here, like Nikki said, and no one to watch her or keep her company. We'll have to start the search for a home all over again, and it wasn't easy the first time. I'm worried about Benny, who I can see from here is getting his fractions all wrong. I'm worried about Nikki, who gets hurt so easy by her surroundings, who holds everything up to such a strong fierce light, and I'm worried about Pauline because I never worry about her at all.

There's a class I took one time at the kids' school, yoga meditation. Pauline's teacher taught it to me and a couple of the other teachers, though it was meant for parents. She tried to teach us how to use our breath to free our minds from judgment, how to be accepting of the place where you are, to be present for the moment, for your breath. It was hard—I kept thinking about practical Nikki, who would have laughed out loud at me sitting cross-legged on the gym floor with my eyes closed—but I got there, just for a minute, and it was a good, full, peaceful feeling, a little like being high but without the paranoia. It's like you're on the verge of a thought that will explain something, but you don't have to actually think it. I try to put myself in that space now, with all this breathing and pencil scratching around me, and I can't do it. The teacher only ever gave one workshop—lack of interest, she explained—but I think maybe if she'd kept teaching I could've gotten better at it.

At nine thirty we start to bundle up in our warmest coats. Nikki finds an extra hat and gloves for Love, who's lost hers or never had any. Pauline wants to copy out the questions from Benny's extra credit page—maybe she can get extra credit too—but Nikki tells her no. "That's Benny's extra credit," she says. "It ain't yours."

He clutches his page and a composition book against his down parka, a pencil in his gloved hands. "Hurry," he says. "It's hot in here."

Love has her notebook too, and her pack of smokes, and Pauline has brought *her* notebook anyway. We walk out into the dry December cold of blinking Christmas lights and lighted plastic Santas. The bus stop is right there, empty. It's a pretty clear night but the MCI Center, to the south, throws brightness overhead. Light from our living room illuminates our bare little yard and I think how I need to get one of those Santas, or some reindeer.

"Where we supposed to look, my man?"

Benny studies his paper, holding it close to his face in the half dark. "The North Star. Polaris?"

Pauline points for us, and we look. The sky is a washed-out blue-black, the stars we can see faint and few.

"It says it won't start up really until after ten," Benny says. "Maybe we should go back inside."

I tell him no, be patient, we'll see the first ones. Besides, Love and Nikki are already sitting down at the bus stop. Big women, their natural posture is sitting. I'm standing on my little patch of land with my kids, looking at my sister and my wife, their wide, loving backs hunched there close together in the cold. From where I stand they look like strangers to me, like any old tired mamas waiting on the bus. I feel like if I can love them and know them, then I can love and know *anybody,* and then I get that yoga feeling, that peaceful on-the-verge-of-a-thought feeling.

I walk over to sit next to Nikki. I see that she has her flash cards out.

"Baby, you're supposed to be looking up," I say. *Peritoneum,* the one on top says. She flips it over: *the membrane that lines the abdominal cavity.* I take the flash cards from her and hold her sweet soft chin in my hands and point her face up, toward the stars. I watch her dark brown eyes scanning the sky.

"Down South," she says quietly, "you can see so many stars."

It's true—I remember them scattered like salt against a clean black sky. I also remember how I could go months without bothering to check them out. For now, though, we look and look. We stare until our necks ache. The bus pulls up, groaning to a stop, and I wave it on.

"Look!" Benny cries. "I saw one!"

Then Pauline sees one, and they're calling back and forth—there! There! Look!

In the bus shelter Love lights a cigarette and passes it to Nikki. "Down South they stay put. They don't go falling out of the sky."

Nikki nods like she understands perfectly, but she's looking. I start to see them too. It's quiet now that the bus has pulled away. The more you look the more you can see, three and four at a time. I'm not paying attention to anything but that when a boy, twenty maybe, walks up and stands just inside the shelter. He has on a big coat un-zipped over a T-shirt and a do-rag on his head. He looks at his watch and checks the schedule.

"Bus ain't come yet?" he asks.

"Just missed it," I say.

He looks at us skeptically. "What y'all doing then?"

"We're watching falling stars," Nikki says. She points. "Look."

He squints up at the sky like it's the first time he's thought about it all day. "Shit," he says after he sees one. He looks worried. "For real?"

Nikki laughs her big old laugh, the one I remember before the bus shelter came, exhaling a long plume of smoke and coughing at the same time. When she recovers she says, "They won't hurt you, son."

"They're not stars, anyway," Pauline says. "They're meteors catching fire in the atmosphere."

"Oh," he says. "Yeah." But he doesn't look away, he keeps watching like they're stars, every one of them ancient and real, about to come burning down right here at our feet and grant our very wishes.

Youngest Daughter

The old man delivers eggs, not because he has to, not because he needs the money—surely he could do without the few, crumpled dollars it brings, surely the checks sent monthly by his daughters are enough—but because the work of it is a good reason to get up in the mornings, a reason to see people.

It is snowing the first snow. On the passenger seat beside him are three dozen eggs, trembling in their cartons with the engine's rattle, and a letter from his youngest daughter, which he opened and read in the post office. *Dear Dad,* it said, *When are you going to move to L.A.?* He visited her there once, after she and her husband moved from New York, and didn't like it for all the reasons he hadn't liked New York, plus some additional ones. She likes it in Los Angeles, likes her engineering job, likes the sunshine, the palm trees, the beach. She tells him this in her letters. He does not ever try to talk her out of it. Does not say, your sisters live nearby, now why can't you? She calls her hometown, where he and her mother raised her, that place. Calls it Klan country. Refuses to bring his granddaughter there to visit. Hush now, he says on the phone. It's where we brought you up. There's no Klan here.

There is a story she always tells of a man who said to them when she was a girl, there's a turkey not long dead up the road a ways. She always exclaims, at the end of the story, *as if we were going to rush out and scoop it up! Like it was our lucky day!* It's only one story among many, but it's the one she most often tells. She tries to make it funny. She does not say how the man looked at them, how he hitched up his pants and looked down at her father like he was a man who would feed his family with roadkill. That part, and the fact that people used to do such things as collect dead turkey and deer from the road, is a silence between them. He likes to remember how they used to pick dandelion greens and fry them in butter. Now she eats in restaurants, leaves a big tip at the end of the meal.

The snow clings wet to the road and to his car, a metallic green Pontiac. It starts at most once a day, so if there are multiple places to stop he has to leave it running and hope the engine doesn't choke. He drives slow, leans forward into the steering wheel to see the road better. He pulls into the driveway of the oldest house in the town, where the old lady whose family founded the town lives. It is the kind of town where such details matter and are known. She is stubborn, refuses to eat anything but *fresh eggs* from *his chickens*. She is mostly bedridden these days, lives in two rooms with the rest of her house closed up, the furniture covered in sheets. A year ago she had good help, a nurse who kept her moving, but that woman quit and who can blame her. Now she has a sullen woman who lives with her, is abused by her. His tires spin on snow and gravel.

He pulls up behind the kitchen to wait. The woman normally fetches the eggs from his car. He can see his breath coming in white clouds from his mouth, and he gives the car a little gas, both to hurry her and to keep the engine from dying. Snow collects on the boxwoods, which are hundreds of years old, which he tended when he was younger. It does not always snow here. Where is that woman? he thinks.

He grows tired of waiting, takes a carton of eggs and gets out of the car, leaves it running. He almost slips on the way to the back door. He thinks of the eggs all broken and freezing on the flagstones. No one answers. He goes inside to set the eggs in the refrigerator. It is that kind of town.

There is a gasp and muffled sniffling from the next room. It is coming from the sullen caretaker, who sits wide-eyed in the corner. On the daybed is the old lady, propped on her many pillows, covered in afghans and tissues and torn-open mail. The old lady is dead, he can tell. Her face is fragile and still and whiter than the sheets.

The caretaker starts talking all at once. I found her like this! I found her this morning! I haven't touched her!

The old lady's son and daughter-in-law are on a Disney cruise. There is no 911 service in the town; 911 gets a busy signal. You have to dial a seven-digit number for help. The caretaker says she couldn't remember the number, couldn't think what to do but wait. She was already dead!

The old man gets the caretaker a glass of water from the tap and calms her down. He is on the phone holding for the sheriff's office; there is music on the line, a country station, and he can hear his car shuddering in the drive, the idle increasing and decreasing. The snow is turning to sleet, striking windowpanes, oil drums, car hoods.

He thinks of what he will tell his daughter.

Good riddance, she'll say.

Acknowledgments

I would like to thank each of the following people for helping and encouraging me over the years: Michelle Latiolais, Geoffrey Wolff, Mona Simpson, Marita Golden, Gary Sange, Patricia Hoppe, Sally Doud, Jennifer Hill, Susan Keller, Dan Kois, Rosemary Sabatino, my parents, Buttons and Terry Boggs, my brother, Sky Boggs, my grandmother, Jean Haynes, and especially my husband, Richard Allen, who submitted *Mattaponi Queen* for the Bakeless Prize and is the first reader of almost everything I write. For the time and knowledge she shared with me, I thank Minnie-haha Custalow of the Mattaponi Indian Tribe.

I will always be grateful to the Bread Loaf Writers' Conference for giving me this opportunity, and to Percival Everett for choosing the book. I can't imagine a better home for my book than Graywolf Press or more thoughtful, exacting readers and editors than Fiona McCrae, Katie Dublinski, and Polly Carden. Frances Pelzman Liscio created the marvelous image for the cover.

I am also grateful for the generous support I received from the University of California at Irvine and the International Institute of Modern Letters.

Bread Loaf and the Bakeless Prizes

The Katharine Bakeless Nason Literary Publication Prizes were established in 1995 to expand the Bread Loaf Writers' Conference's commitment to the support of emerging writers. Endowed by the LZ Francis Foundation, the prizes commemorate Middlebury College patron Katharine Bakeless Nason and launch the publication career of a poet, a fiction writer, and a creative nonfiction writer annually. Winning manuscripts are chosen in an open national competition by a distinguished judge in each genre. Winners are published by Graywolf Press.

2009 Judges

Linda Gregerson
Poetry

Percival Everett
Fiction

Sue Halpern
Creative Nonfiction

Belle Boggs has published work in *Glimmer Train*, the *Oxford American*, *At Length*, and the *Paris Review*. She holds an MFA in fiction from the University of California at Irvine and grew up in King William County, Virginia.

Mattaponi Queen has been typeset in ITC Legacy, a typeface designed by Ronald Arnholm in 1992. Book design by Ann Sudmeier. Composition by BookMobile Design and Publishing Services, Minneapolis, Minnesota. Manufactured by Versa Press on acid-free paper.